"I can't go with you."

Kelly hiked her hands on her hips and continued. "I have a prior commitment."

"Well, that's too bad." Will's voice was unsympathetic. "Because, you see, it's the first rule of hostage taking that the hostage has to cancel all prior commitments."

"Is that what I am? A hostage?"

"Bingo, lady. For once you got it right."

"Will you stop calling me lady!" Kelly shouted. "Look, I'm on assignment. If I don't show up, people—like my employer—will wonder where I am."

"We'll deal with that on the way. Get dressed. And no lip." Will nodded toward her nightshirt. "You've got two choices. Either you dress yourself, or I'll dress you."

Kelly had no doubt he would make good his threat. Scowling, she marched into the bathroom and slammed the door. "You won't get away with this, you know," she muttered.

ABOUT THE AUTHOR

This is Sandra Canfield's seventh Superromance novel.
This popular author has won numerous awards, and
two of her recently published Superromance titles were
finalists in the RWA's Golden Choice Award for Best
Romance of the Year.

The Louisiana author is particularly excited about *Snap
Judgement* and its spin-off, *Proof Positive,* that will be
published later this year. "It's the first time I've worked
with connected books," she says. Sandra lives with her
husband, Charles, in Shreveport, Louisiana.

Books by Sandra Canfield

HARLEQUIN SUPERROMANCE

Snap Judgement

Sandra Canfield

Harlequin Books

TORONTO • NEW YORK • LONDON
AMSTERDAM • PARIS • SYDNEY • HAMBURG
STOCKHOLM • ATHENS • TOKYO • MILAN
MADRID • WARSAW • BUDAPEST • AUCKLAND

Published April 1993

ISBN 0-373-70545-X

SNAP JUDGEMENT

CHAPTER ONE

THE SUCCESS OF his escape plan depended upon his remaining cool-headed and steady-nerved, Will Stone thought as he glanced around the workroom of the California State Prison at Folsom. Everything, everyone, seemed monotonously the same. Fellow inmates, clad in blue pants and blue chambray shirts, milled around making license plates, many of which now hung drying on ceiling-suspended wire racks. Finished plates, boxed and ready for transporting, were being loaded, as usual, via forklift and man, into the back of a delivery truck. As Will caught sight of the truck—his ticket to freedom—his heart began to race.

"Hey, Stone, you just gonna stand there, or you gonna bring me that packing list?"

At the caustic query of the guard, a tall, spindly, thin-faced man whom the prisoners called Froggie because of his cigarette-scratchy voice, Will forced his heartbeat back into a normal rhythm. Wordlessly—it was pretty much the way he did everything—he stepped forward and offered the clipboard. The man, disliked by the inmates because he abused the power the penal institution granted him, looked Will over. Will met the look head-on. After a round of eye-to-eye combat, the guard was first to lower his gaze. He reached for the clipboard, studied the list of figures, and, initialing the top of the page, passed the material back to Will.

"See that those plates get loaded, then take that paperwork to bookkeeping."

Will said nothing. He simply turned away. As he did, the guard spoke again.

"Hey, Stone Man, you still ain't got much to say, do you?"

The Stone Man was what the San Francisco press had dubbed Will during the trial that had ultimately netted him a fifteen-year sentence for murder six months ago. The appellation was appropriate since he hadn't spoken a single word during the trial. Not a word acknowledging his guilt or proclaiming his innocence. Will had had a good reason for not speaking. That reason notwithstanding, he probably still wouldn't have said anything. After all, who in hell would believe a worthless jerk like him? Nobody ever had. Nobody ever would. William Randolph Stone— a fancy name for a nobody, a fancy name for a loser extraordinaire.

"No," Will said, his voice sounding as vacant as his heart felt.

To one degree or another, Will's heart had always felt empty. It had felt particularly so for the past two weeks—ever since the private investigator he'd hired had informed him that his brother had at last been found. Dead. That information had motivated Will to plan his escape. Before that, he'd tried to be the model prisoner his lawyer pleaded with him to be, insisting that good behavior would earn him an early parole. In light of his brother's death—his brother's *murder*— Will no longer cared about being a good boy.

"No, *sir,*" the guard goaded.

Refusing to rise to the bait, Will gave a sardonic half smile and said, "No, *sir.*"

Into the silence that fell between the two men came the tinny clanging of license plates, the whirring of the machinery that drilled holes into the metal, the shuffling of cardboard boxes, the mechanical calling of one forklift to another.

"Get to work," the guard ordered finally.

Will said nothing, turned and approached the truck. He willed his steps to be unhurried, to show no evidence of the anxiousness eating at him. Once at the vehicle, which was already a quarter loaded, he climbed aboard and began to match the numbers on his clipboard with those on the boxes. Surreptitiously, he searched for a box, a box with a certain set of numbers which he knew didn't appear on the paperwork. The box wasn't there.

For the first time, Will entertained the notion that his escape attempt might fail. He couldn't carry through his plans without the box. He needed the pair of metal cutters he knew it contained. Refusing to give up yet, he discreetly arranged the existing cartons so that a man-sized gap remained in a back corner of the truck.

Fifteen minutes later the vehicle was three-quarters full and the special-numbered box still hadn't shown up. Will began to panic. It was a cool, quiet panic, but a panic nonetheless.

"C'mon, get this thing loaded," the gaunt-faced guard called, slapping the side of the truck. "We haven't got all day."

One of the prisoners called back, "Speak for yourself, Froggie, I've got the next twenty years."

Laughter crackled, while Froggie croaked, "Very funny, Winters, but save your act for the Geraldo Show. C'mon, Stone, get outta there and let them finish loading."

With a litheness that defied his six-foot, four-inch height, Will jumped from the truck. As hard as it was, he forced himself not to look back at the space he'd left for himself. He continued checking box numbers, as though it were the only thing on his mind. Load... check...load...check...load...check. Where in hell was Glover and those cutters he'd promised him? And even if Glover did show up now, how could he get the box into the truck without being seen? More important, how could he himself get back into the truck? Froggie obviously meant to baby-sit this shipment.

With a growing sense of despair, Will watched the delivery truck fill to near capacity. Only one stack of boxes remained to be loaded and those, under the vigilant eye of the guard, were soon placed aboard. Heartsick, Will continued to record the numbers. Suddenly, his hand stopped. The third from the last box bore the numbers he'd been searching for. Relief washed through him, as did a frustration bordering closely on anger. There was no way he could execute his plan now, not with half the prison acting as an audience.

"C'mon, Stone, whatcha waiting for, your parole?" the guard asked, closing one door of the vehicle as he reached for the other. The guard nodded to the driver, a young man who didn't look comfortable being in a maximum security prison and was obviously anxious to leave.

The relieved driver slid behind the wheel and slammed the door shut, while the guard finished closing the back of the truck. At the same moment, all hell broke loose. One forklift collided with another; the latter seemed to come out of nowhere. Metal crunched against metal, sending up a sickening sound. A jumble of voices followed.

"What the hell?"

"Did you see that?"

"It's Glover!"

"Glover?" the guard asked, starting off toward the mayhem unfolding in the center of the room. Everyone, even the now curious truck driver, followed suit. Everyone, that is, except Will, who remained where he was. By the truck. By the abandoned truck.

Billy Glover, a strapping black man, emerged from the massive machine that now sat idling, a deep dent clearly visible on its side. Billy and Will had locked horns Will's first week of incarceration, with the result that each had come away with a respect for the other. They weren't friends—no one in stir really was—but they trusted each other in a cautious way. When Will had made his request of Billy, a request Billy could fulfill because he worked in the license-making division of the prison where tools were numerous, Billy hadn't asked any questions. His eyes now briefly met Will's, telling Will that he hadn't needed to ask any questions, telling him that the accident that had just occurred was no accident at all. *Take the gift I'm offering you,* Glover said silently.

"Glover, are you blind?" the guard boomed.

"Hey, man, no wonder you were caught if you were driving the getaway car," a fellow prisoner joked, knowing that Billy Glover was serving time for armed robbery.

Laughter was the last thing Will heard as he opened the truck door and stepped inside the vehicle. Darkness, a surprising coolness that he hadn't noticed before, the crazy thump-thump-thumping of his heart—all these things assailed Will like a crashing wave. Easy, he told himself. Just take it slow and easy. As a precaution, in case someone should take a last look inside the truck, Will moved to the hiding spot he'd left for himself. He squatted, took a deep breath and waited for what seemed like hours, though it couldn't have been more than a few minutes. Both relief and anxiety jolted through Will when the driver returned, started the engine and began to maneuver the truck from the prison grounds. Relief that he was finally on his way; anxiety that this was it, there was no turning back and he would have to bear the full consequences of his act if caught.

But he wouldn't be caught, simply because he couldn't be. Not until he'd done what he had to do. After that, he didn't much care what happened to him.

Will waited until he was sure the truck had cleared the prison gate. Then quietly, he made his way to the back of the truck. The jarring motion of the vehicle rumbled through him. He wished he'd paid more attention to the location of the box he needed, because time was critical. Had the box been in the stack to the right or to the left of him? Was it the third from the top or the third from the bottom? He chose a box and broke into it.

License plates.

Will cursed.

He reached for another box and fumbled it open, wishing he had the pocketknife that he never used to be without. Its absence was just another prison indignity, another invasion of his privacy. Struggling with the box, he wrapped his fingers around a pair of metal cutters. Thanks, Glover! Will rearranged some boxes, climbed atop them and began to hack his way through the top of the truck. Working feverishly, he snipped and snapped, the cutters eating at the ceiling only inches at a time. Precious inches. Precious time. Will had to have a hole cut by the time the truck reached a certain deserted spot, a winding curve that would force the truck to slow down.

In the process of peeling back the jagged triangular sheet of metal, Will gashed his knuckles. Blood poured from the wound, but he paid it no heed. Instead, he poked his head through the serrated opening. With a start, he realized that the bend in the road was just up ahead. Much closer than he'd imagined. With no time to waste, he heaved himself upward, trying to clear the narrow opening. That done, bending low, he rode the truck and the wind, the ragged motion of both threatening to topple him. He dug in his knees...and waited.

They reached the bend in the road. It was now or never. Not allowing himself to think about what he was doing, Will hurled himself from the truck. The ground rose quickly to meet him, slugging him in the back, knocking the breath from his body. He heard himself cry out, a guttural sound protesting the pain that shot through him. You're too old for this, a part of his brain thought. A forty-one-year-old body can't take this kind of abuse. But what choice did you have? he asked himself.

Although he lay only marginally protected by a ditch and overgrown underbrush, Will didn't move immediately. Then, slowly, he began to take stock. Flexing one limb, then another, he determined that nothing was broken. And his breath, though still heavy, struck a steady in-and-out rhythm. He was okay. More important, he was free. Free. He breathed in deeply, savoring the afternoon, savoring the crisp taste of a California autumn. This air, free and unguarded, smelled deliciously intoxicating.

If his luck held, he wouldn't be missed for a few hours—that was the beauty of a job that required you to be in more than one location. Still, he knew he had to make haste. He had a clear-cut destination in mind, one he had to reach that night, because, come morning, every lawman in the state would be looking for him.

Oh, yeah, he had a destination, he thought as he peeled off his prison shirt, leaving only an ordinary white T-shirt to cover his chest. It was a destination he'd plotted and planned with particular care. A certain someone owed him a favor. A whale of a favor. And he was going to see that that someone paid him his due.

KELLY COOPER SAW the world through a short, disheveled maze of copper-colored curls. At present, she was staring down at the empty suitcase sprawled open on the bed of her San Francisco apartment. Mercy, how she hated packing! But, oh, how she loved traveling! It was one of the wonderful perks of her job as a photojournalist. That, and the endless parade of people she met and photographed. She didn't always like people—they could be unkind and selfish, sometimes without knowing they were being either—but she was always fascinated by them, always intrigued with capturing on film their unguarded moments, moments of the soul, she called them.

Kelly thought about the assignment that lay before her. Bright and early in the morning, her trusty camera slung over her shoulder, she would be off to Europe to film its children, children from the countryside, children from the cities, even the christening of a wee royal monarch. From there, she'd travel to Africa to photograph the hopeless faces of that continent's starving youth. All would be part of a layout called

"Children of the World," a UNICEF project to which she was donating her services. Kelly knew the assignment stood a good chance of earning her an award. Perhaps even another Pulitzer Prize. Winning came easily to her—failure, or even mediocre success, was intolerable. She'd long ago programmed herself not to fail. More to the point, her father, a famed journalist himself, had programmed her to succeed.

Yes, she thought, glancing at the bedside photograph of the man she'd loved dearly, but had hardly known, people could be unkind and selfish without even knowing they were being so. People could also be totally illogical. Namely herself, for in her heart of hearts she knew that she worshipped perfection simply because she was trying to live up to her father's idea of it. She was trying to make herself so special that he couldn't ignore her . . . even though he'd been dead for five years.

As always, thoughts of her father brought thoughts of her mother, who'd died when Kelly was an impressionable twelve-year-old. From there, thoughts of Kelly's recently failed marriage intruded. These latter thoughts stung like angry bees, and she forcibly ejected them from her mind.

Raking her hair back from her forehead, Kelly stepped forward and turned on the television. With the Wednesday-evening news as a background, she began to give serious attention to the inevitable packing. Khaki slacks? Yes. Tennis shoes? Definitely. A scarf, a jacket, for sure. Red sweater? Kelly shrugged. Maybe it had seen better days. She'd take the ivory sweater instead. She'd...

"This afternoon, Suzanne Andriotti, the daughter of prominent businessman Edward Andriotti, was married to Emmanuel Echieverra, the son of the Mexican politician, Rodriqué Echieverra."

At this announcement, Kelly glanced toward the television, taking in the film footage of the lovely garden wedding she'd attended earlier. *San Francisco Today,* a glitzy local magazine, had hired her to cover the event. Actually, it had been more than an event. It had been *the* event of the year. Edward Andriotti was more than a prominent businessman. A resident of Knob Hill, or Snob Hill, as Kelly referred to it, he was a scion of a social dynasty that dated back to the founding of the city. Furthermore, Rodriqué Echieverra was far from being your run-of-the-mill politician. A wealthy mover and shaker, he wanted to be the next president of Mexico, if you could believe the political rumors rumbling south of the border.

The assignment had proven to be more difficult than Kelly had expected. Upon arrival at the Andriotti mansion—*house* simply would not describe the mammoth, castlelike structure—she'd learned that only a limited number of journalists had been cleared for entrance. Undaunted—there were those who said that if spunkiness could be sold, she'd be wealthy—Kelly had literally scaled a brick wall, had made quick friends with a Doberman pinscher and had procured—*stolen*— a tray of drinks, which she proceeded to serve to the guests as though she were a servant. All this without so much as having incurred a run in her panty hose.

While there, Kelly, careful not to attract attention to what she was doing, had taken a little over a roll of film—photos of the bride and groom, the proud parents, the guests. Most of this last group vainly hoped that their pictures would show up in the press so that all of San Francisco could be impressed with their social connections. Knowing she was leaving town the next day, Kelly had already developed the roll of film. She'd reasoned that the few shots on the second roll were probably duplicates of what she already had. Later, if any of the photos were singularly outstanding, she could always mail them to the magazine.

Anything to keep from packing, Kelly walked to the bathroom that doubled as her darkroom and, fighting panty hose and a colorful assortment of underwear drying hither and yon, she checked the wedding photographs. The prints, clipped to a sagging line, were dry. Collecting them, studying the integrity of each as she did so, Kelly walked back into the bedroom. She stopped short at the news bulletin coming from the television.

"This just in from the State Police. Earlier today, William Stone escaped from the California State Prison at Folsom. The Stone Man, so called because he refused to speak at his trial, was convicted of a drug-related murder and sentenced to fifteen years. A local resident, a renowned photojournalist, was instrumental in his conviction."

The newscaster continued with more details concerning the photojournalist who had played such a major role in the trial, but Kelly heard nothing beyond the wild pit-a-pat of her heart. Easing to the side of the bed, she recalled an autumn day almost a year ago. Like today, that day had blossomed with the full promise of fall. Leaves—gold, russet and tangerine—had rustled in the chilled, whispery wind that blew off the bay. Kelly had awakened early, in part because it was her habit, in part because she had an assignment to complete. A nature magazine had commissioned her to photograph a butterfly indigenous to the area. While jogging in a nearby park, Kelly had seen such a butterfly a number of times, always early in the morning, always near a bed of yellow-and-purple pansies.

That morning, however, she'd found more than a butterfly. She'd found a man—she'd later learned that his name was Will Stone—kneeling over a body. Kelly had seen instantly that the man slumped on the ground, the man with the gaping bullet hole in his chest, was dead. As a war correspondent, she'd seen more than her fair share of death. As grim as the sight of the dead man was, however, it was Will Stone who had captured her attention. Blood smeared across the knuckles of one hand, he'd been holding a gun. With the other hand, he'd been wiping the weapon free of fingerprints. He'd stopped when he'd noticed her.

The moment he'd turned to face her, fear had exploded inside Kelly. She had been certain that he was going to kill her, too, but as second after second passed and he made no move toward her, fear had given way to an intense awareness of his eyes. A dark tobacco-brown, they had intrigued her. There was something fathomless, even mysterious, about Will Stone's eyes. Ever the photojournalist, Kelly had reached instinctively for her camera. She hadn't been trying to record his guilt, only to satisfy the hungry pangs of her own creative curiosity. A couple of clicks of the camera, however, and she had sealed his fate. Even as he fled the scene, she knew that she'd sealed her own fate, as well, for she knew that the pictures she'd taken would forever haunt her.

At the trial, she'd been called to testify to what she'd seen that morning. Her photographs had been introduced into evidence. Day after day, she'd listened to Will Stone say nothing in his defense. Day after day, she'd wondered why he'd chosen this destructive path of silence. Day after day, she'd seen the secrets in his eyes give way to a blankness. Although initially she'd been fascinated, the blankness now frightened her. It said clearly that here was a man who had nothing more to lose. And this man, who'd had nothing to lose then and probably even less now, was free.

"...possibly armed...should be considered dangerous...do not approach...direction of travel unknown at this time..." the newscaster said as a mug shot of a rough-looking Will Stone appeared on the television screen.

A shiver skipped down Kelly's spine as she realized that his eyes looked as blank as she remembered them. The shiver intensified when an unsettling thought occurred to her. Don't be ridiculous, she told herself.

You're just being paranoid. Will Stone had far more important things on his mind than revenge. Like putting as much distance between himself and the police, between himself and the state of California, as possible. Besides, come morning, she'd be gone, well beyond the grasp of anyone plotting revenge, well beyond the grasp of the man with the frightening eyes. Furthermore, she thought, her spunkiness returning, surely the guy wouldn't be stupid enough to tangle with her. After all, she'd taken care of herself in far more dangerous situations, namely, a volcano eruption, a mountain-climbing expedition that had almost cost her her life and a couple of bloody coup d'états.

Holding tight to this last thought, Kelly finished packing, setting both the suitcase and the camera bag by the door. She then collected the photographs of the wedding, placed them in a stamped manila envelope, which she took downstairs and dropped in the mailbox to be picked up the following morning. Next, she showered, washed and dried her naturally curly hair and donned a faded nightshirt. It was then that the phone rang. It was the police, informing her that, though they in no way suspected Will Stone would seek her out—after all, he'd made no threats against her—they'd nevertheless have a patrol car drive by her apartment several times throughout the night. Feeling better, she locked up, set her alarm and crawled into bed.

But sleep eluded her. She tossed and turned, twisting the sheet beneath her until it draped about her ankles like seaweed. Furthermore, her brain seemed to have kicked into overdrive. It seemed intent upon dredging up every memory, particularly every painful memory, from her past. She thought of her mother's dying, of her father's never being there when she needed him. Like at night when she was frightened ... or when she needed someone to explain to her again why her mother had died ... or when she just needed a loving pair of arms to hold her.

"You've got to make me and your mother proud of you, Kelly," her father would say when he was home. *"She's watching you from heaven, you know. She's telling all the angels how special you are."*

And so Kelly had set out to make her parents proud of her, to prove that she was as special as they believed her to be. She couldn't just be special, though. She had to be the best of the best. And she had been. She had garnered top grades, had graduated *summa cum laude* from Bryn Mawr and had gone on to win one photo-journalistic accolade after the other. Yes, everything she touched turned to gold, Kelly thought. Everything, that is, except relationships. Those she hadn't a clue how to maintain. They all translated to loss for her.

"You know what I think?"

"No, what do you think, Gary?" Kelly had asked her husband, a man she'd lived with for a year and been divorced from for a year.

"I think you set this marriage up to fail. I think you're so hung up on people never being there for you that you've decided to leave me before I can leave you."

Kelly couldn't dispute the accusation. She, too, feared that was exactly what she'd done, that she'd shattered the marriage before her husband could. Somehow it would be easier to clean up the messy pieces if she did the breaking. Her husband hadn't fought her decision, however. In fact, he'd let her walk away with minimal opposition. For a reason she couldn't explain, his lack of protest had hurt.

Groaning, punching her pillow, Kelly willed away thoughts of both her father and her ex-husband. That left thoughts of... No, she wouldn't think of Will Stone. But she found that she couldn't help herself. He was the last thing on her mind before she fell into a fitful slumber. She saw his eyes, dark, secretive, blank. Just as before, they intrigued her, frightened her.

Where was he now?

Was some woman waiting for him?

Why had he remained so stubbornly silent at his trial?

Her dreams had no answers. Neither did the clock that ticked faithfully at her bedside, marking the hour as early morning. Kelly moaned, turned, buried her sleep-filled head deeper into the downy pillow. Without warning, the nightmare began. It was a nightmare that didn't end when she awoke. Which she did the instant the rough hand clamped over her mouth.

"Do as I tell you, and I won't hurt you," a masculine voice whispered in her ear.

CHAPTER TWO

ON SOME intuitive level, Kelly acknowledged that she'd finally heard the Stone Man speak. During the trial, even long after it, she'd wondered what his voice sounded like. Well, now she knew. It sounded gravelly—gravelly and dark. As dark as his eyes, as dark as his temperament.

"Be still!" the voice growled, and it was only then that Kelly realized her survival instinct had kicked in, and she was fighting her captor. No match for his superior strength, her struggle was futile.

At his clipped, uncompromising command, Kelly froze.

"That's it," he whispered, the words, steel-sheathed in satin, spilling into the silence. "Just take it easy."

The hand continued to press against her mouth. The warm voice continued to rasp against her ear. He was near, so near that his body, hard and muscular, crushed her into the pliant mattress.

"I'm going to take my hand away and, when I do, I don't want to hear a sound out of you. You got that?"

Kelly made no response.

"You got that?" the voice snarled softly.

Kelly nodded, a quick bob of her head. Slowly, the pressure of the hand began to lift. Kelly gave a deep sigh, pushed to her elbow and blinked when the figure on the bed beside her turned on the lamp. In the span of an uneven heartbeat, she was staring into familiar eyes, eyes that she'd been unable to forget even though she'd done her best to do so.

Will Stone looked as she remembered him, tall and slender with dark brown hair and piercing darker brown eyes. But he seemed older, wearier, as though the past six months had been not merely unkind, but downright hostile. She recalled that the time in the park and all during the trial, he'd been neatly, if modestly, dressed. Now, he was disheveled. Dirt streaked his white T-shirt, which hung carelessly over his pants. A tear sliced the fabric at his knee. His hair, in need of a cutting, slashed across his creased forehead, while stubble shaded his cheeks and chin. Blood caked the knuckles of one hand, reminding Kelly of the first time she'd seen him. He'd had blood on his hand then, too. Another man's blood.

Will followed both the direction of her gaze and the direction of her thoughts. Derision twisted his mouth. "I didn't kill anyone to get here, if that's what you think."

Kelly wasn't certain what she thought. She noticed his eyes were no longer blank. They were now filled with rage.

"You don't seem surprised to see me," Will said.

"You made the news."

"Ah, the press. They always did like me," he said, adding, "Tell me, were you frightened when you heard I'd escaped? Were you afraid I'd show up on your doorstep demanding a pound of flesh?"

Kelly tilted her chin in defiance. She'd die a thousand cruel deaths before she'd let him see that, indeed, she had been, and still was, concerned about precisely that.

"What do you want from me?" she asked, ignoring his question. Typically, her inquiry went straight to the point.

Will pulled no punches, either. "Compensation, though not in the form of a pound of flesh."

"Compensation for what?"

"For the six months I've spent in that stinking prison."

"I didn't put you there."

"The hell you didn't!"

"I didn't!" she retorted, her green eyes sparkling with a cold fire. "I simply testified to what I saw. I was subpoenaed. I had no choice in the matter. It was the jury who decided you were guilty. It was the jury who sent you to prison. And, I might add, you did nothing to help yourself. You never said a single word in your own defense."

Will was in no mood for logic. "Yeah, well, lady, you still owe me."

"What do I owe you?" Kelly asked, uncertain she really wanted to hear just what Will Stone had in mind. He didn't seem intent on harming her, though, and, because of that, her heart beat steadier—if only a little.

"Right now," he said, an overwhelming exhaustion claiming him as he bent to untie his boots, "you owe me a place to catch a few hours of sleep. In the morning, we'll discuss the rest of your debt."

Two things struck Kelly simultaneously: One, Will Stone was dog-tired; two, he was getting ready to crawl into bed with her. Even though she'd been trained to remain calm under stressful situations, everything from bullets to Bengal tigers, this latter realization panicked her.

"Hey, wait—"

"Go to sleep!" Will growled, shutting off the lamp, stretching out atop the cover, and throwing his arm across Kelly's waist. He lay on his side, his mouth once more so close to her ear that his breath fanned against her bare skin. "And don't try to get up," he warned, his voice reverberating through her. "If you do, I'll know it. Being in prison teaches you to sleep with one eye open. And believe me, you don't want to wake me up quickly. Especially not after the kind of day I've had."

Kelly was uncertain which upset her more, that he was so near, as in body to body, or that he'd just threatened her again. He hadn't harmed her, but he obviously wasn't dismissing the idea altogether, especially if she defied him.

Forty-five minutes later, Kelly surmised that Will Stone was dead to the world, a fact evinced by his deep, even breathing and the lead-heavy weight of the arm draped across her waist. Besides, he hadn't moved, not so much as a twitch, from the instant he'd lain down. Yeah, the man was out like a light. With this realization, and the knowledge that the police were patrolling her apartment, came a return of her spunkiness. She had no intention of taking this situation—she smiled ruefully at the pun—lying down.

Angling her head, she once more checked the bedside clock. It was nearing four o'clock. Her gaze lowered to the telephone that was only inches, only one good reach, away. What should she do? Ease from the bed, take the phone into the bathroom and call the police? Or was that too risky? Yeah, too risky. She'd just ease from the bed, sneak from the house and... And what? Flag down the police car? Don't be stupid. Chances are slim that it would be passing by at just that moment. Okay, then what? Go to a neighbor's house? No, even that was too risky. She'd get out of the house and make a beeline for the car that was tucked away in her garage. Then, she'd find a pay phone and call the police. Yeah, that's what she'd do, she thought with confidence. That would teach Will Stone to mess with her.

Slowly, carefully, Kelly edged one toe, one foot, from the cover. Ever so slightly, she lowered her foot to the floor, stopped, waited, and, when the man beside her didn't stir—thank heaven, he *was* dead to the world!—she trailed the second foot from the blanket. The real problem was how she was going to get out from under the encumbrance slung across her middle. With an unhurriedness that made a snail look swift,

Kelly proceeded to slip her body from beneath Will's arm. By the first stirring light of dawn, she idly noted that the sleeves of his T-shirt had been rolled back in a James Dean-like fashion, revealing substantial biceps. She didn't have time to dwell on these trivialities, however. There were far more important things on her mind. Like moving slowly, slowly, slowly—

Will moaned.

Kelly halted.

He rolled, shifted, settled, pinning her more securely beneath him. The mouth that had once been at her ear was now poised at her neck, inspiring ticklish little feelings that at any other time would have made her want to laugh. At the moment, she'd never felt less like laughing.

Her heart pounding, a prayer at her lips, Kelly closed her eyes and held her breath. She counted one minute, then another, that was followed by yet another. Long, long minutes that seemed to go on forever. When ten such endless minutes had passed and Will again lay silent and still, Kelly allowed herself a swollen sigh of relief. Dare she try again? The answer came quickly and clearly. She had no choice.

Once more, slow second by slow second, unsteady heartbeat by unsteady heartbeat, she began to ease herself out of his confining embrace. An inch here, a milli-inch there, the arm, like a sun-lazy snake, began to slither away. His wrist, his palm, his fingers, the knuckles of the latter crusted with dried blood, trailed over her stomach, over her side. At the same time, Kelly slid from the bed and to the floor. She crouched on her knees on the carpet to give her heart time to travel from her throat back into her chest. As she waited, she watched Will for any signs that she had awakened him. There were none.

She had done it!

Now all she had to do, was to rise cautiously, grab her purse and get the royal heck out of the house. She could do that. Easily. In fact, it would be a piece of cake after what she'd just managed to pull off. Yes, a piece of—

The hand that moments before had slithered like a lazy snake now struck like an angry one. Fingers gripped Kelly's wrist without any thought as to whether they were inflicting pain. In heart-stopping seconds, before Kelly could even think to fight back, she found herself being dragged onto the bed, then pushed onto her back and pinned beneath a very heavy, very irate man, his face thrust into hers.

She became aware of myriad things all at once: the firmness of muscles; the roguelike beard that now scratched her chin; the lethal look in his eyes.

"Do that again, and I promise you'll regret it," he threatened through gritted teeth. "Do you understand me?"

Kelly said nothing. She simply stared at the man who'd unceremoniously invaded her life.

Will tightened the fingers around her wrist, which was now held high above her head. "Do... you... understand... me?"

Kelly grimaced at the pain. "Y-Yes," she whispered, the fear she'd been fighting scoring a mighty victory.

Will saw the fear flash across her face. Curiously, the victory tasted bitter, for he intuitively realized that part of this woman's charm lay in her free spirit, her unwillingness to be easily tamed. It was a conclusion he'd reached as he'd watched her during the trial. It was a conclusion he'd just had confirmed.

Despite her fear, Kelly managed to maintain her dignity. Her voice quiet and even, her eyes meeting his fully, she said, "You're hurting me."

Will's gaze raised to the wrist he was still encircling. He relaxed his fingers, surprised at the reddish imprint they'd left. Shocked even. He knew that he ought to apologize, but the words wouldn't come. They hadn't for a long time. Not since he'd spent his childhood apologizing to his old man, and his adulthood apologizing to society. Apologizing to both for not being what they expected him to be.

Will pushed himself up, rolling to sit on the side of the bed. His anger, the only loyal companion he had, returned. He welcomed it. "Get ready to leave," he said, pulling on his boots and tying the laces with a vengeance.

Kelly had also sat up and was rubbing her wrist. "What do you mean 'get ready to leave'?"

"We're taking a trip."

"A trip?"

"That's what I said, lady," he repeated, standing and tucking his T-shirt into his pants. "I could have used a little more sleep, but seems you like getting up early."

"Listen," she said. "I can't go anywhere. I mean, I'm already scheduled to leave on a trip in the morning...this morning." She glanced at the bedside clock. Her plane left at 7:43. "In fact, I have to be at the airport by—"

Will glanced over at her, hiking his hands onto his hips. "I don't think you quite grasp the situation."

Unknowingly, Kelly mimicked his pose and hiked her hands onto her hips, drawing attention to their shapely slimness. "No," she said. "I think you're the one who doesn't grasp the situation. I can't go anywhere with you, because I have a prior commitment."

"Well, that's just too bad, because, you see, it's the first rule of hostage-taking that the hostage has to cancel all prior commitments."

Again, she ignored his sarcasm. "And that's what I am? A hostage?"

Will smiled, though the action lacked any warmth. "Bingo, lady, for once you got it right!"

"Will you stop calling me *lady?*" Kelly shouted. Before Will could do anything more than acknowledge that this woman had a temper to match her flame-colored hair, Kelly said, "Look, I'm on assignment. I'm on a job. If I don't show up, people—like my employer, like the people at UNICEF, like the people I'm supposed to photograph—are going to wonder where I am."

"We'll deal with that on the way," Will answered, nodding toward her nightshirt. "Get dressed."

"On the way to where?"

"I'll tell you when we get there. All I want from you is your car and your company. And no lip," he added, nodding again toward her nightshirt. "You've got two choices. Either you dress yourself, or I'll dress you."

Kelly had absolutely no doubt that he would make good his threat. He *would* dress her if he had to. Scowling, she grabbed a pair of jeans and a sweater, marched into the bathroom and slammed the door behind her. She snatched a pair of black bikini panties and an equally scanty bra from the shower-curtain rail. Propelled by her anger—how dare he do this to her!—she yanked on the clothing, jamming the zipper of the jeans, an act that caused the sacrifice of a full five minutes. Their loss did nothing to sweeten her sour mood. As forcefully as she'd closed the bathroom door, she now threw it wide open. She tramped back into the bedroom, a frown on her makeup-free face, her hair in a wild tangle of blazing disarray.

At her entrance, Will, who'd discreetly been staring out the window, glanced up. His eyes roamed over her, but he said nothing. Not about her appearance. Not about the handful of underwear she carried to, and thrust inside, the suitcase, along with sundry toilet articles.

"I'm going into the bathroom to wash up, so talk to me," he said.

"Talk to you?"

"Yeah, so I'll know you're in the room. And you better keep talking, because the minute I hear you stop, I'm coming out. Finished or not, if you get my drift."

"Crude," Kelly commented, fingering the hair from her eyes.

Will smiled, again mirthlessly. "I haven't exactly been away at finishing school." The smile faded, as he headed for the bathroom. "Now start talking. And stay by the door and away from the telephone." With that, he disappeared into the other room.

Kelly toyed with the idea of making a run for it, but concluded that she couldn't move that fast. She was willing to take a risk, she was willing to take a dare, but being foolish was something else altogether. She might make it down the steps, maybe even as far as the garage. In the end, all she'd accomplish was angering Will Stone again and, frankly, she wasn't all that wild about the idea. Her wrist still ached from the last time she'd provoked him.

"I don't hear you," Will called out.

"I'm here," Kelly hastened to reply, adding, "You won't get away with this, you know? Why don't you make it easy on yourself and give yourself up? Surely they'd take that into consideration." She heard the toilet flush and water begin to run in the lavatory. "I mean, turning yourself in would surely look good. Besides, how far can you get with every Tom, Dick and Harry searching for you? Every policeman in the state—across the nation... breaking out of a federal prison is a federal offense—is going to be looking for a man..." Kelly trailed off as the reason for his having involved her struck her like a bolt of lightning.

The bathroom door opened. Will's eyes met hers. "Bingo," he repeated. "Everyone's going to be looking for a man, not a couple."

Though the plan was clever enough, Kelly felt compelled to speak her mind. "Even so, you're not going to get away with it."

Some indefinable emotion streaked across Will's eyes. "I don't have to get away with it forever."

To say the least, his remark was cryptic. "I don't understand—" she began.

"You don't have to understand," he interrupted, his voice once more abrupt.

He stepped past her, walked to the window and again looked out. The world, huddled on the brink of dawn, appeared quiet, still, sleepy. Nothing, no one, stirred, except for a cat stealing a slow journey home after a night of carousing.

"Pack your things," Will ordered, turning from the window to once more face Kelly. "By the way, the patrol car went by a few minutes ago. I doubt it'll be back for a while."

Kelly's stomach fell at her feet. Had she really thought the police car would miraculously save the day? She refused to give Will the satisfaction of seeing her dismay. "I'm packed," she retorted.

"Let's go, then." He reached for her suitcase as Kelly picked up a denim jacket and her camera. "You won't need that," Will said of the camera, as though he considered it a mortal enemy whose presence he wasn't about to tolerate.

Kelly stopped, holding her ground both literally and figuratively. "I don't go anywhere without it."

Belligerent brown eyes and defiant green eyes met and held. A park scene a year ago flashed into two minds, a dramatic park scene that had changed lives.

"Yeah, I remember," Will said, his voice devoid of any emotion. "Just keep the damned thing away from me."

IT HAD BEEN a long while since he'd been behind the wheel of a car, and he'd never been behind the wheel of a car this classy, Will thought as he backed Kelly's sports car from the garage and down the driveway. He thought of his own car, a secondhand, in-need-of-repair contraption that he'd sold to get the money to hire a private detective. The two vehicles were as different as night and day, as different as he and the woman who sat beside him. That her car was crimson-red in no way surprised him. A sassy lady would own a sassy car, and there was no doubt in his mind that Kelly Cooper was sassy.

"I'd appreciate it if you wouldn't strip the gears," Kelly said over the loud grinding noise.

In fact, maybe she was just a little too sassy, Will thought. "You're certainly getting brave, lady."

She glanced over at him, looking a little less courageous than she sounded. "I figure if you were going to kill me, you'd have done it by now...and don't call me lady."

As before, he ignored this request. "Don't press your luck, lady. The day isn't over yet."

Kelly gave him a scathing look, which Will ignored. His thoughts were elsewhere. As he'd cleared the driveway and pulled out onto the street, he'd noticed a car parked alongside the curb, across the street one house away. Even though he could see no one inside the car—the interior was as dark as the night—the back of Will's neck tingled. He told himself he was being foolish, but he knew that he couldn't afford to take any chances, and so he watched in his rearview mirror until the car, a pale shade of blue, dwindled in size. Obviously the car wasn't following him, Will assured himself. The tingling at his neck eased.

Even though he had been in San Francisco only once before, Will negotiated the streets as though he'd lived there all of his life. The long hours spent in the prison library, studying maps of the city until they'd been committed to memory were paying off now. He had one particular goal in mind. When he pulled into the cemetery, Kelly glanced over at him, her surprise clearly evident. As was his habit, Will offered no explanation.

Will was less familiar with the narrow meandering pathways of the cemetery than he'd been with the city streets. Creeping here and there through the warren, he advanced from one landmark to another, all of which he'd heard about from the private detective he'd hired, none of which he'd seen. A gnarled tree, an angel with spread wings, a pink granite mausoleum. Moving into a more modest section of the cemetery—here there were no elaborate gravestones, here there were no flowers, no trees to create shade and break the monotony of the grim landscape—Will drew the car to a slow halt. Shutting off the motor, he opened the car door and pocketed the keys as though they were his.

"C'mon," he ordered Kelly in a tone that once more brooked no opposition. Curiously, though, he'd spoken softly, as though out of respect for their location. It was a softness that seemed totally incongruous with his usual harshness.

Kelly followed obediently, seemingly cowed by his insistence.

After several minutes, during which he seemed to forget Kelly's presence, Will found what he'd been searching for. Hunching down onto the balls of his feet, he stared at the mound of earth. Carefully, he brushed aside the weeds from the simple gravestone, a gravestone which read: John Doe.

John Doe.

The anonymity angered Will, and he vowed before a God that he'd long ago renounced that one day he'd replace this obscene, no-nothing tribute with a proper one, a proper one that read: Stephen Andrew Stone.

"Hey, man, come on out to San Francisco for a while. We got lots of hot sun and lots of hotter women."

Will could hear his brother's voice skipping through the silence of the cemetery, through the silence of the early-autumn morning. He remembered well the phone call he'd gotten a year ago. He remembered, too, thinking that something was wrong. Not that his brother's request to come for a visit was unusual—over the years the requests had been numerous and sometimes Will had complied—but what was unusual this time were the strange vibes that Will was picking up on. On the surface, Stephen sounded fine, but below that surface Will detected anxiety. Maybe even something more. Something like downright fear.

"Is everything okay?" Will had asked.

"Sure, everything's okay. It's even better than okay. That's why I want you to come out. I've got this great job, a new apartment, a new car. Hell, yeah, everything's perfect. That is, if you'd come on out."

Will had gone to San Francisco, as he'd known he would the moment he'd suspected his brother needed him. He'd never turned his back on Stephen and he never would. He was the only family he had. Both of them were products of a Chicago ghetto, products of a dysfunctional family and each had clung to the other. Interestingly, Stephen, older than he by two years, was always subordinate to Will. From the beginning, Will had known that Stephen was their father's favorite. At least their father hadn't put the same demands on Stephen that he had on his younger son. Stu Stone had said it was because Stephen was incapable of meeting them.

Deep in his heart, Will knew this was true. Stephen was weak-willed; his eye was often caught by the flash of fool's gold. For all that, however, Will loved his brother, protected his brother, would have given his life for him. Which, ironically, was the very thing he did, Will thought as he meticulously began to pull the weeds from the gravestone.

Yeah, he'd gone to San Francisco. And had had his suspicions confirmed. Something had been wrong. Stephen hadn't acted normally. He'd spent a lot of time, when he'd thought Will wasn't looking, taking quick glances out of the window, as though he'd been watching for someone. He'd seemed to be waiting for something to happen, a fact borne out by his jumping out of his skin every time the phone rang. Stephen's jitteriness aside, Will would have suspected something was out of kilter, simply because Stephen was living well beyond what should have been his means.

Will had wondered just what kind of high-paying job his brother had at Anscott Pharmaceuticals. The truth was that neither he nor Stephen had more than a high school education, with unimpressive grades at that. Stephen, because he just didn't have the mental prowess; Will because he hadn't applied himself. When Will had asked his brother about his job at Anscott, Stephen had been vague, though he did acknowledge how ironic it was that he was working for a drug company. As a child, Stephen had had a tonsillectomy. The anesthetic and pain medication had frightened the young boy. Woozy, he had believed that demons were chasing him. From that time on, he never took medication unless it was forced down him. As an adult, he even refused all alcohol, including beer.

Two days into the visit, Will found a gun in the nightstand by his brother's bed. Holding the weapon with its distinctive silver handle he'd really begun to worry.

"What's this?" he'd asked, confronting his brother.

Even now, Will recalled the unadulterated fear that had flashed upon Stephen's handsome, suntanned face. *"Where did you get that?"*

"From your nightstand."

"Ah, man, what are you doing? Spying on me?"

"I wasn't spying on you. I was looking for the newspaper. The nightstand drawer was open. I couldn't help but see the gun."

Stephen had raked his fingers through his wavy black hair. *"Hey, look, it's no big deal. Everyone has a gun out here. For protection."*

"For protection from what?" Will had asked, adding before his brother could answer, *"What, who, are you afraid of?"*

"No one," Stephen answered. *"Look, man, get off my case, all right?"*

It had been the first time since childhood that Will could remember his brother raising his voice at him. It had hurt then and the memory hurt now. Will's hand hesitated in the act of pulling away weeds. Instead, he carefully, gently, traced the deeply gouged letters that formed the name John Doe. *Ah, Stephen, why couldn't you have trusted me? Maybe if you had, I could have prevented what happened.*

Somewhere in the distance, a bird cawed, a shrill sound that reminded Will of the telephone which had awakened him early in the morning following his discovery of the gun. The phone had been answered quickly—on the first ring. When Will had arisen minutes later, the apartment was empty. His brother was gone. As was the gun. A notation on a pad, which appeared to have been nervously, perhaps even unknowingly, jotted down, bore the name of a nearby park, with the additional words "pansy bed." An uneasy feeling clawing at him, Will had gone to the park. He'd found a pansy bed with little problem. He'd wished to God that had been all he'd found.

When he'd realized that a trail of blood led into nearby brushes, he'd followed it and had discovered a man dead from a gunshot wound to the chest. To Will's horror, he recognized the gun lying beside the body. It was Stephen's. Without thinking, acting only on pure instinct, Will had picked up the weapon and had begun to wipe it clean of prints. While he'd been doing this, the redhaired woman had appeared.

KELLY WATCHED from the sidelines, a spectator observing a man in a form of worship. Even the way he knelt suggested a reverence, as did the way he plucked away weeds and grass from the gravestone, and the way he gently fingered the engraved generic name. Whoever was buried here occupied a lion's portion of Will Stone's heart. This insight startled her. That this man was capable of such caring startled her. All she'd seen of him was a rock-hard harshness, a winter-chilled coldness. After all, he was a criminal, a man convicted of murder. Such a man wasn't supposed to feel. Was he? And yet, this man did. At least for whoever was buried here in this ignominious plot of earth.

"Who is he?" Kelly asked, surprised at her own question, but unable to curtail her curiosity. "Who is this John Doe?"

Will glanced up from where he knelt, mirroring a pose that was almost an exact replica of the one he had taken a year before. This time, however, the red-haired, green-eyed woman didn't have a camera in her hands. What she had, though, was just as deadly. Maybe more so. What she had was a question that would force him to bare his soul. He'd stopped doing that a long time ago, because baring your soul made you vulnerable. And when you were vulnerable, people, the vultures of society, moved in for the kill.

The really crazy thing was, though, that he had a sudden urge to answer this woman's question. He had the urge to tell her that this John Doe was his brother, the guy he'd played stickball with, the guy he'd protected when their father had gone on a drunken rampage, the guy he'd taken a fifteen-year rap for. The guy he'd loved. Will wanted to tell her that he'd waited to hear from his brother throughout the long weeks before the trial, throughout the trial itself. But there had been no word. Stephen seemed to have vanished from the face of the earth.

Of course he never told anyone about his brother. As a result, with his drifter status—he never stayed long in one place, though he'd always kept in touch with Stephen—it had just been assumed that he'd wandered into San Francisco and had gotten involved in a bad drug deal, a theory corroborated by the fact that the dead man had drugs on him. The prosecution had also established Will as a loner, a brawler, a malcontent with a chip on his shoulder. It was even learned that he had a criminal record for breaking and entering. Will didn't bother to explain the circumstances, circumstances that had led him several years before to break into a garage in some small town in North Carolina one cold night in search of shelter.

In light of the evidence piled against him, and in light of his own silence, the guilty verdict had come as no surprise to Will. He'd tolerated his loss of freedom by telling himself that he was protecting his brother, whom he'd come to believe was dealing drugs. He'd believed then and now that Stephen had sold the dead man drugs and had used the money he'd received to disappear. Will had hired a detective. Stephen had to be found. He had to be helped. He had to accept responsibility for what had happened in the park that fateful morning. But none of that would ever come to pass now. Stephen was dead . . . from an overdose.

Yeah, he had the urge to tell Kelly Cooper this and more. Like how angry he was that his brother had once again been drawn to the flash of fool's gold, angry that his brother had fled, leaving him to clean up his mess, angry that someone had taken his brother's life, because, in the end, the heart defying all logic, he'd loved Stephen.

"Who is this man? Who is this John Doe?"

Though the urge might be strong, Will wasn't stupid enough to share what lay hidden in his heart. He couldn't trust this woman any more than he could trust anyone else. In fact, she'd already betrayed him once, unwittingly and unmaliciously perhaps, but nonetheless thoroughly. Besides, he'd learned a long time ago that people didn't really care what Will Stone thought, or felt. Why should Kelly Cooper be any different?

Will stood and stared at Kelly, once more with hostile eyes. "None of your business," he said, starting for the car without another word.

Kelly watched him go. Although his curt, evasive reply stung, it hadn't surprised her. It only reinforced what she already knew. Will Stone was a complex, troubled man, who felt much more than he was prepared to admit. There was no doubt that he'd cared deeply for a man named John Doe.

CHAPTER THREE

"MAKE THE CALL," Will ordered, adding, "And no funny business."

Only seconds before, Will had stopped the car in front of a pay phone. As Kelly dug through her purse for change, she prayed that he would remain in the car while she made the call, but, even as she was praying, she knew she was wasting her time. Sure enough, he'd accompanied her to the phone and now stood at her side like a prison warden.

Removing the phone from the hook, Kelly glanced up at him. "And what do you suggest I tell them? That I've been taken hostage, and that I'll get back to them when my captor comes to his senses and realizes that he can't outrun the long arm of the law?"

Will ignored her sarcasm. "Tell them you're sick. Tell them that you've got the flu, a cold, anything. Just keep it short and to the point. Tell them you'll be in touch when you're feeling better."

"How original," Kelly commented under her breath.

"Just do it," Will said, grabbing the quarter from her fingers and depositing it in the slot. It tinkled as it fell, a hollow sound that matched the hollow feeling in

Kelly's stomach. When she still hesitated, he said, "Now!"

Kelly checked her address book and punched in the number of the United Press International office, which had helped to coordinate the UNICEF project. Even as the phone was ringing, she wondered how she could slip some kind of coded message to them. And would they be clever enough to pick up on it if she did?

"Rachel, please," Kelly said when someone answered the phone.

"No funny business," Will mouthed, repeating the warning.

"I heard you the first time, Stone. I'm not deaf— Oh, Rachel," she said into the phone.

"Sound sick!"

Kelly coughed, a faked croup that blared through the telephone like a blast of thunder. When she spoke, her forced hoarse voice sounded as though it belonged to someone calling from the grave.

Will, his eyes thin slits of displeasure, glared at her.

She looked away, and spoke into the receiver. "This is Kelly. Yeah. Yeah. Sick. As a dog." She coughed again, with no more authenticity than the first time. "Flu, cold, something. Oh, yeah, fever. Lots of fever. Hot as a firecracker. Yeah, called a doctor. In fact, he's here now. Made a house call and everything. A regular saint this man is," she said, glancing up at Will with a look that defied him to silence her.

He slid his palm over the receiver. "Watch it," he whispered.

"No, no, I'm here," Kelly said when Will removed his hand. His don't-mess-with-me look remained in place, however. But then, so did her look of defiance. "Just the doctor. Telling me to watch it. You know how they are, not wanting you to overdo. Right, antibiotics. No, a few days in bed, he says, and I'll be good as new. Look, I'll fly to Zurich as soon as I can. Yeah, sure, I'll take care. Right, right, okay, bye."

In grand finale fashion, Kelly coughed once more, a long hacking spasm that sounded like a wild animal in heat, and hung up the phone.

Will's glare had turned into an out-and-out glower. "That was the worst job of acting I've ever heard."

"Yeah, well, you should have taken Meryl Streep hostage," Kelly retorted as she brushed a bobbing red curl from her forehead and pranced back to the car.

Will watched her, thinking that Meryl Streep, or anyone else, for that matter, would probably be a much easier hostage. But it was too late. He was stuck with this brassy redhead who didn't seem to understand her subordinate position. Climbing in beside her, Will looked in her direction. She stared straight ahead, as though he didn't exist.

"Watch your p's and q's, lady," Will warned.

Still, she kept her eyes averted.

"This is no picnic we're on," he said.

Kelly continued to face straight ahead, with not so much as a single word slipping from her lips.

Will mumbled something about uncooperative hostages and started the car. As he pulled away from the curb, he ground the gears.

This time, Kelly didn't notice. She was too busy hoping that Rachel was wondering why she'd mentioned flying to Zurich when she'd been scheduled to fly to London. Kelly smiled inwardly. Will Stone had underestimated her.

"GIVE ME SOME MONEY," Will said, twenty minutes later as he pulled into the parking lot of a fast-food restaurant.

"What do you mean give you some money?"

"Just what I said. Give me some money. Five bucks will do."

"Terrific," Kelly said, as she once more flung open her handbag. "A cheap kidnapper. Not even a Dutch-treat kidnapper. Oh, no, I have to get a moocher, a bum, a—"

"Will you just shut up and give me the money?" Will said, extending his hand. "And I'm not a bum. You just remember that."

It struck Kelly as odd that Will Stone didn't refute being a murderer, but jumped to defend himself against being a bum. She said nothing, however, except an acerbic, "Well, excuse me, Mr. Trump."

Will wondered if the woman beside him had any idea how difficult it was for him to be beholden to anyone for anything. Money had been a scarce commodity in his life, but he'd always managed to make his own way, to stand on his own two feet. Now, however, he had no choice. His wallet was pauper-thin, except for prison coupons, which had no value in the real world, and a couple of tattered-edged snapshots, which had no value at all—except to him.

Kelly slapped a crisp five dollar bill into the palm of Will's hand. "There," she said. "But I'm keeping a tab of every dime you owe me." As she spoke, she rummaged through her purse for a piece of paper and a pen. Once she'd found them, she began to write. "And don't think I'm not including that phone call, too."

"You do that," Will said, directing the car to the carry-out window. "What do you want?"

"Nothing," she said stubbornly.

"You've got to eat."

"I'm not hungry."

Kelly's stomach growled, belying her words. Will glanced in her direction. As was becoming habit, they engaged in a battle of wills. He won. Without asking her again, he ordered her a biscuit and sausage sandwich and a cup of coffee. He ordered the same for himself. Once it had come and had been paid for, Will pulled the car into a parking slot at the restaurant and, without a word, began to eat.

Only then did Kelly realize how ravenous he was. Though he ate slowly, it was obvious that he was making an effort to do so. It showed remarkable self-control. Funny, self-control wasn't a trait she'd ever associate with a murderer. For the first time since the Stone Man had broken into her apartment, Kelly looked at him, really looked at him, and wondered just who, and what, he was.

"Eat!" he barked, drinking the last of the coffee and crushing the disposable cup in his large hand.

His voice jarred her back to the reality of the situation. It didn't matter who or what he was; he'd taken her hostage. He was her enemy.

They headed north. Kelly didn't bother asking their destination, because she knew she'd be wasting her breath. Instead, she took her cue from her captor and didn't say a word, not even an hour later when he pulled into the parking lot of a discount store.

"Get out," he ordered.

"Do you ever say anything nicely?"

Will scowled and said, sarcasm dripping from every word, "Would you please do me the honor of accompanying me into the store?"

"I just can't think of anything I'd like more," Kelly said as she opened the car door and got out.

Instantly, Will was beside her, planting his hand at the small of her back as a reminder of his presence.

"Behave," he cautioned as they started toward the building.

Because the store had just opened for daily business, there was a limited number of shoppers. Kelly tried to make eye contact with each one she passed, hoping to signal her situation. No one, however, seemed the slightest bit interested.

The hand at her back tightened. "Cut it out," a dark voice growled.

Maintaining the pressure on her back, Will guided her to the section of the store he wanted and, within minutes, he had selected a pair of jeans, a shirt, a change of underwear and socks, and a brown corduroy jacket.

"Geez, is there anything else you'd like? Perhaps I could buy you a home in the suburbs or send you on a European vacation? What if I just send your kids to college?" Will ignored her. She nodded toward the bundle in his arms, "Don't you think you ought to try those things on?"

"How stupid do you think I am?" Will asked. "You'd be halfway to Oregon before I got out of the dressing room."

"I doubt that," Kelly retorted, angling her head in the direction of a policeman who had just come into view. "But I'm quite certain I could make it to him."

"Don't even think it," he said, his voice once more low and gravelly and giving no hint that his heart had stumbled into an erratic rhythm at the sight of the policeman.

"Then don't give me the chance," she answered, her voice dead serious as she made her position clear. "Now or anytime, because I promise you I'll take it."

"Your point is taken. I'll just have to make certain you don't get the chance, won't I?"

"Can you do that?"

"You had better believe it."

By the time they reached the cashier at the front of the store, the officer had left.

Will's unmitigated gall, his high-handedness angered Kelly, just as his nearness disturbed her. The sensation of it reminded her of something that she didn't want to be reminded of. Namely, that she was a woman, a woman who hadn't fully recovered from the breakup of her marriage. In an ironic way, both she and Will Stone had spent time in prison. The only difference was, he had broken free. In many respects, she was still incarcerated.

Forcing her mind from the painful subject, she retreated behind a sullen anger of her own. "You won't get away with this," she felt compelled to restate.

But get away with it he did. At least at the discount store. Not only did he return them safely to the car, he once more got Kelly to pay for the items he'd purchased. The first thing she did was record $54.99 in the running tab she was keeping. It gave her a tremendous sense of satisfaction, since it seemed the only thing at present that she had any control over.

"THE POLICE STILL have no clue as to the whereabouts of convict Will Stone, who made a daring escape from Folsom Prison yesterday in a delivery truck. Authorities urge extreme caution be exercised, stating that the prisoner is dangerous. It's unknown whether he's armed. If you see someone who matches this description, please notify. . ." The announcer went on to give a vivid description of Will.

Will turned the knob of the radio, bringing blessed silence once more to the car. He glanced over at Kelly, who stared straight ahead, as though she'd heard nothing. Even so, Will could tell she wasn't unmoved by the news bulletin, nor unmoved by the fact that he was watching her.

Convict. The word sounded strange to Will's ears. Even now, after six months behind bars, he could never think of himself as a convict. Technically, though, he was. Being a convict had nothing to do with being guilty of a crime. It referred to a person found guilty of a crime and sentenced by a court. And that he had been. Twelve jurors, all supposedly fair-minded citizens, had heard the evidence and pronounced him guilty. Guilty! There were times he wanted to shout his innocence from the rooftops. Most of the time, however, he didn't give diddly-squat what people thought. Let them think him guilty, let them think him dangerous, let them think him kin to the devil. Hell, maybe he *was* the son of Satan!

Convict. The word sounded strange to Kelly's ears. She'd never met a convict before. She wondered how he had fared in prison. What sort of man had he been before he went in? Thoughts of prison led to thoughts of the trial. In turn, that led to the question never far from her mind.

"Why didn't you say anything?" she asked. "At the trial, I mean?"

"I didn't have anything to say."

Kelly gave a short laugh of disbelief. "You were on trial for murder, for your life, and you didn't have anything to say?"

Will looked at her and then back toward the road, and Kelly saw his jaw muscles clench. "What was the point? Everyone had already made up his mind."

"I hadn't."

Again Will looked in Kelly's direction. "Oh, yes, you had. You made your mind up the moment you saw me hunched over that body."

Kelly started to deny his accusation, then stopped. Had she thought him guilty? It had all happened so quickly that she hadn't known what to think. In retrospect, she supposed she *had* believed him guilty—she remembered fearing for her own life—and yet, during the trial, she longed to hear him deny that guilt. What did that mean? Did she have doubts, after all?

Obviously so, because she heard herself asking, "Did you kill that man in the park?"

The muscles in Will's jaw tightened again until his profile looked chiseled from granite. Silent second after silent second passed. When seconds led to minutes, Kelly knew that, just as before, he had no intention of confirming or denying his guilt. Once more, he had become the Stone Man.

"WHAT ARE WE stopping for?" Kelly asked. They were three hours into the trip, still heading north with no declared destination.

"What do you usually stop at a service station for?" Will asked, bringing the sleek sports car to a halt in front of a self-service gas pump.

Throwing open the door, he unwound his long, lean legs and stepped out. The muscles he'd abused the day before when he'd jumped from the moving truck continued to scream for attention. What he wouldn't give for a hot shower!

Kelly had noticed his stiffness earlier, the way he favored one shoulder, the way he dragged one leg.

"What's wrong, Stone?" she asked, easing out of the car and stretching like a feline. "You getting too old to break out of prison?"

Will glanced up from where he was pumping gasoline. He couldn't help but notice the way the rays of the sun struck Kelly's hair, weaving gilded threads among the russet corkscrew curls. "You want to keep your voice down?"

"Not particularly," she said, her reply saucy, her green eyes shimmering with impertinence. She couldn't help but notice the way the sun played in Will's hair, highlighting the brown until it was almost black. A black that, like a bolt of satin, begged to be touched.

"Well, do it anyway."

"Sure, Stone, but you're absolutely no fun as far as kidnappers go."

"Yeah, well, as far as hostages go, you leave a lot to be desired, too. Give me some money," he added, returning the hose to its slot on the gas pump and screwing the lid back on the gas tank.

"Why not?" she said, reaching inside the car for her purse. "I mint this stuff on my day off, you know. Oh, no, guess I didn't mint enough this week. All I've got left is a ten." This she waved in the air with obvious pleasure. "Now, what are we going to do? I know. How about we rob the joint? C'mon, this is our chance to be Bonnie and Clyde."

"You're real mouthy, you know that, lady?"

Kelly grinned. "Guess you should have kidnapped Marcel Marceau. And as I keep telling you—stop calling me lady. I have a name. Kelly Cooper. Can we say Kelly Cooper?''

Will was not amused. Grabbing the purse from her hands, he ransacked her wallet, his fingers finally coming to rest on a credit card. Retaining the card, he tossed the purse back into the car and grinned mirthlessly. ''I accept all major credit cards.''

Kelly's grin turned sarcastic. ''What a peach of a guy.''

Will encircled her upper arm with his fingers. ''C'mon,'' he said as he headed for the office of the station.

Kelly balked. ''I'll wait here.''

''I don't think so,'' Will said, tightening his grasp. ''Besides, you'll have to sign the credit card receipt.'' Will saw the idea flash through Kelly's mind as if it had appeared above her head like a caption in a comic. ''Don't even think it. I'm going to check everything you write on that receipt, and it better be nothing more than your name.''

''Spoilsport,'' Kelly groused.

The sign above the door of the service station proclaimed that the town was Redding and that the owner of the establishment was Bo Boggess. Bo—Kelly assumed it was Bo—smiled as they entered the building.

''Hi,'' the large-framed, bald-headed man said.

''Hi,'' Will returned. ''We want to pay for the gas.'' As he spoke, he placed the credit card on the old, but meticulously clean counter.

''Sure thing,'' the man said, reaching for the credit card and beginning to process the purchase. That done, he pushed the slip, along with the pen and card, toward Will.

Will waited for Kelly to step forward, which she took her own sweet time doing. Will knew that her slowness was designed to irritate him. It did.

"Tell me, Bo—" Kelly glanced up and smiled. "—you are Bo, aren't you?"

The man smiled back. "Yes, ma'am."

"Do you need a phone number?"

"No, ma'am, you look like honest folks to me."

Oh great, Kelly thought, this Bo Boggess must be half-blind. There she was with not a dab of makeup on and with her hair looking as if she'd used an eggbeater to comb it. By comparison to Will, however, she looked as though she'd spent hours on her toilette. A lock of his hair fell down over his forehead, while a stubble sprouted on his face, giving it a tough, mean look. To complete the picture, the knuckles of his left hand had scabbed over, suggesting that he'd been in a doozy of a brawl. No, there'd be no counting on Bo Boggess. If Big Foot himself came in, Bo would probably think him well-groomed and honest-looking.

"Oh, we are that," Kelly said. "Honest folks, I mean. Aren't we?" she asked, turning to Will.

To his credit, Will did a reasonably good job of hiding his scowl. "You bet we are," he said, as he checked Kelly's signature, tore off the customer copy and pocketed it. "Thanks," he said to the owner of the station and fitted his hand at the small of Kelly's back. He discreetly gave her an insistent nudge.

"Oh, wait a minute," Kelly said, as though the idea had just occurred to her, although Will recognized the thin performance for what it was. "I think I'll go to the rest room while I'm here." She smiled up at Bo as she reached out her hand. "That is the key hanging there, isn't it?"

Bo turned around and plucked a key from over the cash register. "Yes, ma'am, gotta keep them locked. People trash them if I don't."

"What is this world coming to, Bo?" Kelly asked, taking the key that was offered to her.

Will intercepted it. Kelly scowled.

Once more, the service station owner seemed to notice nothing out of the ordinary. "Oh, by the way," he said. "The key fits both rest rooms."

"Thanks," Will said, shoving Kelly ahead of him in the same way that a huge wave pushes forward all in its path. Once outside, he snapped, "You'll be lucky if I don't throttle you here and now."

"Hey," Kelly said. "Is it my fault I have to go to the bathroom? My kidneys aren't impressed with this hostage situation."

"Then go," Will said, propelling Kelly toward the rest room. Once there, he jammed the key into the lock, threw open the door and thrust her inside. He then closed the door behind her and locked it.

Locked it?

Kelly heard the key turning and couldn't believe her ears. She tried the door, but found it exactly as she knew she would—securely fastened.

"Hey!" she shouted, pounding on the door.

"Be quiet or I'm coming in," he growled.

"You can't do this. This is inhumane. This is against the Geneva Convention. Will Stone?" she cried. "Unlock this door. Now!"

Nothing. Silence. Except for someone—Will—in the adjacent rest room.

Calling him a most unflattering name, Kelly slammed her palm against the door one last time. She was mad. Madder than hell. This was the final indignity in a long line of indignities. Brushing a spiral of hair from her forehead, she considered her options. Which, at best, seemed limited. She could leave a message on the bathroom wall if—how she hated that word!—her purse with the ballpoint pen inside it, hadn't been left in the car. Maybe she could scratch a message with...with...with what? Her nail? She looked at the pitiful nubs she called nails. Forget that idea. Maybe she could find something in the rest room she could use.

She checked the toilet, for anything, some metal doodad perhaps, that could be unhinged or disconnected, and used to scratch a message. Nothing. Absolutely nothing. She checked the floor—maybe someone had dropped something. Then she examined the mirror, the radiator, the sink, the window—

Kelly stopped.

The window?

Over the radiator was a window. A horizontal, skinny... beautiful window.

All right!

Without hesitating, Kelly climbed on top of the radiator, balancing like a tightrope walker. After a few tries at wrestling with a lever, she managed to throw open the window. It swung outward, creating an escape route. It would be a narrow escape, but a narrow escape was better than none. Using the brick wall to gain a toehold, she began to crawl upward as she used her hands to haul herself forward. An inch...slip back two...gain another inch...scrape her palm...knee to wall...hand to window ledge. There! She pushed her head through. Please, dear God, let her hips fit. *No more brownies, I promise, if you'll only help me get through this window.*

She had just started through when something grabbed a fistful of her behind!

Even as she prayed that some guardian angel was giving her a boost, she knew that the hand more probably belonged to the devil. And this devil had a specific name: Will Stone.

With a yank that ripped the pocket on her jeans, Will hauled the squirming Kelly from the window. On the way to the floor, she ricocheted off the wall and struck the radiator. Once on the floor, tremors of pain sluicing over her body, she blinked, focused, blinked again. Suddenly two legs came into view. Since she needed something to focus on to prevent herself from passing out, she visually followed those legs up a pair of snug-fitting blue pants torn at the knee, up muscular legs, up a masculinely impressive pelvic juncture, up a dirty T-shirt peeking from a jacket, up past a mouth set in a thin, grim line.

Her eyes stopped at Will's eyes. At Will's narrowed eyes. He said nothing. Not a word.

Two things crossed Kelly's mind: One, she was going to be sore as heck from this scuffle; two, this time she quite possibly had pushed Will Stone too far.

SHE'D MADE him angry.

Buried deep in the passenger seat, Kelly kept stealing glances at the taciturn man beside her. She kept stealing glances because she was afraid anything more would attract his attention. And, if she did that, he might actually look at her directly and she'd be burned to cinders by his wrathful fury. Hours and miles—they were now in Oregon—had passed since the incident at the service station, and not a word had been exchanged between them. Just a hostile silence that was colder than an Arctic iceberg.

Yeah, he was angry, with a capital *A*, and she was... She was what? Angry, too? She tried the word on for size, seeing if it fit. Yeah, she was angry, darned angry that Will Stone had invaded her neat, orderly, perfectly controlled life, a life that, except for a broken marriage, was based on the solid ground of success. Success. Failure. Maybe that was what was really eating at her. Since Will Stone's arrival, she'd known nothing but failure, and she just wasn't accustomed to its bitter taste.

Kelly stole another glance at her captor, noticing in the process that the fray back at the service station had caused his knuckles to bleed once more. Good, she thought! Served him right! Suddenly feeling smug, she vowed to find a way to best him yet. Sooner or later, he'd come to realize just who he was dealing with. After all, she was—here the sleepless night and stressful morning caught up with her and she yawned—special. Special, she repeated silently, as the monotonous motion of the car, combined with the warmth of the sun streaming through the window, danced lazily through her. She closed her eyes, intending to rest them. Yeah, she was special, all right. Special as in can't make an error. Special as in got to be perfect. Special as in got to make Daddy proud.

HE *WAS* ANGRY.

Will stared straight ahead, not daring to look at the woman beside him. He was afraid of what he'd say or do if she gave him any more lip. She'd just about pushed him to the limit. Okay, okay, so he didn't have a right to expect her complete and heartfelt cooperation, but, that aside, shouldn't she have enough common sense to know when she was outgunned? Obviously not. She'd tried to escape twice now, and there was no doubt in his mind that she'd try a third, a fourth, a fifth time—whatever it took. This woman just didn't know when to throw in the towel. This woman had no knowledge whatsoever of the meaning of the word *quit*.

Despite himself, Will couldn't help but respect her determination. Maybe, he thought painfully, the reason he admired it so was because he possessed none of it. No, that wasn't entirely true. He wasn't that quick to give up...on anything except himself. Why was that?

He'd asked this question a thousand times over the years. Each time he did, he always arrived at the same answer. If you're told something often enough, you begin to believe it. If you're told you'll never amount to anything, that's exactly what you amount to. At least in your own mind.

At the soft sigh that interrupted the silence, Will glanced over at Kelly. She was asleep. Sound asleep. Alternating his gaze between her and the road, he allowed himself his first real look at her. With her head slumped to the side, she looked so peaceful and so...vulnerable. Another realization stole through his consciousness like a swift thief. She also looked pretty.

Why hadn't he noticed this before? He'd seen her red hair—its flaming color wasn't something you could miss—but he'd failed to observe, at least consciously so, the dozens of short curls that coiled about her head in a bewildering, beguiling kind of bedlam. Her hair—both its color and style—suited her. It was as feisty, as unmanageable, as she.

Will let his gaze drift to her fair-complexioned cheeks, her small nose that threatened to turn upward, but never quite did, her cinnamon-hued eyelashes that formed delicate half moons against her pale skin. His eyes moved lower...to the denim jacket gaping open to reveal a maize-colored sweater...to the small swell of breasts that mounded beneath the clinging fabric...to the waist that was small enough to be doll-like.

Beneath her clothing, was she wearing the tiny scraps of lace and satin that he'd seen her shoving into the suitcase? Though the question surprised him, he made no attempt to fight against it. An image flashed through his mind, an image of his hand splayed wide across her backside only seconds before he dragged her back into the rest room at the service station. It had been a long time since he'd thought of lace and satin, a long time since he'd thought of feminine backsides. More to the point, it had been a long time since he'd allowed himself to think of them. It seemed futile when all a man saw were bars and more bars, stretching before him into fifteen endless years.

It was still futile, he reminded himself. He was going back to prison. That is, if he wasn't killed first. Besides, the woman seated next to him wouldn't give a man like him the time of day. Which was fine with him. He had more important things on his mind than a woman. He had a mission to fulfill. Unfortunately, he needed this woman to fulfill it, which meant that he couldn't allow her to escape. He knew she'd try again, but he couldn't allow it. He had to come up, and quickly, with some way to guarantee that she wouldn't.

He pulled the car to a halt at a red light. They were in some small town that he didn't even bother to check the name of. All the little towns, with their faceless people and look-alike stores, had blended together. Stores. There was the usual smattering, a drugstore, a couple of fast-food places, a hardware store, and a dress shop whose window was filled with fall fashions unimaginatively arranged on stiffly posed mannequins.

Adjacent to the dress shop stood a pawnshop. This was one type of establishment he hadn't seen a lot of in these pass-through-in-a-blink-of-an-eye towns. Perhaps because of that, Will's gaze wandered over the sign out front advertising some of the wares within. There was a like-new guitar, an upright vacuum cleaner, a one-carat diamond pendant necklace, and genine (the *u* was missing) police handcuffs.

The light changed from red to green.

Someone honked.

Instead of moving on through the light, however, Will hooked a sharp, unplanned right-hand turn. Maybe, just maybe, things were beginning to look up.

CHAPTER FOUR

"WHERE ARE WE?"

The stillness of the car and the silence of the engine had awakened Kelly, who bolted to an upright position, her vision blurred, her mouth tasting like a wad of cotton. Even though groggy, she was angry with herself for falling asleep. She had to stay alert. She had to stay vigilant.

Will gave a shrug and said, "I don't know. Just another little town."

"Why are we stopping?" Kelly raked her fingers through her hair. She looked through the windshield. "A pawnshop?"

"Get out," Will said by way of an answer.

Kelly was growing accustomed to, if not appreciative of, her abductor's imperious attitude. If he'd graced her with a civil reply, she probably would have dropped dead on the spot.

"Yes, sir," she said, giving him a clipped military salute.

Will grabbed her wrist in midair. "Listen to me, and listen real good. I'm tired, I'm hungry, I'm under a lot of pressure, and frankly, lady, you've pushed me to the limit of my patience. If I didn't need you as cover, I'd dump you on the side of the road in a New York minute. Maybe quicker. Now, we're going into that store, and I don't want to hear a word, not a word, out of you. You got that?''

As though his question didn't deserve an answer, Kelly said nothing. She simply pulled her hand slowly, scornfully from his grasp.

Her eyes burned into his, his into hers, before he said, ''Let's go.''

The inside of the pawnshop was reminiscent of a clean, but cluttered, attic. Musical instruments abounded. A set of drums crouched by the door, guitars gathered on one wall, a saxophone slumped in a corner ready to wail its throaty notes. Contained within a glassed-in counter winked abandoned diamonds and a variety of colorful gemstones. These were followed by row upon soldierlike row of watches, some gleaming in gold, some shining in silver. Necklaces and bracelets lay next to a silver-handled hairbrush and a silver baby cup.

The thick smoke of failure wafted in the air, reminding Will how much he hated pawnshops. The few times he'd been in them had only served to point out that he'd failed—again. These were not establishments frequented by winners.

''Can I help you?''

''Yeah,'' Will answered, ''I'm interested in the handcuffs you have advertised.'' He noticed Kelly look up with a frown. He hoped she wouldn't make a scene.

"Yes, sir," the shopkeeper said, "I've got one pair left. Those handcuffs sold like a house afire. Go figure, huh?"

As he spoke, the clerk had placed a pair of metal handcuffs on the counter. "Genuine police handcuffs," he confirmed, adding, "I keep the key in a desk drawer in the back. I'll just get it." With this, the man disappeared through a doorway.

Kelly charged like a wounded rhino. "You creep! You jerk! You . . . you lowlife!"

Will whirled, his glacier-cold eyes reminding her that she wasn't to speak a word. She took perverse pleasure in disobeying him.

"How dare you—" she began.

Will cut her off by abruptly encircling her upper arm with his hand, his fingers digging deep into her flesh. He drew her to him until they were standing nose to nose. Their breath, uneven and coming quickly, mingled, an intimacy both were acutely aware of.

"I'll dare what I have to," Will snarled. "Now shut up!"

"Make me," Kelly ordered, spitting the words back at him. She knew she sounded like a ten-year-old on a school playground and didn't care in the least. Nobody, but nobody, was going to tell her to shut up. Nobody, but nobody, was going to put her in handcuffs. Certainly not a two-bit hoodlum with a bad attitude and no social graces.

"You've got five seconds to zip your lip, lady."

"Five . . . four . . . three . . ." she said tauntingly, her eyes as hot as a blistering sun.

Will had the sinking feeling that he was losing control of the situation. And it was all his fault. You never issued an ultimatum unless you were in a position to follow through with it.

"...two...one...so, what now, Stone? Gonna wrestle me to the floor? Gonna cuff me? Gonna—"

"Here's the key," the shopkeeper said, walking back into the room.

In an attempt to salvage the situation, Will spun around, jerking Kelly to his side. Their hipbones bumped together, the unexpected jarring motion almost throwing Kelly to the floor. Will steadied her by tightening his powerful arm—powerful was her interpretation—around her slim—slim was his interpretation—waist.

The clerk, who'd missed the whole fracas, smiled and said, "Let me show you how the key works."

"Oh, he knows all about handcuffs," Kelly said, smugly looking up at Will. "Don't you?"

If Will had sensed earlier that he was losing control, he knew now that he'd lost it completely. All hell was about to break loose, and there was no way he could stop it...her. There would be no silencing this woman. He had warned her, threatened her, and had even thought that he'd made a convert out of her back at the service station, but now he saw how wrong he'd been. Temporary silence, temporary acquiescence, was the best he could ever hope for from her.

Will realized that the shopkeeper was looking at him expectantly, obviously awaiting some kind of explanation as to his familiarity with handcuffs.

When Will said nothing, the clerk placed the key on the counter. "If you know how they work, I won't waste your time."

Kelly smiled suddenly, a huge smile that curved into the visual definition of maliciousness. "Oh, Aunt Tillie is going to be so pleased with the handcuffs."

As hoped, the statement ensnared the shopkeeper's attention. Along with Will's. The gleam in Kelly's eyes told Will that the situation had already gone to hell in a handbasket.

"Aunt Tillie's a little—" here Kelly lowered her voice, as though divulging a family secret "—strange. Kinky, even. If you know what I mean." She didn't give the shopkeeper time to answer. "Personally, I think it's Uncle Walter who's kinky, but that's neither here nor there. They have this little game they play. Uncle Walter pretends he's just broken out of prison and takes Aunt Tillie hostage."

Kelly smothered a cry as the arm around her waist squeezed the breath out of her.

The shopkeeper stared, his expression saying that he was wondering just what kind of customers had wandered into his shop.

Will was wondering something, too. Would a jury convict him of murder again if he strangled this woman right here. Somehow he didn't think so, not if the jurors were forced to spend a few frustrating minutes with her.

"How much are the handcuffs?" Will asked abruptly.

The man told him. "Will that be all?"

"Yeah," Will said, reaching into the pocket of his jacket, removing Kelly's credit card, and placing it on the counter.

Kelly frowned. She hadn't realized that Will hadn't returned her card at the service station. She'd been too intent on escaping.

"No, wait!" Will cried suddenly, scattering thoughts of the credit card from Kelly's mind. "Let me see that," he said, pointing at the glass-encased cabinet.

That turned out to be a gold wedding band, a gold wedding band which Kelly stared at as though it had just landed on earth from another planet. Why in the world would Will Stone want to purchase a wedding band?

"The wedding ring?" The clerk was clearly as surprised as Kelly.

"Yeah," Will said. Taking the ring the man offered him, he studied it, and announced, "The size looks about right."

For what? Or rather for whom? Kelly thought. Inexplicably, even as the question flitted through her mind, an uneasy feeling settled about her. The feeling was nothing tangible, but rather a dark shadow that played hide-and-seek with her consciousness.

The dark shadow pounced. It took the form of Will's smile, which was every bit as smug as Kelly's had been earlier. He hugged her close. "The little lady and I were married yesterday. Sort of spur of the moment. There wasn't time for a ring."

Kelly's head whipped around, her gaze crashing into Will's.

"Was there, darling?" Will asked, his eyes daring her to contradict him.

A dozen thoughts raced through Kelly's mind, a dozen feelings through her heart. The charade he was suggesting scared her. It dredged up old feelings of failure. She could hear herself telling her ex-husband that she wanted out of their marriage. She shook her head. That marriage had nothing in common with this one. Will was only securing his safety. The police were looking for a man alone, not a man with a woman, certainly not a man with his wife. Despite herself, Kelly could still hear the echo of his softly drawled "darling."

Stay tough, she told herself, noticing the disparity between the warm smile at Will's lips and the cold look in his eyes. She angled her head to a position that could only be called stubborn. "No," she said unyieldingly, and Will understood exactly what she meant. A flat refusal to wear the ring. "And furthermore—"

Her "and furthermore" lingered in the air. Afraid of what revelation Kelly was on the verge of making, Will had to stop her and, short of risking that trial he'd been thinking about only seconds earlier, he knew of only one way to do it.

Kelly never saw the kiss coming. She saw the flash of fire, hostile fire, in his eyes; she saw the tilt, the lowering of his head. And then, the world was reduced to nothing but feeling, the feel of his mouth settling on hers (no, his mouth didn't just settle over hers; it took possession of it), the feel of bristly beard, the feel of his warm breath, the feel of anger. This latter expressed itself in the punishing firmness of his mouth. The kiss ended as abruptly as it had begun. The sudden absence of his lips surprised her as much as their sudden presence had.

For long moments following the kiss, Will simply stared at Kelly, as though he, too, had been surprised by something. Just what, she had no time to ponder.

"We'll take the ring," Will announced.

They were back to square one, an angry square one.

Minutes later, two car doors slammed shut.

"I won't wear the ring," Kelly said.

"Oh, yes, you will," Will retorted.

"I won't!"

"You will!"

With that, Will reached for her hand and jammed the slender gold band onto her finger. "And don't take it off until I tell you to."

Will gloated.

Kelly seethed.

Neither mentioned the kiss.

THEY ARRIVED in Seattle at sunset. Kelly had no idea if the city was their final destination. And she really didn't care. She was hungry and tired. The stress of the day's events had taken its toll, both physically and emotionally, leaving her little more than a zombie. She knew that Will, too, was exhausted. Not that she cared. In fact, if he fell flat on his face, she'd cheer...if she could muster up enough energy.

Will stopped at a fast-food restaurant, where he purchased hamburgers, fries and shakes which he placed on the seat between them. This time Kelly had the money ready—her last ten dollar bill, she reminded him with a haughty look. Will said nothing. Instead he drove to a nearby motel. Cutting off the engine, he turned to her.

"I suppose separate rooms would be out of the question?" she asked.

"Yes. Now get—"

"I know the drill," she said as she slung open the car door wearily, parroting him. "Get out, get out, get out."

Thoughts of food, a hot shower and a soft bed pushed all other thoughts out of Kelly's mind. She allowed Will to drag her inside to register. Not only did Will want the clerk to know that he wasn't traveling alone, he also wanted him to know that the woman with him was his wife.

His fourth wife, Kelly inserted, the sight of the ring on her finger momentarily reviving her spunk.

"At least you didn't mention Aunt Tillie and Uncle Walter," Will muttered on the way to their room minutes later.

"You didn't give me time."

Decorated in mauve and gray, the room looked like heaven to Kelly. Dropping her camera and suitcase on the floor, she plopped down into a chair, closed her eyes and made a noise somewhere between a grunt and a sigh. Yes, even though the devil stood nearby, this was heaven.

"Here," the devil said.

Kelly opened her eyes just in time to catch the sack sailing toward her. The smell of food danced beneath her nose, making her stomach growl in anticipation. She'd—they'd—had nothing to eat or drink since early that morning. Not even so much as a can of soda or a cup of coffee.

"Eat," Will ordered.

Kelly needed no prompting. The food tasted wonderful. From the side of the bed, Will devoured the hamburger and fries. It dawned upon her that he'd had nothing but institutional food for a long time, that this, along with what he'd had for breakfast, was his first reacquaintance with "civilian" food.

"What's prison food like?" she asked.

Will, still wearing his jacket, looked over at the woman who was still huddled in hers. He downed the last of his shake in one gulp. "Lousy," he answered. "Everything about prison is lousy."

"Yeah, well, I think that's the point. The wages of one's sin and all."

Will's eyes hardened. "Yeah." Standing, he shed his jacket and carelessly tossed it on the back of a chair. He reached for the handcuffs. "I need a shower. What do you want to be cuffed to?"

"A policeman?" Kelly suggested.

Will ignored her remark. "Get on the floor here by the dresser."

Kelly's hackles rose. "You're not really serious about these handcuffs?"

"Dead serious," he answered, unceremoniously hauling her, her half-eaten hamburger in her hand, from the chair onto the floor and securing one of her wrists to the massive dresser. Without looking back, he grabbed the pair of new jeans they'd bought, and started for the bathroom, saying as he did so, "And no calling out for help. My hearing is excellent."

"You're a real jerk, Will Stone!" she shouted after him. The last glimpse she had of him before the bathroom door closed was of him stripping off his T-shirt. His back, rippling with muscles, was tanned a golden brown. An image of the notorious chain gang came to mind, shirtless men manacled together, sweating in the sun. Though the image was archaic, Kelly could easily imagine Will in the scenario, a man who would remain a loner though bound to others, a man who wouldn't offer a single word of protest.

His shower seemed to run forever. Kelly finished her hamburger and spent the rest of the time trying to loosen the handcuffs. Although she knew perfectly well she wouldn't be able to get free, she felt obliged to try. The only thing she managed to accomplish was to tire herself out more. Anger flowing in her veins, she prayed to live long enough to get even with Will Stone.

The shower stopped. The sound of the curtain being drawn followed. Then came the rough rustle of what Kelly assumed was denim being unfolded. Less than a minute later, the door opened. Will stood on the threshold, barefoot, bare-chested, holding a towel which he passed repeatedly through his wet hair.

Kelly had seen men in her day, clothed and un-clothed, but there was something about the semiclad Will Stone that grabbed her attention. He was the most photogenic person she'd ever seen. This quality had intrigued her in the park; this quality intrigued her now. The crow's-feet around his eyes, the creases and shadows of his face, fascinated her, begged her to pick up a camera and capture what lay hidden beneath the surface of this complex man.

At this particular moment, however, she saw more. Something in the diamondlike beads of moisture glistening in the dark hair foresting his chest, something in the skintight fit of his jeans, something in the way the zipped, but unbuttoned, waist of the jeans lapped open—each and all defined masculinity. As did the rugged, beginning growth of beard. The beard also did one other thing: It called specific attention to the lips it framed.

Harsh lips.

Angry lips.

Lips that kissed punitively.

From out of nowhere came a question. Would the same lips know how to kiss softly, lovingly, passionately? Kelly only had time to register her surprise at the query—where in the world had it come from?—before she realized Will had spoken to her.

"What?"

"I said do you want to shower?"

Kelly pushed the thought about his lips out of her mind. "Aren't you afraid I'll escape down the drain?"

"Is that a yes or a no?"

"That's a yes," she answered, too eager for what he was offering to defer it any longer, however much her pride might demand otherwise.

Taking the key from the nightstand, Will crouched before her, the balls of his feet burrowing into the gray carpet. Her position necessitated that he lean into and across her to unfasten the clasp of the handcuffs. In so doing, the hair on his chest brushed against her nose, tickling her. She turned her head to the side.

"Will you be still?" he said gruffly.

"Will you hurry?" she replied just as curtly.

In the time it took her to rub her wrist, glower at Will, and shed her clothes in the corner of the bathroom, Kelly stood beneath the deliciously hot water of the shower. It sluiced over breasts and belly, running in rivulets down her legs. Turning, she angled her head backward, letting the water tunnel through her hair before escaping down her back and buttocks.

Escape.

She had to escape. But perhaps she should get a good night's sleep first. Tomorrow she'd be more alert, ready to take advantage of any opportunity that presented itself. Yeah, that's what she should do; she should get a good night's sleep. A vision of the downy-soft bed danced in her head more sweetly than any sugarplum fairies.

As she reached for the soap, the sight of the gold ring on her finger caught her eye.

"I won't wear the ring."

"Oh, yes, you will."

"I won't!"

"You will! And don't take it off until I tell you to!"

Once more, she resented Will's high-handedness. Once more, she thought of her failed marriage and her ex-husband. Gary and Will were vastly different. The former was a respected science professor, while Will was an escaped prisoner, a man convicted of murdering another human being. Gary had never raised his voice to her, while Will had done nothing but. Her ex-husband had no knowledge of what a threat was, while Will seemed to delight in delivering them. And yet, Will Stone had one thing over her ex-husband. Will Stone never would have allowed his wife, his woman, to walk away from him.

Dressed once more in her jeans and sweater, Kelly opened the bathroom door to make yet another observation. Gary had never made her as mad as Will Stone could without even trying, a fact he proved the instant he opened his mouth.

"You've got two choices," Will announced in the way of a greeting. He'd been watching the news on television, which he cut off abruptly after learning that Seattle newscasters didn't care enough about his escape to even mention it. "You can either share the bed with me, or I'll handcuff you to the dresser again."

Kelly told herself that it was his arrogance, not his bare chest, that made her chin tilt upward. "I'll take the handcuffs."

Without a word, Will stepped forward, dragged her to the floor, and once more handcuffed her to the leg of the dresser. He threw her a pillow and a blanket, then crawled into bed though it was barely seven o'clock. He turned off the lamp.

"You know, Stone," Kelly said, "I don't like you."

"Yeah, well, we're even, lady. I don't like you, either."

THE PALE BLUE CAR sneaked into the motel parking lot. After selecting a location that offered a measure of seclusion, while at the same time allowing a clear view of Kelly's red sports car, the driver shut off the engine. Slumping back, Mitch Brody rested his sandy-haired head against the seat and shut his sky-blue eyes. It was the first time he'd closed his eyes in hours. Tailing was hard on the old eyesight, harder on the old nerves. One careless moment and hours of discreet work could be lost by an unobserved turn, an unexpected stop. The police academy had trained him well, however. He hadn't lost his quarry, not at the service station, not at the pawnshop.

The police academy. He remembered being there as though it were only yesterday. He remembered graduation, his first beat as a police officer. He remembered the years of growth and maturity, years during which he was decorated and commended. He remembered being respected by his peers. Then suddenly one day, all of it was gone. He was no longer a police officer; he was no longer commended or respected. He had become an outcast, an officer who'd been given a chance to resign before being fired. The humiliation was the same. Either way, everyone knew that he'd been accused of taking a bribe.

The bitterness, always present, welled up in Mitch's throat. With his dismissal from the San Francisco Police Department, he'd lost everything—his career, his wife, his kid, most of all his self-esteem. Yeah, Connie couldn't wait to believe the worst of him, couldn't wait to boogie out of his life. Had she just been looking for a reason to leave? He'd known that things hadn't been great between them for a while, but he'd naively thought that every marriage suffered from such growing pains. Her leaving had been bad enough, but to worsen matters, she'd taken Scott out of state. Memories of bedtime stories, collecting baseball cards, and pitching to his ten-year-old son came flying at him like dark ghosts out of the past. The memories hurt. So much that he'd sell his soul for a good stiff drink.

Mitch opened his eyes, giving a wry snort of laughter. That was a joke. He no longer had a soul to sell. He'd already used it to purchase enough alcohol to sink a battleship. Yeah, nine months ago he'd lost everything, everything but a long-necked, full-hipped siren, one with punch and fire and capable of bringing about blessed forgetfulness. The bottle had become his friend, his lover, something he couldn't get through the day, and particularly the night, without. But this was different. Sweats and shakes be damned, he'd promised himself that he wouldn't take another drink until he found out what Will Stone was up to. Alcohol and driving didn't mix, and he certainly had no death wish. Or maybe he did and realized that he had to guard carefully against it. Either way, he'd nixed liquor for the present.

Mitch studied the door through which Will and Kelly had disappeared. Unless he was mistaken, they were settled in for the night. If he were Will Stone, he'd hole up for the night, too, hole up and get a few hours of shut-eye. And then what? It was the and-then-what that intrigued him.

Sighing, Mitch closed his eyes in earnest. He, too, needed a little sleep. He needed sleep, but what he wanted was a drink. Or, more to the point, several.

CHAPTER FIVE

SQUATTING BESIDE HER, Will stared at the sleeping Kelly. Nothing about her looked comfortable. She was sprawled on the floor on her belly, one knee drawn upward, her head half off the pillow. The blanket had slipped or possibly been kicked off, leaving her exposed, particularly her rear end, which hiked slightly in the air. The torn pocket on her jeans, the pocket he himself had ripped at the service station, stood out like a neon sign. It should have reminded him of how little he could trust this woman. Instead, it reminded him of the feel of her backside. Which, in turn, reminded him of other things.

He shouldn't have kissed her. However, at the time, it had been the only way he could think of to silence her. It should have been a simple, meaningless act. But it hadn't been, and he couldn't figure out why. True, it had been a while since he'd kissed a woman. Could that account for his reaction? And what exactly was his reaction? He wasn't sure of anything, except that he'd been surprised.

Kelly, her cheek buried in the pillow, whimpered, diverting Will's attention away from thoughts of the kiss. Kelly had tossed and turned, moaned and groaned all night. For all that, though, she'd never asked to be released from the handcuffs, a fact he couldn't help but admire. Also, he couldn't help but feel guilty.

Kelly moaned again. This time her sleep-hazed eyes fluttered open. For an instant she didn't know where she was. Watching her, Will could tell the exact moment reality struck.

"I was hoping you were a bad dream," she mumbled.

The mouth that spoke these words looked as soft as Will remembered it feeling, while the tip of the tongue that moistened the lips looked too tempting to even consider. He replied gruffly, "You can keep hoping, lady, but it isn't going to do you any good."

"Kelly. My name is Kelly."

As always, he ignored her as he nodded toward the handcuffs. "Do you want out of those things?"

"Gee, let me think about it. Do I want out of 'these things'?" She considered the question before shaking her head. "Naw. Probably not. I've grown accustomed to no feeling in my hand. I like having a meaningful relationship with a dresser. I'm thrilled to be playing the lead role in *The Prisoner of Zenda*."

Will ignored her outburst. Standing, he walked to the bed, picked up the corduroy jacket and shoved his arms into it. He headed for the door, still giving slightly to the leg he'd hurt when he'd jumped from the truck. After a night of letting the injury settle, the muscles had stiffened and he was in worse shape this morning than yesterday.

At the sight of his leaving, surprise twined its way through Kelly's voice, along with threads of panic. "Hey, where are you going?"

Will said nothing. He just kept walking.

"Hey, wait!"

Will reached for the doorknob.

"Stone, you can't leave me like this!" The threads of Kelly's panic had woven themselves into a full tapestry of fear.

Will stopped and angled his head over his shoulder. "You want out of those handcuffs? Yes or no? And I mean just that, yes or no."

This was no time for pride. "Yes," she said.

Will knew how much her answer had cost her. Just as he knew one sometimes had to practically sacrifice pride to survive. The trick was to know when to do it.

Stepping forward, he bent before Kelly and unfastened the handcuffs. When he held out his hand to help her up, she refused his offer. He let her hold on to that handful of pride.

"Do what you have to," he ordered, indicating the bathroom. "And make it quick."

Kelly pulled to her feet, grimacing at the pain that streaked through her. The night spent on the hard floor, combined with the incident at the service station, had done nothing for her thirty-six-year-old body. It helped her immensely that Will didn't seem to be getting around any better than she.

"C'MON, hurry up in there," Will called ten minutes later.

Kelly emerged from the bathroom, looking fresh in a pair of clean jeans and an ivory turtleneck sweater. Though she still wore no makeup, she had brushed her hair, bringing a temporary measure of control to the usual chaos.

Will glanced up as she reentered the room. She didn't look any the worse for wear for the fitful night she'd spent. How could she look so bright-eyed and bushy-tailed, when he felt as if a herd of cattle had stampeded over him—twice.

"I need some cash," he said curtly.

"And good morning to you, too," Kelly said, adding, "I told you that ten dollar bill was the last cash I had."

"Can you write a check on your credit card?"

"Nope," she said, stooping to shove her toilet articles back into her suitcase. When she rose, she was smiling, triumphantly. "Gee, Stone, what do we do now?"

What Stone did was take her purse and dump its contents into the middle of the rumpled bed.

"Hey!" she cried as he began to riffle through her personal property as though it were his own.

He started with her wallet, which he satisfied himself was, indeed, empty of cash. He ignored Kelly's smug I-told-you-so look and proceeded to make his way through a compact, a comb, an address book. When he came to the Swiss army knife, he slipped it into the front pocket of his jeans without a word of explanation or apology.

"Help yourself," Kelly said snidely.

Will said nothing, but reached for a small leather case.

"There's nothing in there," Kelly said quickly. Too quickly.

Will glanced up, his eyes meeting hers.

"I mean besides my passport . . . and my press credentials . . . and . . ." She stopped as Will, with a deliberate slowness, slid his thumb between the slit and flipped open the folder. A cache of traveler's checks tumbled onto the bed.

"Bingo," Will said. "I didn't think you'd be traveling out of the country with no money."

Kelly shrugged. "I'm obligated to make things as difficult for you as I can. Captive's code and all."

"Yeah," Will said, thinking that seemed to be the role of everyone in his life. "Here," he said, shoving two twenty-dollar checks in Kelly's direction, "Sign these."

She did without fuss, though, as always, it seemed imperative that she have the last word. "I'll just add these to your tab. Your growing tab. Oh, and Stone, I am prepared to take you to small claim's court for reimbursement."

"Wow, lady, I'm shaking in my boots."

"Just don't say you weren't warned."

Ten minutes later, Kelly couldn't say that she, too, wasn't warned. From the moment she asked the question, she had the sinking feeling that she wasn't going to like her captor's answer. It had everything to do with his arrogant look.

"So, where are we off to this morning? Another town? Another motel? The nearest police station to turn yourself in?"

"*We're* not off anywhere. *I'm* off to get breakfast."

"Let me hazard a wild guess," Kelly said. "You're not going to free me with a heartfelt thank-you for my participation up to this point."

"Bin—"

"—go," Kelly finished.

Will left Kelly handcuffed to the bed, the phone well out of her reach, her mouth gagged so that she couldn't cry for help. Then he put a Do Not Disturb sign on the doorknob. There was no doubt in Will's mind as he stared into flashing green eyes that, if looks could kill, he'd be pushing up daisies.

SEATTLE AWOKE that Friday as it did every morning, with a start. By nine o'clock, people were going about their business. The whistle of ferry boats pierced the waterfront stillness. Tall buildings sculpted the nearby landscape, shrouded in a gauzy mist that heralded another day of rain.

Though Will had never been in Seattle, he maneuvered Kelly's sports car through the streets with the same competency he'd displayed in San Francisco. Glancing at street names to confirm that his photographic memory of the map he'd studied in prison hadn't failed him, he crossed through the heart of the city and out into the suburbs. He hadn't lied to Kelly when he'd told her that he was going for breakfast.

He'd just failed to mention that there was something he
had to do first.

Some twenty minutes and twenty miles later, Will
exited the freeway. He took an asphalt road that wove
its way deep into a thick forest of spruce and fir. It was
like being inside a green cathedral, Will noted. The
trees muffled all sound. Catching sight of closed iron
gates up ahead, Will slowed the car, edging it onto the
shoulder of the road. Meticulously, he studied the scene
before him. Beyond the iron gate, which operated
electrically, stood a guard station. Will could see the
shadowy movements of a man inside the small glass
cubicle. Well beyond the gate and guard station
stretched an orange-brick building surrounded by a
stone wall. On the front of the building, black letters
spelled out: Anscott Pharmaceuticals.

At the sight of the company name, anger knotted
Will's stomach. He was certain that the corporation
was somehow responsible for his brother's death. To
keep from losing his mind after he'd received news of
Stephen's death, he'd spent every free moment re-
searching the drug company. He'd quickly learned that
the business was headquartered in San Francisco, but
that there was a branch in Seattle, a branch that kept a
very low profile.

"Yeah, very low profile, but very high security,"
Will muttered, noting the rows of barbed wire strung
along the top of the stone wall.

A mean-and-lean patrol dog appeared briefly in
front of the gate, then disappeared. Rain had begun to
fall, a persistent drizzle. Will turned on the windshield

wipers. Yeah, he thought as the blades slashed their wide arc, Anscott-Seattle had gone beyond the usual precautions that drug companies took against industrial espionage, far beyond the measures they'd taken at the San Francisco location. Now why would they do that, unless there was something inside Anscott-Seattle that warranted that kind of security?

The knot in Will's stomach tightened. He'd made a promise to himself that he was going to keep, even if it was the last thing he did. He was going to find out the truth behind his brother's death and make the person, or persons, responsible pay. Now was not the time, however, he thought, as he maneuvered the car into a slow U-turn and started back down the asphalt road. His time would come, though. He'd see to that. And soon. It had to be soon, because he didn't have much time left. The law would see to that.

THIS WAS the perfect cover, Mitch Brody thought as he stared at the asphalt road. Minutes before, he had pulled the car into a small stand of trees. He hadn't worried about damaging the vehicle because, frankly, with its dents and scratches and internal injuries, it was beyond damaging. It, like his life, was on the verge of falling apart. It was a real toss-up which was going first, his sanity or his transmission. He looked around. Yeah, the trees provided the perfect shelter. And the slate-gray rain trickling downward helped. Still, it wouldn't hurt to be extra cautious, Mitch thought, starting the car and backing it deeper into the forest's greenery. Under the circumstances, Will Stone's eyesight would be sharper than that of a hungry hawk's.

For the next few minutes, Mitch waited, watched and wondered. What was Will Stone up to? Mitch wished he could have a drink. Maybe then the trembling in his hands would stop. He usually had a couple of shots of Jack Daniel's to get the day started, then a couple of others every hour or so to make certain that the day passed without a whole lot of clear thought. The nights were for celebrating, again with liquor, the fact that he'd made it through the day. This morning, though, all he'd had was a cup of coffee and the caffeine hadn't even begun to meet his special needs. He'd hardly finished the coffee before he'd seen the door to room 110 open. Will Stone had emerged alone, had placed a Do Not Disturb sign on the doorknob and had driven off in the red sports car.

What was Will Stone up to? came the question once more, followed by yet another: Why was he himself getting involved in something that wasn't his business? If he had any sense, he'd turn the man over to the proper authorities.

Suddenly, Mitch saw the red car doubling back. After Will had passed by, Mitch started his own dilapidated vehicle and drove ahead to see what had been the object of Will's interest. Somehow, though he realized it only at that instant, he wasn't surprised to discover that Will had sought out Anscott Pharmaceuticals. He wasn't surprised because it was exactly what he himself would have done. He and this Will Stone thought a lot alike, which Will's showing up on Kelly's doorstep had already proven. They were alike in another way, too. Both were innocent of the crimes of which they'd been accused. In Will Stone's case, Mitch had nothing to go on but gut instinct. But then, gut instinct was the only thing that had never failed him. Everything, everyone else had. Most of all, he'd failed himself.

RAIN WAS FALLING in earnest by early evening. Drawing back a corner of the drapery, Kelly peered through the motel window at the pellets of water striking the glass. As the drops splattered, they reminded her of spider webs. Spider webs. How appropriate, she thought, for she felt caught in a web. Caught and waiting to be devoured.

The spider had returned at midmorning and now sat propped against the headboard of the bed...whittling, of all things...with her Swiss army knife. At first, she hadn't known what to think about the tree branch he'd brought back with him—and she certainly hadn't much liked the idea of her captor with a knife. As the day had passed, however, the act of putting knife to wood had seemed to calm Will's nerves. Now, if only she could find something to calm her own.

Kelly let loose the drape and stepped back from the window. She walked to the dresser and fidgeted with the carry-out carton containing the remains of their now-cold dinner, sweet and sour pork. Then she moved to straighten a picture on the wall. She was headed back to the window when Will spoke.

''Will you light somewhere?''

Kelly turned and glared. "And what if I don't? Are you going to bind and gag me again?"

The question blazed with Kelly's usual spiritedness. It burned, too, with fear, though this she hoped her abductor didn't notice. The truth was that, tied up and unable to do more than mumble garbled sounds, she'd been scared half out of her wits. What had frightened her most was that he'd left her alone. All of her life, she'd feared being left alone. This morning had been one of the worst experiences of her life. Alone and virtually helpless, she became the emotional prey of all kinds of stalking demons.

"Sit down," Will said in answer to her query. The slow patient strokes he made with the knife contrasted dramatically with Kelly's restlessness.

Kelly plopped down in a chair, crossed her legs and began to swing her foot in an agitated fashion. She forced the morning's episode from her mind. As well as the fact that she had been relieved—who would believe one could be relieved at the return of one's captor—when Will had returned with breakfast. Instead, she concentrated on the question that had kept repeating itself all day: Where had he gone? He certainly could have gotten something to eat in a fraction of the time, a fact borne out by the ten to fifteen minutes it had taken them to go for the Chinese food. She'd been afraid that he was going to leave her behind again, but, thankfully, he hadn't, probably because he'd wanted to be seen in her company. Which once more raised the subject of where he'd gone that morning. What was so important that he'd been willing to risk traveling alone? It wouldn't do to ask the question head-on, however.

"So, are we staying here in Seattle?"

She'd already decided that the city was his destination, but it was a good opening gambit. Then again, maybe it wasn't, since he made no pretense of supplying an answer.

"So, what do we do now that we're here?"

She thought he wasn't going to answer this question, either, but finally he said, "Wait."

"For what?"

"You ask a lot of questions."

As he offered the terse reply, he brushed coiled shavings of wood from his lap and onto the floor. The twisted slivers reminded him of the dozens of ringlets of Kelly's hair, ringlets that had been damp from sweat when he'd returned that morning. His first thought was that she'd perspired from struggling to free herself, but it didn't explain the look in her eyes. He could have sworn he saw fear there. But that was impossible. Kelly Cooper feared nothing. Hadn't she been defying him ever since he'd taken her hostage? Her defiance wasn't that of a frightened woman. And yet, he couldn't forget the look that had filled her eyes.

"So, what are we waiting for?" she asked again.

"Night."

The fact that he answered her at all surprised her, but not nearly as much as the answer he gave. "Night?"

"Night," he repeated, adding, "And don't ask me anything else."

Kelly stood and walked back to the window. This time Will said nothing about her fidgetiness. Once more staring out at the rain, she wondered exactly what he had planned for the night. Did he know someone here in Seattle? Was he returning to wherever he'd gone this morning? And would he again leave her behind? This last thought brought drops of perspiration to her forehead, and so she forced herself to think of something else. Something positive. Or at least something potentially positive. Had Rachel picked up on the clue she'd given her that afternoon?

Out of the clear blue, Will had ordered her to contact her office again, to inform them that she was still fighting some bug and couldn't travel. With the same stern warning, he had monitored her every word, giving the same disapproving look at her performance. Kelly's mind had raced a mile a minute trying to come up with something that Rachel might get suspicious about. In the end, Rachel had handed her the opportunity on a silver platter. When the young woman announced that a co-worker had just become engaged, Kelly pretended to have no knowledge of the co-worker's fiancé's name, a fact which Kelly could tell surprised Rachel. But had it signaled that something was wrong?

Kelly turned away from the window, expecting to feel a full measure of animosity toward her captor. What she felt instead was the same sense of fascination that she'd experienced the first time she'd seen him. Once more, she longed for the camera that lay on the floor beside her suitcase.

But maybe there was no way to capture the essence of this complex man. His strength, the way he concentrated on running the knife through the raw wood, or his gentleness. Gentleness? How odd that this man, who'd been nothing but brusque and bearish up to this point, had another side to his nature. A very disconcerting side, Kelly thought as she watched the way his fingers caressed the wood. Another thought occurred to her. What if *this* was the real man? This thought was more than disconcerting; it was downright disturbing. A harsh Will Stone might be difficult to forget, a gentle Will Stone, impossible.

"Where did you learn to whittle?" she asked, fleeing these thoughts for the security of a safer subject.

Will didn't look up as he pointed out, "That's a question."

"A harmless one."

He shrugged. "I don't know where I learned to whittle. I can't remember not knowing how to."

"Were you raised in the country?"

"Hardly. I was born and raised in the middle of downtown Chicago."

Kelly slid her hands into the back pockets of her jeans. A slight smile danced across her mouth. "I didn't know they had trees in the asphalt jungle."

For a fraction of one second, it looked as though Will was going to smile. Kelly found herself hoping that he might. What would his lips look like with a smile nipping at them? The question remained unanswered, however, for no smile materialized. Instead, a frown appeared.

"Despair was the only thing that grew where I lived. And we always managed to have a bumper crop."

Kelly sensed that Will didn't want her pity, that he wouldn't tolerate it.

"So, how did you start whittling?"

Will drew the blade downward through the wood. "Broom and mop handles. We used them for playing stickball. I don't even remember the first time I put a knife to one." He glanced back at her. "It just felt good. I couldn't always control what was happening around me, but I could control the wood."

"Yeah," Kelly said, thinking about the lonely hours she'd spent. Photography had been her comfort. "What about family?" she asked.

"What about them?"

"Did you have any?"

"Doesn't everyone?"

"Not really."

Kelly could see her answer surprised Will. And seemed to make him uncomfortable. Did he not want to talk about family in general or did he not want to know about hers? What was he afraid of? Kelly wondered if he was deliberately avoiding learning anything about her. Maybe that was why he never called her by name. If she was a nameless, unknown means to an end, would it be easier for him to . . . ?

"Yeah, I had family," he said, grudgingly, interrupting her thoughts.

"Brothers? Sisters?"

"Anybody ever tell you that you ask a lot of questions?"

"Yeah, you did. A little while ago."

"Yeah, well, I was right."

"I take it that I ask questions that you don't want to answer."

"You got it, lady," Will said, closing both the conversation and the knife, the latter with a flick of his thumb. He crawled from the bed in one long, fluid motion and brushed past Kelly—as though she didn't exist, Kelly thought.

WATCHING THE RAIN as it pattered a thick and arrhythmic beat against the pane, Will listened to the thunder. It sounded, he thought, like a drunken man stumbling against a row of trash cans. A drunken father returning home. Now, just as in his childhood, the night crept in to comfort him, to conceal him, to hide his tears.

Night.

It was time to set his plan into motion, time to start paying back.

"I've got to go out," Will said, threading his fingers through his hair and reaching for his jacket. Shrugging his shoulders into it, he picked up the handcuffs and Kelly's scarf, which he'd used as a gag. He turned toward Kelly, who stood beside the bed.

"No," she said.

The word, spoken somewhere between a cry and a whisper, sounded defiant. But the look in her eyes was the one Will had seen before. It was definitely one of fear. And it made Will uncomfortable, for it humanized, personalized this woman and forced him to admit he was beginning to admire her. Although Kelly's fear was real and powerful, he saw clearly that she had no intention of begging him not to handcuff and gag her.

Stiffening her shoulders, angling her chin, she announced, "I'm going with you. And that's that."

CHAPTER SIX

KELLY SMELLED a story. It was as pungent as the lofty firs lining either side of the narrow, curving roadway. Yeah, there was a story here, and she'd give a hundred bucks for her camera, which Will had forbidden her to bring along. She hadn't argued with him, lest he change his mind about taking her with him. She was still lamenting the absence of the camera when Will rounded a curve, cut the headlights of the car and glided the vehicle to a stop on the side of the road. Up ahead, she saw an iron gate and an occupied guard station. Beyond, sprawled a brick building lush with outdoor lighting.

Anscott Pharmaceuticals.

Kelly recognized the name. It was one of the best-known drug companies on the West Coast. She'd had no idea that there was a branch here in Seattle, but then she'd had no reason to know. The Stone Man had known, however, and with the same certainty that she sensed a story, she sensed that this—Anscott—was where Will had gone that morning. It was also the reason he had traveled to Seattle. All Kelly had to do was find out why.

When Will shut off the engine, the sound of peppering rain enveloped the car, making the interior seem a quiet, sheltered haven in the stormy night. Kelly glanced over at Will, who stared straight ahead with an intensity that suggested he was attempting to memorize everything he saw.

"What's so interesting about Anscott Pharmaceuticals?"

"Nothing you need to concern yourself with," Will answered, never once taking his eyes off the scene before him.

"Oh, well, excuse me. You abduct me, take me to Seattle, and now we're sitting in the middle of nowhere in the middle of the night. I foolishly thought that perhaps I had the right to know just why all of this was happening."

Will looked over at her. He could barely see her in the darkness, but he could make out the tilt of her chin. "Hostages don't have rights, lady. The less you know, the better," he said, shifting his gaze back to the building and the grounds. "Besides, *you* asked to come along."

Kelly overlooked this obvious fact. "Yeah, well, just tell me this. Are you about to commit another crime, this one that I'll be an accessory to?"

"Like I said," Will replied, "you asked to be here."

Kelly ignored his answer and asked another question. "Does Anscott have anything to do with what happened in the park a year ago?"

Will avoided any eye contact, an action about which Kelly drew her own conclusions.

"Does it?" she insisted.

He gave her an irritated glare. "Everything in my life for the past year has had something to do with that day in the park."

"What? I mean, what does Anscott—"

Will threw open the car door, lighting the interior of the car. "C'mon," he ordered, stepping outside.

"It's raining," Kelly called after him.

"Believe me, you won't melt. Now, get your rear out here."

Grumbling as she slung open the car door, Kelly did as ordered. She turned up the collar of her all-too-thin denim jacket against the rain. At the same instant, Will hiked up the collar of his jacket, slipped his hands into his jeans pockets and, careful not to be observed, started crossing to the other side of the road.

Kelly rounded the front of the car, hastening to catch up with him. When she did, she asked, lowering her bare head to keep the wet wind out of her eyes, "Did you have a psychiatric evaluation in prison?"

"I didn't need one until I hitched up with you."

"Cute, Stone. Real, real cute."

Neither spoke again, Will because he was preoccupied, Kelly because she had to fight to keep up with his long stride. Using the tree line as cover, he edged closer to the gate. As it loomed nearer, he angled off into the woods.

"Will you slow down?" Kelly called at one point.

"Will you shut up?" Will hissed back. "The whole point is for no one to know we're here."

"Then why did you leave the car parked out there in plain sight?"

The question was a valid one. It angered Will that he hadn't considered it. He excused his negligence by telling himself that he wasn't accustomed to playing cloak-and-dagger games.

Clearly, Kelly would have said more on this topic, but her foot slipped going up a slope. She cried out as she struggled to keep her balance. The guard dog barked. Had the animal heard the sound? It was hard to believe it had at this distance, in this weather, but Will couldn't afford to take a chance on anything. He reached for Kelly, grabbing her hard by the hand and yanking her up alongside him.

"Will you be quiet?" he gritted.

"Will you slow down?" Kelly whispered, vaguely realizing that they'd simply repeated the questions of moments before. She realized one other thing, as well. Even though Will's hand gripped hers roughly, his touch was nonetheless comforting, his touch said that there was someone there. Kelly closed her hand tightly around his, as though trying to keep him by her side.

A stone wall rose to meet them, a stone wall topped with layers of knife-sharp barbed wire.

"Someone means business," Kelly whispered, surprised by the extent of the security. Barbed wire always suggested a war zone to her. At the very least, it suggested a hostile attitude meant to keep people at bay.

"Yeah, and besides the guard up front, there's a dog that patrols the grounds."

"I thought I heard a dog."

"You did. A Doberman pinscher."

"Ah, my favorite breed of guard dog. They can be such pussycats."

"You haven't seen this dog."

"You haven't seen me in action."

Will was about to say that, if anyone could scare a Doberman, Kelly could, when she, still holding to his hand, deliberately dropped to the ground, pulling Will down with her. Before he knew what was happening, he was lying flat on his belly on the leaf-strewn, wet ground. She was lying in a similar position beside him.

"Shh," she whispered, only seconds before a set of bright headlights speared the black night. Will hadn't even heard the approaching vehicle, which turned out to be a van. Once more, he found himself admiring this woman, a fact she seemed to sense because she added, "I've covered a couple of wars. You learn to listen for incoming artillery."

The van, marked with the logo of a florist, pulled up to the guard station; the driver and the guard exchanged a few words, which filtered back to Will and Kelly as nothing more than a jumble of sound, although Kelly could have sworn she caught a few words of Spanish. In seconds, the gate opened and the van drove through.

"Nine-thirty is an odd time for a floral delivery," Kelly whispered.

"Yeah," Will answered. "Real odd."

Rain was still falling. An uncomfortable dampness had seeped into Kelly's jeans. She imagined that a super-duper cold was in her future. But she gave only cursory thought to the state of her appearance or to her health. She was too busy acknowledging the quickening of her pulse. Yeah, she smelled a story. The truth was that even if Will would have allowed her to walk away, she wouldn't have gone. The photojournalist in her wouldn't allow it.

She watched as Will crawled closer to the wall. Once there, he stood, but, even on tiptoe, he was unable to see over the wall. "Come here," he whispered, motioning for Kelly to join him.

She guessed at what he wanted—actually, she, too, was eager to know where the van was headed—so when he called, she came creeping on her hands and knees. Planting his hands at her waist, he hoisted her up. Keeping her head low, she peered over the top of the wall.

Meanwhile, the only thing that Will could see was Kelly's backside. The rain had caused the denim to cling to her like a second skin, snagging his attention although he didn't want it to. He told himself that his reaction was normal. That it meant absolutely nothing. In particular, it meant nothing personal. He would have reacted in a like manner had it been any other woman.

"What do you see?" he growled under his breath, illogically angry at Kelly.

The sudden sharpness in his voice didn't escape Kelly, but she attributed it to nothing more than his mercurial nature. "Give me a minute, will you?" she whispered back in the same cutting tone. "I can't see—No, there's the van."

"Where's it going?"

"It disappeared around the back of the building," she said, adding the question that Will was silently posing, "Why would they deliver flowers at the back of the building?"

Without warning, Will lowered Kelly to the ground.

"Hey, wait—" she began as she turned around, only to have the words come to an abrupt halt.

She was literally pinned between Will and the wall. The latter she felt as a hard presence behind her, while the former, his thighs flush with hers, seemed an even harder entity. Her hands sought his chest in an effort to steady herself. It, too, felt unyielding, ungiving, warrior-strong. She could feel her body responding to his nearness, a kind of superawareness of the opposite sex. She told herself that her reaction was normal. Had Will felt the same awareness? She didn't know, but she could feel his eyes full on hers. The intensity in those eyes made her breathless, so breathless that she withdrew her hands, then stepped away from the wall, away from Will.

"Why would they deliver flowers at the back of the building?" she repeated.

"Maybe they're not delivering. Maybe they're collecting, instead." Will's voice sounded oddly husky.

"Collecting what?"

Will said nothing. How much could, should, he trust this woman?

When Will didn't reply, Kelly said, "What do you think is going on at Anscott?"

Again Will didn't answer. This time he turned away from her.

"Will?"

It was the first time she'd called him by name. Oh, she'd called him Stone, in a distancing kind of way, but she'd never called him by his given name. For that matter, neither had anyone else for an entire year. Maybe longer. In prison he'd been only a number, a sharp-spoken, "Hey, you!" or "Hey, Stone!" Then again, maybe no one had ever spoken his name as Kelly just had—softly, femininely, as though she really gave a damn about getting his attention.

He turned, watched her through the falling rain, then said, simply because he couldn't help himself, "The illegal manufacture and trafficking of narcotics."

His answer didn't surprise Kelly. She'd suspected it herself. "Do you have proof?"

"No, but I'm going to get it," he said.

"How? By breaking into Anscott?"

"Exactly."

Kelly didn't miss a beat. "Then what you need is an accomplice, not a hostage."

"I thought you were afraid of being an accessory to a crime."

"I'll risk it."

"Why?"

"Because I think there's a story here."

Will wasn't certain what he'd expected her answer to be. Had he thought she'd believed so vehemently in his innocence that she'd cast in her lot with his despite all odds, despite the danger? Had he really been that naive? He laughed angrily.

"Just like you thought there was a story that day in the park? No, thank you very much, lady. I don't need your help."

At this, he started working his way through the thicket of trees and back to the parked car. His anger, which Kelly hadn't expected, startled her. So much so that it took her a few seconds to gather her wits about her.

Racing after him, she caught him by the arm.

"You do need my help," she insisted.

"Oh, yeah?"

"Oh, yeah."

"How do you figure that?"

"It's pretty simple to see that you don't know the first thing about breaking and entering."

"I would remind you that I'm the criminal in this duo."

"And you got caught, didn't you?" she said smugly. Before Will could do more than frown, Kelly pushed on, "Look, you're going to go in there and botch everything before you even get started."

"Your vote of confidence is touching."

"For heaven's sake, you left the car parked on the roadside!"

"Ten to one, nobody even noticed it."

"Oh, it was noticed."

"Then, they'll just think it's out of gas."

"Forget the car. You didn't even hear the van coming."

"I would have."

"And you don't know the first thing about getting past that guard, past that dog, and into the building."

"And you do?"

Proudly, as though taking credit for the greatest of achievements, Kelly replied, "Yes, I do."

Both of them drenched and chilled to the bone, they stared at each other. They were still standing in the same position when Kelly, again without warning, grabbed Will's hand and dragged him downward. Before he hit the ground, headlights cut through the dark. Both watched as the van pulled from the gate. After the vehicle had passed by them, Kelly rose, wiped at her pants, though the action didn't remove a speck of the mud, and started for the car.

"Without me," she whispered over her shoulder, "you're going to get yourself caught before you even get started."

Will didn't reply. He simply got into the car and headed back to the motel. Halfway there, he saw the pale blue car, kept it in his sight for a while, then was relieved when it turned a couple of miles from the motel. Thank heaven, he thought. He didn't need anything more to worry about. The law and the woman beside him were quite enough. And not necessarily in that order.

THE HAIR DRYER in her uncuffed hand, Kelly sat on the floor of the motel room, sending a shaft of warm air through her wet hair. Thirty minutes earlier, she'd showered in water practically hot enough to scald. Even so, she'd still felt chilled and had donned her long-sleeved nightshirt. It hadn't helped that the room's radiator appeared to be on the blink. On his way to the bathroom, after he'd handcuffed her to the dresser, Will had tossed her a thick blanket, which she now curled beneath in an attempt to get warm.

A dozen thoughts fought for equal footing. She could hear the shower running and suspected that Will was in no hurry to get out from under the hot water. When he'd gotten out of the car at the motel, his limp had been worse. As for his knuckles, they'd oozed blood again.

A mental picture of steam rising like a primordial mist, filling the bathroom and smoking the mirror, rushed at Kelly. Steam that coiled around a naked Will like a shapeless serpent. Somehow the image of Will unclothed fit the primitive scene in her head. To her, he represented first-man, man without cultural trappings, man without civilized trimmings. He didn't try to be what anyone wanted him to be. He simply was what he was. And was that something a murderer?

This question led to thoughts about Anscott. Was Anscott producing and distributing narcotics? If so, Anscott's possible involvement in drug trafficking surely had something to do with what had sent Will to prison. Otherwise, why his interest in it? And hadn't the murder he was supposed to have committed been drug-related? Which brought Kelly right back to the same question. *Had* Will killed the man? If so, had he done it coldbloodedly or in self-defense? And who was the man buried in the grave Will had visited? Who was this mysterious John Doe?

She had so many questions and so few answers.

Kelly rose to her knees, and searched the top of the dresser for her hairbrush. She had just reached for it when something far more interesting caught her eye. Will's wallet. Her first thought was that she had no right to invade his privacy, her second that she had every right. Hadn't he invaded her privacy in a major way when he'd taken her hostage? Not to mention when he'd rummaged through her purse as though he owned it and its contents? Thus motivated, Kelly picked up the wallet and studied it.

The wallet, black in color and worn with age, was inexpensive. No genuine cowhide here, no imported exotic skin. Just a cheap imitation. What struck her even more forcefully, however, was its thinness. He carried very little with him. It crossed her mind that, perhaps, he'd sacrificed a lot of its contents at the time of his incarceration. She had no idea what prisoners were allowed to keep. Obviously, no money, she thought, remembering all he'd hit her up for.

Intrigued, she opened the wallet in an effort to discover if it held anything at all. She had just decided that it contained absolutely nothing when her fingers, which she'd run into one last pocket, came into contact with something. She pulled out a social security card with the name William Randolph Stone. Beneath it she found two snapshots, one of a gray-haired woman, who looked tired and as worn as the wallet, another of a dark-haired, bright-eyed young man. The young man's smile covered his handsome face. It was a smile that said he owned the world and dared anyone to try to take it away from him.

Who were these people? Were they family? Friends?

"What are you doing?"

Will's curt voice thundered through the room, causing Kelly to jump. When she looked up, her heart began to pound, not only because of the scowl plastered across Will's lips, but because of his near-naked state. He stood bare-chested, a towel knotted about his waist. For a series of erratic heartbeats, all she could think about was being pinned earlier that evening between this man and the wall. The heartbeats became even more irregular when another image came to mind, an image of her being pinned between him and a bed. Her thoughts were interrupted by Will's next words.

"Put them back," Will ordered, indicating the snapshots she continued to hold.

His voice had grown toneless, his face expressionless. Both were more frightening than the anger he'd first displayed. Kelly had the curious feeling that the photographs were the only things of value in his life.

"I was only looking at them," she said, suddenly feeling the need to explain herself, suddenly feeling that it was she who was the criminal.

"Put them back," he repeated. He still spoke the words atonally, but his eyes had hardened once more, as though he was growing impatient at seeing his treasures in another's hands.

"Who are they?" Kelly asked. She knew she should be complying with his demand, but she simply couldn't keep the query from coming.

"None of your business," he said, and moved so quickly to snatch the photographs out of her hand that she never even saw him coming. She flinched. "And stay out of my wallet. You have no right to mess around in my things."

His words were like a tall flame to a short fuse. "*I* have no right to mess around in *your* things? And just what kind of right do you have messing around in mine? Just what kind of right do you have messing around in my life? I've been battered and bruised, handcuffed and gagged, and now I'm probably well on my way to catching pneumonia, and you have the gall to stand there and tell me that I have no right to mess around in your things."

Pursing her bottom lip, she blew a strand of hair from her eyes. "And let me tell you something, William Randolph Stone, if you want to break into Anscott, you can damn well do it on your own. I'd like nothing better than for you to get your rear end caught and thrown back into the slammer. It would serve you right."

By this time, Kelly was breathing fire like an angry dragon.

The snapshots hidden away, Will tossed his wallet back onto the dresser and said, as though she hadn't spoken a single word, "Stay out of my things."

"You . . . you . . ." Kelly called him a scathing name that would have made half the sailors on the high seas blush scarlet.

Will stepped to the lamp, turned it off, and plunged the room into total darkness. In the silence that followed, Kelly heard him strip the towel from his waist. Again, an image streaked through her mind, an image of him unclothed, an image of a bare rear end, the same rear end she'd seconds before hoped got caught and thrown back into prison. She still hoped it. In fact, she double hoped it!

"Do you think I could have a pillow?" she asked, as she tried to spread the blanket out with one hand. "Or would that constitute messing with *your* things?"

The wrist in the handcuff ached already, but she'd die and go to hades before she asked to be uncuffed. Besides, given a choice between the bed, with a naked Will in it, and the floor, she'd take the floor every time.

Out of the clear blue, a pillow whopped Kelly upside the head.

"Gee, thanks, Stone!"

Predictably, Will said nothing.

An hour later, Kelly was still awake. The floor had never seemed harder or the handcuffs more abrasive, and she was freezing to death. At long last, exhaustion overcame her, and she tumbled into a fitful slumber, during which she dreamed of Will standing in a primeval swamp, shower steam rising all about him, and of a florist van delivering gigantic tree-sized poppy plants, from which a Spanish-speaking Doberman pinscher extracted white-powdered opium.

THANK HEAVEN she had quieted down!

Will had listened to her toss and turn until he didn't think he could stand anymore. Or perhaps it was his own thoughts he couldn't stand much more of. He knew he'd acted like a heel. Worse, he'd been exactly what Kelly had called him. Truthfully, he hadn't seemed able to help himself, however. The evening had been unsettling.

As though reinforcing this sentiment, Kelly moaned. As it had all night, the sound knifed at Will. He waited to see if she was going to start up again, and was relieved when she didn't.

Yeah, he thought, allowing his mind to roam again, the evening had been unsettling, beginning with what he'd seen at Anscott and ending with the sight of Kelly holding the photographs of his mother and brother. A dozen things in between had upset him, too: Kelly's offer to help him break into Anscott, her admitting that the offer was purely professional, the soft way she'd spoken his name.

"Will?"

The memory of the one word laced itself about his heart and tugged—hard. Why should her calling his name have affected him so profoundly? Why did it sound differently on her lips than on any other lips that had ever pronounced it?

This time, Kelly's moan turned into a full-fledged groan.

Will turned his back to her, hoping to shut out her misery, hoping to feel his usual nothing. But he did feel; he couldn't shut out her suffering. In fact, he could no longer define what was her pain and what was his. The two of them seemed inseparable. Just as they'd seemed inseparable for that brief moment tonight when they'd stood in the rain, staring at each other, that brief moment when she'd stood between him and the stone wall. He had felt her thighs brushing against his, her hands flattened against his chest. He'd felt the same oneness when he'd stepped back into the room following his shower. For one heartbeat, as he'd viewed her sitting on the floor, her hair curling wildly about her head, her fleecy long-sleeved nightshirt hugging her curves, he'd felt as though they'd merged.

And then he'd noticed the photographs in her hand.

In retrospect, he didn't know why he'd been so angered by the sight. Except that he viewed her intrusion as a violation. Without asking, she'd taken something that was his. She'd taken something else, too, something far more valuable than the snapshots themselves. She'd taken advantage of him. She'd treated him as though he were so worthless that she could just rummage through his things, his life, at will. As though he wasn't worth respecting.

And have you treated her with respect, Will ole boy?

Kelly started to moan, but the sound turned into a pathetic whimper, instead. A whimper that eloquently answered Will's question. Of course he hadn't treated her with respect. If he had, he'd never have kidnapped her, never have forced her to be part of his revengeful scheme, never had bound and gagged her and left her scared half out of her mind. If he'd treated her with respect, she wouldn't be on the floor now—cold, chained and emitting sounds he could barely stand to hear.

As though to taunt him, Kelly whimpered again, this time to the accompaniment of the rattle of the handcuffs.

He had his reasons for treating her as he had, as he was doing, he told himself quickly. Namely, she, and the rest of the world, too, for that matter, owed him! Didn't they? Didn't she?

Kelly groaned...

Of course, they did! Of course, she did!

...moaned.

Don't listen to her! Don't you dare listen to her! Don't you dare remember what it felt like to be shackled!

...whimpered.

Will cursed...and accepted as gracefully as he could that he'd just been defeated.

IT WAS a strange dream, a dream in which the world was cold, the floor hard. The steel handcuff at her wrist bit into Kelly's flesh, just as the gruff voice telling her to be still bit into her consciousness. In the face of all this severity, the tender touch seemed totally out of place. As though it belonged in another dream. Yes, that was it. It must be part of another dream. But, if it was, how come it seemed so real?

"Be still," came the rough voice again as gentle hands removed the handcuffs.

Wake up, Kelly, she commanded. Wake up and see who has the rough voice and the gentle hands. She did as she bade herself. She awoke with a start as a pair of strong arms hoisted her up from the floor. In one quick motion, she felt herself anchored against a bare chest. Will's bare chest.

Confusion. "What are you—"

"Be still."

Barely awake and certainly unable to think clearly, Kelly seized on the first panicky thing that crossed her mind. He intended to carry her to the bed, handcuff her there, and gag her, then leave her alone again. Probably to return to Anscott. Had she been fully awake, she would have clung more tenaciously to her pride, but, as it was, she sent her pride scurrying.

"Don't!" she began to plead, to fight. "Please don't leave me alone! Not tied up!"

"Will you..."

"I'll go with you! Anywhere!"

"...be still?"

"Please take me with you! Please—"

Kelly's plea turned to a pathetic cry as Will irreverently tossed the struggling woman into the middle of the bed—tossed her and followed her down.

CHAPTER SEVEN

THE WEIGHT of Will's body crushed her, making it difficult for her to breathe. He was going to tie her down! This frightening knowledge tore through Kelly, causing the adrenaline to pump at a head-swirling, heart-churning rate. Sweat broke out across her forehead despite the chill of the room.

"No!" she begged again, fighting and kicking with all her might.

"Stop it!" Will ordered, manacling her wrists with his hands and drawing them above her head.

Only minutes before, one of the same wrists had been secured in a metal prison. Despite Will's strength, despite his obvious intention to hold her still, the fingers encircling her wrists continued to contain a gentleness that Kelly found as confusing as the moment. She felt as though she were being held in a satin bondage, a bondage she wasn't altogether certain she wanted to be freed from.

"I'm not going to tie you down. I'm not going to leave you," Will said, his voice a soft growl purring against her ear. "Just stop fighting me, and I'll let you go."

Kelly had no idea why she believed him, but she did. Perhaps it was the sincerity with which he spoke. Perhaps it was the fact that he could have had her tied a dozen times by now had that been his intent. Perhaps it was because, on a gut level, she knew that Will Stone wasn't a liar.

True to his word, Will released her wrists.

He could not, however, release himself from the feel of her. It was as though, in that brief time, all of her had been imprinted, branded upon him—the clean smell of her, the way her breath fluttered across his cheek, the way her body, her breasts, her belly, her thighs and legs, molded with his. Most of all, he could not free himself from the sudden urge to protect her, to create a safe harbor where she could dock all her fears. He had an overpowering need to take her in his arms. A need so strong it perturbed him.

He pulled away from her.

"Get under the covers," he said, his voice once more short and clipped as he fought to make sense out of what he was feeling. He yanked back the sheet and blanket. "Get in," he repeated.

Kelly did, simply because he gave her little choice. Before she could do anything more than register what was happening, he crawled in beside her and arranged the bed covers over them both. Two things crossed her mind: The bed was invitingly warm and soft. And Will wasn't naked as she'd believed him to be. He wore a pair of tight-fitting cotton briefs, which did little to mask his masculinity. Even so, she was grateful for them.

"Go to sleep," he said, again curtly, rudely.

As he spoke, he drew her chilled body to his, spooning it tightly against him. His chest cushioned her in its strength, while his legs entwined with hers. He draped his arm about her waist. The man was a real dichotomy. His voice screamed harshness, while his body whispered a gentleness that he couldn't mask.

Yes, she thought, as the bed and Will's nearness lulled her into sleep, a gentle Will Stone would be a dangerous thing.

For the second time, Kelly awoke abruptly. Where was she? Certainly not the floor. No, she was somewhere warm and soft and . . .

Memories of the night came charging forward. Kelly angled her head to the spot where Will had lain. His warmth still cuddled there, his pillow still bore the indentation of his head. Where was he? The question had but barely surfaced when a slight noise at the window drew her attention. He stood with his back to her, holding the pair of rain-soaked jeans over the slight heat coming from the radiator.

She propped on an elbow and watched him. Despite the chill in the room, he wore no shirt and no shoes. Only the dirty, torn pants that he'd been wearing when he'd broken out of prison. Some something—her sigh? The rustle of bed linen? An intuitive feeling?—alerted him that she was awake. He turned. Time, the world, stopped as the two stared at each other.

Does she have any idea how sexy she is with her wild hair and wanton lips? Will thought, accepting the fact that he was attracted to this woman. He wasn't, however, stupid enough to think that the attraction could ever be acted upon. Theirs was not a normal man-woman relationship. He was an escaped convict living on borrowed time, she was his prisoner and, as such, she was his enemy. Even if the circumstances had been different, their relationship never could have been actualized. Successful Kelly Cooper wasn't a woman who would align herself with a loser.

Does he have any idea how sexy he is with his scruffy clothes, his shaggy beard, his incredibly sensual mouth? Kelly thought, admitting what she'd known from the first. Or almost from the first. She was attracted to the man who'd taken her hostage. She was attracted to this man who seemed to have a grudge against the world. She was attracted to a fugitive from justice.

He's not so different from me, Kelly thought. In a real sense, she was a fugitive, as well, a fugitive from relationships. She'd fled her marriage with the same haste, the same desperation, that Will was fleeing the authorities. Like Will, she was running for her life. Unlike him, however, she had no concrete goal. Her goal was simply to keep running, to keep traveling, to keep avoiding any emotional commitment.

With a start, Kelly realized that Will had spoken to her.

"I'm sorry—" she began.

"I said, stay in bed. The room's cold."

"The heater still isn't working?"

"Just barely," he said, laying the jeans directly on the radiator vents. The smell of damp fabric drifted upward.

"Can't you ask someone to repair the radiator?" Kelly asked.

"It doesn't matter. I'm changing motels today."

"Oh."

Something in the way she said the one word, as though suddenly unsure of what would happen to her, caused Will to glance back at her. "*We're* changing motels today. We don't want to stay too long in one place."

She nodded, and watched as Will reversed his jeans, attempting to dry the other side. "I have a traveling iron. It'll dry them quicker," she said.

Will crossed the room, squatted before Kelly's suitcase and started to plunge his hands inside. He stopped, pivoted on the balls of his bare feet, and met Kelly's gaze squarely. "May I?"

Kelly noted two things simultaneously: One, the waistband of Will's pants drooped in the back, allowing a brief glimpse of white skin, skin untouched by the sun. Two, what he'd just asked might be as close to an apology as she'd ever get for what had happened the evening before. Yes, she was certain of the latter. Will Stone wasn't a man to whom apologizing came easily.

"Yes," she answered. "I think it's on the right-hand side."

A few minutes later, Kelly watched Will wrestle with the jeans and the iron. He sat on the floor and, as fast as he ironed one wrinkle out, he ironed two in. In addition, he was getting a slow nowhere toward removing the moisture. She threw back the covers and climbed from the bed.

"Here, let me."

"I can do it," he protested. "I iron jeans all the time."

"Wet ones?"

Will looked up. "Let me guess. You're not only an expert at breaking and entering and turning guard dogs into pussycats, you're also an expert at ironing wet jeans."

Kelly smiled and again thought for a second that Will might join in, but, as once before, he didn't. Also as once before, Kelly felt cheated.

"Yep," she said, dropping to the floor beside him and taking the iron from him. "I'm a woman of many talents."

Will said nothing. He just rose and moved over to the piece of wood that lay on the room's small table. He pulled out Kelly's knife and began to whittle. After a few moments of silence, he spoke. "Ironing reminds me of my mother. It's all she seemed to do when she was at home."

Kelly, who decided to take a new tack in getting him to talk about himself, said nothing. She merely went back to ironing.

The ploy worked. "She was a fanatic about my brother and me looking good for school. Sometimes our shirts were faded and threadbare, but they were always clean and freshly ironed. Even if she had to stay up all night getting them ready."

Mother? Brother? The people in the photographs? Kelly didn't dare ask again. Instead, she said, "Memories are wonderful things. Even if they're bittersweet."

"Yeah," came Will's standard monosyllabic reply.

"I wish I had more memories of my mother," Kelly said, applying both the iron to the pants and a little psychology to Will. When he showed some interest in her remark, she added, "She died when I was young. That just left me and my father or, more to the point, just me and a series of nannies."

The quick look that Will gave her before returning his attention to the wood indicated his unspoken question.

"He was a journalist...traveled all over the world...spent very little time at home." She wondered if Will could hear the bitterness in her voice, the bitterness and the loneliness, neither of which the years seemed capable of diminishing. Would they ever?

Will did hear the bite in her reply. Beyond that, he heard a wistfulness, a little girl's need for her father. He also knew that he was being duped into revealing something about himself. It was a something he seemed incapable of holding back, however, especially given this particular subject.

"Yeah, well, mine traveled, too. Unfortunately, he showed up occasionally." As though to emotionally emphasize a point, and that this specific conversation was at an end, Will ran the knife's blade in a long cut down the wood. The cut proved too deep.

Will cursed, while Kelly considered. Were the snapshots, indeed, of his mother and brother? And did his just-spoken comments regarding his father explain why there wasn't a third photograph?

"How many awards have you won?"

The question, which came a full five minutes later, was so unexpected that Kelly thought surely she'd misunderstood Will.

"What?"

He glanced up from the whittling, a shaving of wood curled around his finger. "How many awards have you won?"

"How do you know—"

"You have a lot of free time in prison."

The remark was cryptic, though it indicated that he'd researched her, which his next comment verified.

"Two Pulitzers and what else?"

Kelly didn't go into the dozens of other awards that lined the shelves of her office. "That's about it."

"You're being modest," he said, then spoke again before she could deny this charge, "Tell me, were you always the Golden Girl?"

Kelly didn't back down from an answer. Looking him full in the eyes, she said, "Yes. I wasn't allowed to be anything less."

Will smiled mirthlessly. "Funny, I wasn't allowed to be anything but a disappointment. While you were busy spinning gold, I was busy tarnishing it."

"Yeah, well," Kelly said. "Gold often costs more than a person can afford."

A lingering look passed between them, a look during which each appraised the other and what had just been said. As if by mutual agreement, neither spoke for several minutes. Kelly went back to ironing, Will to whittling, both to wondering about the other's past.

Shortly, Kelly turned off the iron and placed it on its end to cool. Picking up the jeans, she checked them one last time for damp spots, then stood.

"Here," she said, handing the jeans to Will, who, at her approach, had laid aside both knife and wood and risen from the chair.

Will took the jeans, without a thank-you, which again didn't surprise Kelly. She had just started to turn back around when she unexpectedly found her wrist once more caught by Will. She looked up, only to discover that Will's attention was directed to the underside of her wrist. His brow furrowed into a frown. Kelly's gaze lowered to the object of his interest. It was a coin-sized, bluish-purple bruise. Despite the ache, an ache she had begun to think of as commonplace, she hadn't noticed the bruise. Slowly, so slowly Kelly's breath ebbed, Will stroked his thumb back and forth against the blemish.

"I never meant to hurt you," he said, clearly disturbed that he had.

No, he hadn't meant to hurt her. Kelly knew this more surely than she'd ever known anything. Like a bolt of lightning striking her, another realization struck her, as well. She wasn't afraid of Will. She knew Will Stone wouldn't hurt her purposefully.

"I know," she said.

Did she? Will thought. Yes, she did. He could see that fact plainly in her eyes. He was pleased. No, more than pleased, yet he deliberately didn't give a name to the feeling engulfing him, though he knew that he must release her hand. What holding it was doing to him did have a name. It fell under the heading of burning his senses. Slowly, he let go of her, though he couldn't bring himself to step away from her. Neither could he force himself to break eye contact. Dark brown eyes delved into green, green into brown. When her gaze began to burn as hotly as her touch, Will took one step, then another, backward. The jeans in his hand, he turned and headed for the bathroom.

Kelly watched him go, feeling bereft, feeling that she had to repeat a question she'd asked once before. The need to ask the question had arisen as a result of her seconds-before revelation. If she didn't believe Will capable of hurting her, did she believe him capable of hurting someone else?

"Did you kill that man?"

Will stopped, pivoted, found her eyes with his.

"A camera captures an image and makes a snap judgement. It doesn't necessarily capture the truth," he said.

"Is that a yes or a no?"

"It's a whatever you want to believe it is."

"I don't believe you're capable of that kind of violence."

For a reason Will couldn't explain, he'd wanted her to believe that he wasn't capable of such brutality, yet, in truth, wasn't he? Wasn't that what breaking out of

prison had been about? Wasn't he determined to even
the score for his brother's sake. No, his plans weren't
in the least noble, and maybe this woman should know
he was nothing more than the bad boy he'd always
been, the bad boy he'd always be.

Will's eyes hardened, just as his voice did when he
spoke. "Hide and watch, lady."

He said nothing more. But then, there was nothing
more to say.

"HOW WOULD YOU go about breaking into Anscott?"
Will asked over a bucket of crispy-fried chicken, which
sat on the floor alongside him and Kelly. Will leaned
against the bed, Kelly against a chair.

They had checked out of one motel and into another. At the second, as at the first, Will had insisted
that Kelly accompany him into the office to register,
once more establishing that they were a married couple. The ring on her finger continued to feel odd, yet,
curiously, there were times when she felt as though
she'd worn it forever. She wondered what this meant,
especially in light of the fact that she had never felt
emotionally comfortable wearing her real wedding
ring.

Now, at the question Will had posed so nonchalantly, so unexpectedly, Kelly glanced up. She sniffed
and sneezed, both of which she'd been doing all day.
She reached for a tissue, grumbling something about
dying of pneumonia. The latter she'd been doing as
frequently as she'd been sniffling and sneezing.

"Assuming that you aren't dying of pneumonia.
And assuming that you are still interested in helping me

break in, which, of course, you aren't," Will tacked on. "I believe you said you hoped I got my rear end caught and thrown back into...what was it? The 'slammer?' By the way, I never heard anyone in prison refer to it as the slammer. That's only in old movies."

Kelly swiped at her nose, ignoring his sarcasm and trying to ignore the comment about his rear end. His jeans had fit snugly before they'd gotten wet. They now fit as close as a kid glove encasing a hand; in fact, they fit criminally, so criminally that they alone were reason enough for Will to go back to prison, the hoosegow, the slammer—whatever.

"I *am* dying of pneumonia. Or will be soon. No thanks to you, I might add."

"Sorry, but—"

"Sorry? Did I hear the man say he was sorry?"

"...you insisted upon going with me," Will finished.

"I didn't insist upon being dragged out into the rain."

"What kind of fool would I have been to leave you alone in the car?"

"No bigger fool than the one who's planning to break into Anscott."

After their conversation that morning, which had ended with his hide-and-watch comment, Kelly had felt uneasy. Even more than uneasy. She'd been frightened. Breaking into the pharmaceuticals company to prove illegal drug production, maybe even to prove his innocence of the crime of which he'd been convicted, if that's what he had in mind, was one thing, but she had the feeling that Will was playing a far more deadly game. What game she wasn't exactly sure, but the way he'd negated her claim that he wasn't violent had chilled her straight through to the bone.

"Spare me your opinion," Will retorted. "Except on how to break into Anscott."

"I thought you didn't need my help. I thought you were the one with all the expertise."

"Forget it. I don't want or need your help," Will said, suddenly tired of their banter. He wiped his fingers on a napkin, tossed it in the wastebasket and stood. He picked up a second piece of wood and the knife and, propping himself against the bed's headboard, began to whittle once more. To his right, the radiator hummed a warm song.

Kelly watched him. She'd blown it, she thought. She'd had a chance to learn something, and she'd let the chance slip away. More to the point, she'd thrown it away. Or, maybe she hadn't, she added on a positive note. Maybe it was time to quit beating around the bush. Maybe it was time to be direct.

"Why do you want to break into Anscott?"

"I told you," Will said, never looking up.

"No, you didn't. You simply said you wanted proof that Anscott was involved in the illegal drug business."

"See, I told you."

"No, there's got to be more. You don't break out of prison to prove a company is involved in drug trafficking unless it has some personal impact on your life. Oh, I know you implied it had something to do with what had sent you to prison, but why wait six months before breaking out? And why didn't you say something about Anscott at the trial? No, something else is going on here."

"You don't need to know anything more."

"I do."

He glanced up, a sneer on his face. "For your story?"

"I have a right to know why I'm helping you break in."

"You didn't need a reason the other night. You were volunteering your services all over the place."

"I've changed my mind," she said, adding, "Do you hope to prove your innocence through proving Anscott's guilt?"

Will laughed harshly. "Lady, I don't care about proving my innocence. Besides, nobody would believe me innocent, even if God Himself came down and testified on my behalf."

"If you don't want to prove your innocence, then what's this all about?"

"I told you, you don't need to know anything more."

"What's it all about?" she repeated. When he didn't answer, she shouted, "Dammit, what?"

The air crackled with electricity as the two stared each other down, Kelly with the dogged determination that characterized her personality, Will with the distrust that characterized his. Distrust won out. Kelly recognized the moment of its victory.

Scrambling to her feet, she said, as she began trashing the remnants of their dinner, "You're right. I don't need to know anything more. I don't *want* to know anything more." She bunched up the napkins. "I was crazy for asking in the first place. Your business is your business, and—" she grabbed up the cups "—believe me, buster, it's just fine with me if we keep it that way." She crushed the empty bucket. "In fact, I prefer—"

"Someone at Anscott is responsible for my brother's death."

Kelly halted in the act of dumping two coleslaw containers into the wastebasket.

"Your brother?"

"Yeah."

"The man in the snapshot?"

Will nodded, once.

Suddenly, like a blurred camera shot, everything focused in Kelly's mind. "John Doe?"

Will didn't respond right away. When he did, his "Yeah" came out as a rasp. He hadn't needed to say anything, however. Kelly had seen the answer in his eyes, eyes that had turned as dead as the man in the grave. She knew that it would be useless to question Will any further, and so she said nothing. She finished cleaning up the remains of their dinner, then she fiddled with her camera. In the end, she offered Will the one thing she could, the one thing she'd known all along that she would offer him.

"The secret to breaking in anywhere," she said, "is to make it appear that you're not breaking in at all."

CHAPTER EIGHT

THAT NIGHT, Mitch watched as the red sports car pulled into a parking space in front of a convenience store. He had just spent two long boring hours parked outside the Anscott gates observing Will and Kelly. Nothing much had happened. The two never left their car... they'd just sat, watched and waited. Finally, to Mitch's relief, they'd driven off. Now, as Mitch pulled to a stop, both Will and Kelly got out of the vehicle, went into the store, and returned minutes later with Kelly carrying a small paper sack. They got back into the car and drove off. At no time did either look around, leaving Mitch to conclude that they still had no idea they were being followed.

Good, he thought, because he had no idea what he would say if he was discovered. More to the point, what would he be allowed to say? Will—Mitch had grown to think of both him and Kelly in familiar terms—didn't strike him as the patient type. No, Will would not give him a chance to explain. Memories of another time he wasn't allowed to explain came back to him: the voices of his superior on the force, his wife's, his young son's still haunted him.

"You have a choice. You can either resign from the force or be fired."

"How could you disgrace yourself, us, this way?"

"Did it ever cross your mind, Connie, that maybe I'm not guilty? No, I can see that it didn't."

"Daddy, why can't Mommy and me live with you like we used to?"

Mitch turned a deaf ear to the painful memories. Similarly, he turned a blind eye to the fact that beer advertisements blanketed the window of the convenience store. It had been almost three days since he'd had a drink, and he wasn't about to let his defenses down now. He didn't dare. Starting the car, he listened to the transmission grind itself into gear, then, when he considered the red car a safe distance away, he eased back into Saturday-night traffic.

The motel that Will had relocated to was only blocks away, so Mitch, pretty certain it was Will's present destination, headed in that direction. He drove slowly in order to give Will and Kelly a chance to get inside the room. It wouldn't do to be seen now. Possibly later, but not now. Mitch did not relish the thought of spending another cramped night in the car, but since when did what he want count for a thing? The simple truth was that he didn't have money for a room. Or for much else for that matter. He was behind on his child support payments. He was behind on his rent. He was behind on his life. His new job was just about the same as no job at all. Clients weren't exactly flocking to him, and the few that did come were almost as sleazy as his office.

Quit feeling sorry for yourself, Brody, he thought as he directed the vehicle into the motel parking lot. He spotted Kelly's car. Finding an isolated spot, he shut off the headlights and the motor before settling back into the temporary warmth, a warmth that would dwindle all too quickly in the chilly night. Look on the bright side, he told himself, when you were this far down, the only way to go was up. Things simply couldn't get worse.

Mitch never had time to enjoy the thought.

With the speed and unexpectedness of quick-fire shots, the car door flew open. Two hands, seemingly connected to no body, grabbed Mitch by the jacket collar and dragged him out of the car. Mitch stumbled. The hands caught him, pulling him up short and slamming him chest first against the vehicle. One arm was jerked, roughly, mercilessly, behind his back.

"Who are you?" a hostile voice snarled.

Mitch heard the question through a haze of pain.

"Who are you?" the voice repeated.

"Turn me loose and I'll..." Mitch's arm was pushed higher. "Mitch Brody!" he cried out, certain that the powerful hands and angry voice belonged to Will Stone.

Mitch sensed that Will recognized the name from somewhere, but couldn't quite place it.

"I work for you," Mitch grunted out between spasms of pain. "I'm the private investigator you hired to find your brother."

Mitch could actually hear this information sinking in. When it did, he was released as quickly as he'd been seized. Despite the darkness, Mitch could make out Will's too-long hair and his scraggly beard. Most of all, he could make out his somber, suspicious eyes.

In an attempt to restore circulation, Mitch rubbed his arm, saying, "Do you always play hardball?"

"No," Will replied. "I'm not playing games. Why are you following me?" he added without preamble.

"I heard that you'd broken out of prison."

As answers went, this one didn't seem to impress Will. "I repeat, why are you following me?"

"I'm not interested in turning you in, if that's what you think."

"Then why don't you tell me what to think."

"Okay. What I think is that we need to go somewhere and discuss this."

Mitch could tell that Will was still leery. Finally, Will nodded toward the motel, then motioned Mitch to precede him. Mitch did, still massaging his aching arm and wondering not for the first time if he was making a mistake. Maybe he would have been better off if he'd simply minded his own business. Maybe he should have thought twice before entering the lion's den.

KELLY STOOD at the window watching Will and the stranger approach. Earlier, when Will had mentioned that the blue car was trailing them, she'd been careful not to appear too curious. Now she could stare to her heart's content. Who was this man, and why had he been following them? It didn't seem odd that she thought of the man following *them* and not Will alone. She knew this meant something, something significant, but she didn't have time now to interpret it. In fact, she had time for nothing more before the door swung open.

As the sandy-haired stranger walked into the room, he looked over at her with a pair of the bluest eyes she'd ever seen. He stood as tall as Will, give or take an inch, though his build was altogether different. With his wide shoulders and deep chest, Will gave the impression of solidity, of an impenetrable wall, while the blond-haired man, though far from insubstantial, evoked litheness, quickness, a cougar on the prowl. Kelly sensed that the man could be as cunning as that animal, if the situation warranted it. Oddly enough, her internal eye, the one that saw things others didn't, the one that made her such a successful photojournalist, saw that he was hurting. A wounded cougar that kept moving despite its injuries. She admired that kind of courage.

"Hi," he said, one hand buried inside the pocket of his leather jacket. The other he kept flexing, as though trying to restore the circulation.

"Hi," Kelly responded, then sneezed—once, twice. "Sorry," she said, heading toward the bed, sitting down and reaching for a tissue. "I'm coming down with pneumonia. Just one of the perks of traveling with this man."

Will ignored her. "Sit down," he said to Mitch, indicating a nearby chair. "This is Mitch Brody," Will said to Kelly. "The private investigator I hired to find out what happened to my brother."

Kelly looked surprised. "Private investigator? You never mentioned hiring a private investigator."

"Yeah, well, I did, and Mr. Brody is about to tell us why he's been following us."

Us. Will had used the same terminology she had. Again, she couldn't afford the luxury of analyzing this at the moment. Instead, she turned her attention to Mitch and eagerly awaited his response.

"Let's just say I was interested in a man who could break out of Folsom. That's no small feat."

"I don't need a fan club, Mr. Brody."

"Maybe not, but you sure as heck could use somebody on your side. I don't know whether you've heard the news, but everyone and his dog is looking for you. And it isn't to pin a medal on your chest."

"And why should you be the slightest bit interested in what happens to me? Why should you be the slightest bit interested in being on my side?"

"Because, technically, I work for you, and I'm a loyal employee?" The answer was more question than statement.

"Try again," Will said, leaning against the dresser, his feet crossed, his arms akimbo. He looked rough, tough, ready to take up where he'd left off at the car if Mitch Brody didn't supply some decent explanations for his behavior. And soon.

"All right," Mitch said. "I'll lay my cards on the table. I think that you think your brother was killed by someone associated with Anscott. I also think that you broke out of prison to prove this fact."

"Go on," Will said, tonelessly.

"You yourself told me that before your brother's disappearance, he'd worked for Anscott Pharmaceuticals. It didn't take much sleuthing to discover that your brother was living pretty high on the hog. And that he curiously disappeared the day you were charged with murder—a fact, incidentally, you failed to mention."

"You think there's a connection between the guy that was murdered and Will's brother?" Kelly asked, the journalist in her kicking into gear. She sneezed, again apologized, then reached for another of the cold capsules they'd bought at the convenience store. She'd already taken one on the way back to the motel.

Mitch looked from Kelly to Will, then back to Kelly. "I think it curious that the guy had drugs on him, but no money, money which was never found—not even on Will, who should have had it either way. If he'd been buying the drugs, he should have had money, and if he'd been selling the drugs, he should have had money."

"As I recall," Kelly said, "the prosecution contended that Will had set the man up, that Will had never intended to buy the drugs, that he'd only intended to rip off the dealer."

"The prosecution was myopic in their vision. They could never see beyond the smoking gun. I say that someone else got that money, someone who used it to get out of town." Mitch turned back to Will. "What do you think?"

"That it's your show," Will growled.

"By the way," Mitch added, "the gun was registered as the property of Anscott Pharmaceuticals. They claim it was bought for one of their guards and was stolen weeks before the murder. Incidentally, they reported it as stolen, a fact that can be verified by police reports."

This information about the gun clearly came as news to Will.

"Didn't the prosecution know about the gun being stolen, and about its being registered to Anscott?" Kelly asked.

"Maybe. Maybe not. If so, they didn't see the relevance of it, which isn't surprising. In the prosecution's mind, Will found the gun, bought it on the black market, whatever. No, as far as they were concerned, Will had no connection with Anscott. They didn't even know he had a brother, much less one who worked for that particular drug company. Even if they questioned Anscott about Will, it's hardly likely that Anscott would have mentioned his brother being employed there."

"Since he was probably running drugs for them?" Kelly said, cutting to the chase. She sneezed again.

"Exactly," Mitch said, looking over at Will. "That is what you believe, isn't it? That Anscott's involved with illegal drugs? And that they somehow, some way, got your brother involved, too?"

"Yes," Will said curtly. As if he could take no more, he walked to the window and, pulling back the drape, peered out. Silence huddled about him.

Kelly saw, felt, Will's pain. It stooped his shoulders, bowed his head. Even though the subject hurt, there were things that she needed to know, things that she couldn't rely upon Will to tell her.

"What happened to Will's brother?"

"By the time I located him, he'd been dead a couple of months. The city of San Francisco had buried him in a pauper's grave. Prior to his death, it appears he had been living in Los Angeles under an assumed name."

"How did he die?"

"An overdose of cocaine."

"And what makes you think it was murder? Why not an accidental overdose, or a suicide?" As Kelly asked the question, she realized that her head was beginning to feel as though it were stuffed with cotton. The cold medication, she reasoned, fighting to stay alert.

"There was absolutely no evidence to suggest that he was a user."

"To play devil's advocate, few people broadcast their habit," Kelly pointed out. "A lot of users look squeaky-clean. A lot of dealers, too, for that matter."

"My brother wasn't a user," Will snapped, seizing both Mitch's and Kelly's attention. Again, Kelly heard his anguish, particularly when he said, "He might have been..." Will hesitated, as though he couldn't force the words out. "He might have been a lot of things, but he wasn't a user. I'd stake my life on it."

Mitch looked at Kelly, Kelly at Mitch.

"He died in San Francisco?" Kelly asked.

Mitch nodded.

Kelly frowned. "I don't understand. If he fled to Los Angeles, what was he doing back in San Francisco?"

A hesitation punctuated the silence before Mitch said, "I think he returned to right a wrong. I think he returned to tell the truth about what happened in the park that morning."

Will whirled around. "You never mentioned that," he admonished.

"I just found out about it. Seems he placed a call to your lawyer, told him that he needed to talk to him about the case."

Will passed a hand over his tired eyes, fighting to understand what Mitch had said, fighting the emotion that suddenly welled up inside him. His brother *had* tried to do the right thing. "If he called, why didn't my lawyer do something about it?"

"He did. He set up an appointment with your brother, who gave the name he'd been using in Los Angeles. When he didn't show, the lawyer thought he was just some kind of crank. There's always one or two who come out of the woodwork in cases like this. And this one was highly publicized."

"And he didn't show because he was killed," Kelly said.

"Right. In fact, I believe the night before the morning of the appointment."

"How did you find this out?" Will asked.

"The coroner's office called, saying that there were some personal things in your brother's John Doe file, things overlooked when I inquired about the body two months ago. Among the things was a piece a paper with your lawyer's name and telephone number. When I saw them, I called the lawyer.''

''Where are the things?'' Will asked, his voice thick with emotion.

''They're at my office.''

''I want them.''

''I never thought otherwise.''

Throughout the conversation, care had been taken not to refer to the murder, at least specifically in terms of Will's brother's guilt and Will's innocence. Kelly suspected that Mitch Brody was deliberately avoiding such a verbalization out of respect for Will. She liked this display of sensitivity. There was one question that she had to ask, however, and this question she aimed at the blond-haired man that sat opposite her.

''Well, all this is fascinating, Mr. Brody—''

''Mitch.''

''Mitch, then, but it still doesn't answer the question of why you've been following us.'' She reached for the glass of water, took a sip, and thankfully felt the coolness soothe her throat.

''Good point,'' Will said, grasping at any change of subject. He'd noted Kelly's use of the word *us* and had been oddly moved by it.

Mitch answered matter-of-factly. ''Because you're getting ready to break into Anscott, and I want to be a part of it.''

''Why?'' Will asked just as directly.

One silent second sauntered into another as the two men openly considered each other. Finally, Mitch spoke, his blue eyes darkening as he did.

"I have my reasons." A brief hesitation followed before he added, "Let's just leave it at that."

Again, Will sized up the man, sized up the situation. In the end, because he understood the need to keep things close to one's chest, he respected Mitch's request. He also appreciated that Mitch hadn't vocalized the one statement that was screaming to be spoken, namely, that Will had taken the rap for his brother. Even so, there was something that he had to say.

"Give me one good reason why I should let you in?"

"Because you need me." Before Will could reply, Mitch added, "PI's have connections." Again, before Will could say anything, Mitch offered up the pièce de résistance. "I think I can get the floor plan to Anscott."

That got both Will's and Kelly's attention, though Kelly's was not as focused as it should have been.

"How?" she asked, taking the hand that had held the cold glass and planting it across her forehead in an attempt to clear her head.

"A friend—" he didn't mention that the friend was a police officer, his past partner, who was one of a small coterie that believed in his innocence "—is married to a woman who has a sister who works for the architect who built Anscott. See, I told you I had connections."

"I'm impressed," Kelly said, longing to collapse back on the bed and close her eyes for just a few minutes.

In contrast, Will had never seemed more wide-eyed. He wanted the plans to Anscott. Badly. But not badly enough to rush into anything. "Let me think about it."

Mitch stood. "Fair enough." He started for the door. Once there, he pivoted. "If I'd been going to turn you in, I could have a dozen times."

"You know, of course, that what you're doing is illegal?" Will asked.

"You mean planning to break into Anscott, or not turning you in?"

"Both."

"Yeah, I know. But I played by the rules once...and lost."

Without another word, without looking back, Mitch opened the door and walked back into the cold, dark night, toward the car that would once more be his uncomfortable bed, toward memories that hurt worse than the devil, toward a horrendous need for just one drink.

KELLY'S HEAD felt like a stage on which a hazy curtain was being slowly lowered. "What do you think?" she managed to mumble.

Will, who'd just locked the motel room door, thought a lot of things. Too many things to make any sense out of them, though all of them revolved around his brother—the killing in the park, his brother's flight, which had hurt Will despite the stoic face he'd tried to wear, his brother's attempt to make up for his cowardly act, his death before he could do so. No, there was too much to think about.

"I'll tell you in the morning," he answered.

Lithe dancers suddenly filled the stage of Kelly's head, twirling and whirling in lingering, slow-motion pirouettes.

"He's right," she said, smothering a yawn. "He could have turned you in if he'd wanted to. Besides, those floor plans are invaluable."

"I take it that's a yes vote for Mitch Brody?"

Kelly shrugged, or at least started to. The gesture petered out in midmove and became, instead, a sort of halfhearted hunching of her shoulders.

Will frowned. "Are you okay?"

"The cold medicine," she murmured. "It's made me a little groggy."

"I'd say it's made you more than a little," Will said, feeling another protective wave wash over him at Kelly's fragile look. He didn't like the feeling, he didn't want it, and so he responded more severely than he should have. "Lie down."

"I think I will," she said, her eyes closed before her head hit the pillow. She told herself that she'd rest only a minute, that there were things she wanted to say to Will. Those things, however, kept flitting in and out of her mind like swift-winged dragonflies.

Will started for the bathroom, then stopped. Should he restrain her? Seeing her stretched out on the bed, he realized what a foolish idea that was. She wasn't going anywhere, except to sleep. But then, maybe this was just an elaborate ploy to escape. Did he really believe that? No. Besides, if she'd wanted to run, she could have earlier. In his haste to find out who was following them, he'd left her in the motel room alone. She hadn't run then.

Minutes later, after a quick shower, Will, once more dressed in his jeans, stepped back into the bedroom. As though he had no choice in the matter, his gaze went to Kelly. She was sound asleep, with her head rolled to the side in a pose that went straight to Will's heart. His first thought was that, her hair a mad frenzy, her lips parted in such a way that they resembled a Mona Lisa smile, she looked like an angel.

Okay, an angel with a wicked mouth and a short-fused temper and a half dozen freckles across the bridge of her nose, freckles he'd never noticed before. Will smiled...and wondered just when was the last time he'd smiled. Far enough back that he couldn't remember. The smile died as quickly as it had appeared when he realized that he really wanted to kiss that wicked mouth, that Mona Lisa mouth, that he wanted to trace his fingers across a patch of ginger-colored freckles.

Stop it, Stone! You just need a woman. Any woman. Not necessarily this woman. Particularly not this woman. Particularly not now when you've got a thousand things on your mind. Particularly not with your certain past. And your uncertain future.

Even as he told himself not to, he walked toward Kelly and turned out the bedside lamp, plunging the room into darkness except for the faint glow coming from the bathroom light. Again defying his better judgement, he bent over Kelly, drawing the bedspread over her tenderly.

She stirred. Moaned. Opened her sleepy eyes.

"Hi," she whispered.

"Go back to sleep," he grunted and started to move away.

"Will?" she called out.

Don't call me that! "Yeah?" he snarled.

Kelly tried to remember exactly what she'd wanted to talk to him about. It had something to do with what she'd learned that evening, but the dancers in her head were taking their final bow, and the gossamer curtain had floated almost to the stage floor. Floor... ground... earth... park...

"I knew you... hadn't killed that man."

She had all but said this before, but hearing the actual words did funny things to Will's stomach, to his heart. Few people had ever believed in him. For a reason he couldn't explain, Kelly's belief in his innocence meant more to him than he could say, more to him than he fully understood.

"Go to sleep," he repeated. His snarl had shriveled into something that sounded like a hoarse plea. He turned to go.

Kelly grabbed his arm, restraining him. His gaze flew first to where she was touching him, then to her face. She forced herself to concentrate, because she knew what she had to say—to ask—was important.

"You're not going to do anything foolish, are you? At Anscott? You're not breaking in with... some stupid notion of avenging your brother?'' She fought to stay clearheaded. ''We'll just get evidence of illegal drugs, right?'' When Will didn't answer, Kelly repeated, clutching his arm more tightly, ''Right?''

''Right,'' he said, hating himself for the lie.

She told herself to release him, that she'd secured the pledge she'd wanted, but she wasn't at all certain that she fully believed him.

''You're not lying to me, are you? You're really not going to do anything foolish.''

At that moment, the only foolish thing he wanted to do was kiss her. No matter how hard he tried, he didn't seem able to shake this one thought, this one need. He stepped away from her, as if doing so would end his temptation.

Kelly seemed to have forgotten her question. She closed her eyes and mumbled, ''We'll get evidence . . . and give it to the police. Then you'll go free. And I'll get my story. And all's well that ends well.''

''Sure,'' Will whispered, his sarcasm returning at the mention of her story.

With any luck, he would get the evidence he needed, and she would get the story she seemed ready to sell her soul for—dammit, he'd see that she got that!—but she was a bigger fool than he if she thought that all would end well. Nothing ever ended well for him. All he was counting on was finding a little justice. Someone was going to pay for Stephen's death.

On the other hand, Will thought as he snatched a pillow and a blanket and plopped down onto the harder-than-hard floor, maybe he was a bigger fool

than he believed himself to be; for just a second, when
she'd advanced Shakespeare's renowned declaration,
he'd entertained the notion that perhaps this time
things would be different. Maybe this time, he would
win instead of lose.

Fool! he screamed silently.

For believing in miracles.

For believing that Kelly was interested in anything
more than getting a story.

For still wanting to kiss a pair of Mona Lisa lips and
trace his fingers across a patch of freckles.

CHAPTER NINE

MITCH AWOKE the next morning to a tapping on the car window. He had been in the midst of a pleasant dream. He and his son Scott were at Candlestick Park, watching the San Francisco Giants go head-to-head with the New York Mets. It was the bottom of the ninth, with the hometown favorites at bat. Bases loaded, two outs showing on the scoreboard, the Giant's most noted slugger stepped up to home plate. In that surreal way that dreams have, the batter's identity changed and became Mitch. His first thought was that he was in way over his head, his second that no, he thought he could knock the ball out of the stadium. He had to, because he had to make his son proud of him again. He had just drawn back the bat to strike the needed home run when he heard the rapping.

Cold, cramped, and groggy, Mitch opened his eyes and stared into Will's expressionless face. In that instant, not having the least idea what Will's decision would be, Mitch realized just how much it meant to him to be included in the Anscott break-in. Not only did he want to help prove Will's innocence and Anscott's guilt, not only did he want to see justice prevail, he needed to be a part of this in order to restore, if only fractionally, a little of his own self-worth. He needed to hit the ball out of the stadium not only for his son, but also for himself. The question remained, however, of whether Will was going to give him the chance to bat.

Rubbing his eyes, Mitch rolled down the window. He waited for the cold Sunday-morning air to invade the car, but it didn't. It was as cold inside the car as outside it, a fact his stiff, achy joints attested to.

"Get those plans," Will said.

"Does that mean I'm in?" Mitch asked.

"You're in. Under one condition."

"Name it."

"I call the shots."

Without hesitation, Mitch replied, "I can live with that."

HOURS LATER, after a special delivery, three people pored over the blueprints of Anscott Pharmaceuticals. The plans, several pages in content, spread the entire length of the bed. Mitch knelt on the floor at the foot of the bed, while Kelly and Will knelt at its side. Both Will and Kelly, though each would have denied it, were careful not to brush against each other.

The cold medication had left Kelly well rested, but her head felt as empty as a feather-light pillow. She fought to concentrate on the plans before her. Curiously, though, she remembered all too clearly the night before. Or at least snatches of it. She remembered Will tucking her in, then he himself bedding down on the floor, an action which had curiously disappointed her.

She remembered asking if he was planning anything foolish and trying to believe him when he said he wasn't. Above all, she remembered his comforting nearness.

Will, too, remembered more than he wanted to—the fact that he'd lied to Kelly about the full reason for his wanting to break into Anscott, the fact that she'd made it clear that the story was all that mattered to her, the fact that he'd wanted, more than a thirsty man wants water, to kiss her.

"As far as a drug company goes, it looks pretty standard, not that I'm an authority on drug companies."

At Mitch's comment, both Will and Kelly corralled their stallion-wild thoughts.

"It appears, at least on paper, to be on the up-and-up," Will said. "With nothing out of the ordinary going on."

"That's what it has to look like," Kelly said. "Remember I said the best way to break in is to make it appear that you're not breaking in at all? Well, the best way to get by with something extraordinary is to make everything look ordinary."

"Well, it certainly looks ordinary enough," Will said. Using his finger to indicate places on the plan, he added, "Here's the office area, here are the production and packaging areas, here are the holding and shipping areas. My guess is that certain parts of the building, notably this area—" he pointed to production "—is off-limits to unauthorized personnel."

"I'm sure you're right," Kelly agreed. "But then, I'm sure it's that way in any drug company. I'm also willing to bet that, if hanky-panky is going on, most of the employees have no earthly idea about it."

"Yeah," Mitch said. "You couldn't risk more than a few people knowing about something illegal."

"Yeah," Will agreed. "Probably only the chemist or chemists involved and probably somebody in shipping."

"And the administrator?" Kelly asked.

"Not necessarily," Will said. "But I'll go into that later. Right now, take a look at this area." Again, he indicated the production section of the layout. "I thought all along that the legitimate drug production area would be under some form of security system, and I think this proves it."

Written in the corner of the area designated the production room were the words: sec system.

Before anyone could reply, Will, as he flipped to the other pages of the blueprint, went on with, "There doesn't seem to be any specifics regarding it, however."

"There wouldn't necessarily be," Mitch said. "Not on the architect's copy. He'd just be aware that such a system was required and would call in the security company when it was time to install it."

"Is there any indication what kind of system it is?" Kelly asked.

"Uh-uh," Will replied, "It could be a number of things—a number punch-in, a fingerprint read-out, a coded card, something along those lines."

"Would it help if we could determine the security company that installed the system?" Mitch asked.

"I don't know how it would," Will answered. "In the final analysis, we still wouldn't have the number, the card, the fingerprints that would magically gain us entrance into the area."

"Are you sure we even need to get in there?" Kelly asked.

"If that's where the illegal drugs are being manufactured, then yes," Will said. "And my guess would be that's where they're being made. This way they would be hidden amongst the legal stuff."

"I agree," Mitch concurred.

Kelly shrugged her shoulders. "Just asking. So what we need," she continued, "is a means of getting into that room."

"Exactly," Mitch said.

"Bingo," Will answered.

"Actually, though," Kelly corrected herself, "our needs are more immediate than that."

Both men looked at her. "We need to find a way to get inside the building—past the guard and the dog."

"Good point," Mitch said.

"Any ideas?" Will asked.

"I'm working on it," she said. "I'm working on it."

BY LATE AFTERNOON, the three of them were working on a pepperoni and cheese pizza. Kelly had noticed that Mitch, who'd refused the offer of a beer, nonetheless eyed theirs with particular interest. Or maybe it was simply her imagination, she concluded, though she knew that it was not her imaginings that Mitch Brody, private eye, was a man down on his luck. While Mitch had gone for the pizza and beer, Will had told her that Mitch was living out of his car, his old car, at that.

She now heard Mitch saying, "The Seattle branch of Anscott is fairly new. The plans show it was built four years ago."

"I know," Will said, reaching for another slice of gooey pizza. "Do you think that means anything?"

"I don't know," Mitch said, swigging down a swallow of soda. "Whether it means anything or not, it doesn't get us inside."

Kelly sneezed, determined not to take any more of the cold medicine, even if she sneezed herself to death. She couldn't afford a muddled mind.

"Sorry," she said, reaching for a tissue. "So what did you mean when you said that maybe the administrator wasn't involved?"

At the question, which was directed at Will, he glanced up from where he leaned back against the headboard of the bed. Earlier he'd been whittling, which he claimed made him think straighter, made him calmer. Kelly thought he looked tense. More than once, she'd caught him staring at her. Each time, she glanced away quickly, because, in a curious parallel, she spent a great deal of her time staring at him. At his hair, which hadn't seen a real comb in days. At his ever-growing beard, which hadn't seen a razor at all. At his lips . . . She made herself drop this line of thought and concentrate on what he was saying.

"I don't think it's a foregone conclusion that he is. Besides, he has a pretty impressive record in administration. He came to Anscott-Seattle from another well-known drug company."

"How do you know all this?" Mitch asked.

"One has a lot of free time in prison," Kelly answered, repeating the statement Will had once made in answer to her similar question. She tried to make her remark sound flippant, and did, but in truth it hurt to think of Will being incarcerated for a crime he hadn't committed.

"You're not going to do anything foolish, are you? At Anscott? You're not breaking in with some stupid notion of avenging your brother? We'll just get evidence of illegal drugs, right. Right?"

"Right."

Why hadn't she believed him? And, if he was planning something, might he not end up being legitimately, justly incarcerated this time? The thought frightened her. The thought left her with the oddest empty feeling, as though it were she herself who had something to lose if he went back to prison.

"Okay," Mitch said, playing devil's advocate. "Assuming he does have this sterling record, wouldn't that be exactly the image he'd want to project if, indeed, he was involved in the illegal drug business? Wouldn't that be his protection?"

"Or someone else's protection," Will added.

Mitch looked intrigued, while Kelly forced herself to concentrate on the conversation going on around her. The truth was that Will was going back to prison for certain if the three of them couldn't prove his innocence. So far, there were nothing but speculations to go on, and speculations didn't get convictions overturned.

"What do you mean?" she asked.

"Simple. If you wanted to get into the illegal manufacture of drugs, and it's possible that Anscott-Seattle was conceived for that purpose, wouldn't you want someone with 'a sterling record'—your words—heading it?" Will said to Mitch. "Preferably someone who hadn't the foggiest idea what was going on under his nose? Nothing rings clearer than the sound of truth, and no one looks more innocent than someone who *is* innocent."

"What do you know?" Mitch asked.

"It's what I *don't* know that's interesting. What I can't find out."

"Which is?" Mitch asked.

"Who owns Anscott." At the rapt attention that both Kelly and Mitch displayed, Will added, "Government secrets have been uncovered with less difficulty."

"I'm not sure I'm following you," Kelly said, clearly fascinated by what she was hearing.

"Anscott doesn't seem to have an owner," Will said. "Or rather it seems to have a slew of them."

"What do you mean?"

"It's owned by holding companies—a company called Quantex, a company called California Realty, a company called Diamond, a company called Santico. And heaven only knows how many more."

"And who's at the top of this pyramid structure?" Mitch asked, as caught up in these engrossing details as Kelly.

"Ah," Will said, "that's the biggest secret of all. The trail just peters out. A few names keep reappearing as stockholders in all these companies, but it's clear that these stockholders don't comprise the majority. Someone else, maybe several someone else's, hold most of the cards in the deck."

"You said you have connections," Kelly said to Mitch. "Is there any way you can find out anything?"

"Possibly."

They had long ago devoured the pizza, and they were down to the last of the beer. Mitch watched as Will and Kelly consumed the final drops. He rose from the chair, walked to the window and pulled back the drapes. He looked tired, worn out.

Will looked at Kelly, Kelly at Will.

At last, Will said, "I'm staking out Anscott tonight. You want to come along?"

Mitch turned. "You bet."

"Then why don't you get some rest until then. You look tired."

Mitch smiled slightly. "Yeah, I guess I am."

"Get yourself a room," Will ordered.

Hesitating, looking uncomfortable and embarrassed, Mitch said, "I, ah, I don't need—"

"Get yourself a room," Will repeated. "Charge it to me."

Mitch looked as though he'd been slapped hard across the face. "I don't need charity."

"It wasn't what I was offering. You charge all expenses to your clients, don't you?"

"Yes, but—"

"You are still working for me, aren't you?"

"Yes, but—"

"Then get a room and get some rest."

For silent seconds, two strong, proud men studied each other. Suddenly, Mitch grinned. "You do know how to play hardball, don't you?"

Will's grin came quickly, unexpectedly, and with enough power to make Kelly feel as though she'd been struck. Never had she felt quite the way she did at that instant, as though the world had opened up to reveal rainbows, sunsets and a dozen other beautiful things she'd never seen before.

"Don't you forget it," Will said.

Kelly knew the words were meant for Mitch, but they applied equally to what she was thinking. No, she wouldn't forget that smile. Not if she lived to be a hundred.

When Kelly raised her gaze to Will's, he was watching her. The smile on his face died. A frown replaced it, as though he resented being caught smiling, as though it made him uncomfortable.

Giving his attention to Mitch, Will said, "We'll leave around eight o'clock tonight."

Seconds later, both Will and Kelly stood alone in the room. The awkwardly quiet room.

"That was a nice thing to do," Kelly said.

"Yeah, well, don't make me into a saint," Will said gruffly. "And just remember, you're footing the bill for the room."

As always, the tone of his voice stung, but not as viciously as it usually did, maybe because she now knew that the lips that could speak so harshly could also deliver a devastating smile.

NIGHT, like an endless, eternal sea, lapped at the red sports car hidden in the heart of the towering woods. Will, Mitch and Kelly—she sandwiched between the two men, her camera slung about her neck—trudged their way to the tree line. Once more their target was the entrance gate. Kelly felt that time was running out, a sentiment she sensed Will shared. If they were going to make an attempt to enter Anscott, it would have to be soon.

In the silence, an owl hooted. It was the only sound except for the trio's leaf-carpeted footfalls and their chorused breathing. Suddenly, Kelly sneezed.

"Sorry," she whispered, tunneling deeper into her jacket.

"What time did the van come the other night?" Mitch asked.

"About nine, nine-thirty," Will said.

"Do you remember the name of the florist?" Mitch asked.

"The Sunny Buttercup," Kelly said.

"I think I'll put a trace on that, too," Mitch said. "Let's find out who owns it."

"Good idea," Will said.

No sooner had Will made the remark than a set of headlights sliced through the darkness.

"Get down," Kelly said, dropping to the ground and peering around a huge-trunked tree. The asphalt road ran only feet from where the three of them crouched, Mitch on his stomach behind a bush, Will behind a majestic fir tree that seemed to reach to the sky. In the distance, the guard dog began to bark.

A van, bearing the Sunny Buttercup logo, came into view, slowed, then stopped at the guard station. Again, Kelly thought she detected the fluid notes of Spanish, although it was hard to tell from this distance.

"Get a photograph, if you can," Mitch said. "Especially of the license plate."

"You're reading my mind," Kelly said, working quickly to uncap her camera.

Years of experience, countless critical moments that couldn't afford to be missed, paid off and, in virtually seconds, she'd readied the camera, brought it to her eye and begun snapping. Even as she was doing so, the van obviously received clearance, for the guard came forward and motioned for the van to enter. It lurched forward and hastened through the gate. Again, with a speed that was impressive, Kelly snapped—once, twice, three times.

"Got it!" she whispered.

"Good," Mitch said.

Will, who had a clear view of the front of the building, said, "It's pulling around back again."

As they watched, the van disappeared.

"Interesting," Mitch concluded. "It's also interesting that the floral delivery's being made on a Sunday night."

"Isn't it, though?" Will said.

"That kind of conscientious service is downright commendable," Kelly commented.

In less than twenty minutes, the van reappeared, making its way through the gate—the driver waved at the guard just as Kelly took another photograph—and sped on into the shadow-filled night.

"You think it picked up a shipment of drugs ready to hit the streets?"

"I'd say that's a distinct possibility."

"One shipment per night?" Mitch asked.

"Not every night," Will answered. "The van was here on Friday night, but not on Saturday. But then it's back tonight."

"Maybe it comes only when a particular guard is on duty," Kelly ventured.

"That makes sense," Will said. "Surely a guard would be suspicious about a floral delivery made on a Sunday night.... Yeah, a guard would be essential to the operation."

"But it's only going to make our job of getting past the gate harder," Kelly said, taking a snapshot of the guard. "If he's on the take, he's going to be more than careful about who gets in and out."

"Yeah," both men responded.

A short while later, Mitch asked, "What now? Do we call it a night?"

"Let's hang around a little longer," Will said. "It's early yet."

The next thirty minutes passed with only scattered conversation being exchanged. Mitch, sitting on the damp ground, wondered what his son was doing. Getting ready for bed? Looking at his baseball cards for the hundredth time that day? Wondering if his father was guilty of what he'd been accused of, even though his father had sworn to him that he wasn't?

Kelly's mind roamed, too. To Rachel. Had she tried to get in touch with Kelly and, if so, had she thought it odd that a sick woman wasn't home to answer her phone? To Will who sat silently, aloofly, his back propped against a tree. Had he always been a loner? Had he always sought out the separate road in life? Or had he, like her, been forced down a road not of his choosing?

Will, the hard, irregular bark at his back, tried to think of nothing. The ability to do so, to shut his mind down completely, was what had gotten him through the past year, perhaps through his entire life. Tonight, however, he found that blissful state of nothingness hard to achieve, partly because he knew what lay ahead. Revenge was a heavy load to bear. Partly because of the woman who sat only feet away. She had believed in his innocence, believed him incapable of violence. Yet violence was what he was planning, and a part of him hated to disappoint her. But, that was the way it was going to have to be. And why the hell did he care what she thought anyway? All she wanted was a story.

Kelly sneezed.

Mitch muttered a "Bless you."

"You need something for that," Will said, his suddenly rough voice once more reflecting the emotional war being waged inside him.

"I have something, thank you, and it makes me feel as if I've been on a cheap drunk."

At the word *drunk,* Mitch shifted his chilled position.

Will glanced at him. "Mitch, why are you doing this? Why are you getting involved in something that doesn't really concern you?"

"You asked me that before."

"You didn't answer me before."

In the stillness, a needle-sharp breeze blew through the trees, leaving a poignant *whishing* in the air, coupled with the pungent scent of evergreens. The owl, which had been silent for a while, hooted again, then seemed to wait, along with Kelly and Will, for Mitch's answer.

"Let's just say that I know what it's like to be accused of something you didn't do," Mitch replied. The admission seemed torn from him, like an arrow ripping at his flesh.

It was an admission Will could understand. In that crystal-clear moment, under a crystal-clear sky, he wondered if his breaking out of prison and into Anscott had to do with more than revenge. He'd denied that he wanted to vindicate his name, and he'd sincerely believed that was not the reason for what he was doing, but now he wasn't so sure.

Nobody spoke for the next ten minutes.

"I hear something," Kelly announced into the silence.

"I hear it, too," Mitch commented.

Obviously so did the guard dog because it began to run the fence, barking and snarling. As though on cue, headlights again penetrated the inky darkness and, in seconds, a car came into view. The car was a limousine, as black as the ace of spades, as long as the last mile of a tiring journey. It rolled to a stop at the guard station.

"Damn!" Will commented. "The back windows are tinted."

Kelly readied her camera as she spoke. "Do you think there's anyone in the back?"

"I don't know," Mitch said.

"What you want to bet there is?" Will said.

"And what I wouldn't give to get a shot of him," Kelly said, aiming her camera as though she could will the window to lower. Miracle of miracles, as though she'd made a deal with the gods, the window of the back seat inched downward. "C'mon," Kelly whispered, excitement speeding through her.

As the silhouette of a man's face came slowly into view, Will whispered, "Get him!"

Kelly's camera began to click.

Because of the distance, and the dim light of the guard station, it was impossible to make out any of the man's features, except that he appeared to have dark hair. A flick of his wrist, and the glowing butt of a cigarette or cigar arced into the night and landed on the asphalt road.

"Jerk, haven't you heard of an ashtray?" Kelly said.

As though he'd heard her, the man turned his face full toward Kelly.

Click.

And then the window was rising, the man disappearing from view, and the car gliding through the gate.

"I wonder who that is," Mitch said.

"I don't know," Will said, adding, "But, mark my words, he's no casual visitor."

CHAPTER TEN

"HERE'S ONE," Will said an hour and a half later.

From where he sat on the side of the bed, the telephone directory spread open in his lap, he reached toward the nightstand, picked up a pad and pen and jotted down the address of a processing lab. Quick Pic promised to be just that—quick, as in within an hour—or the charges were on the store.

"Does it say what time they open?" Kelly asked as she unloaded the film from the camera.

"Uh," Will said as he perused the ad in the directory. "No...yes! They open at nine o'clock."

"Good. The sooner, the better."

She voiced Will's thoughts. In fact, it was going to be hard getting through the next few hours. He fought the urge to drive to Quick Pic right then and wait the night out there. The urge was ludicrous, he concluded.

He sensed that Kelly and Mitch were going to have as much trouble sleeping as he was. From the time the limousine had appeared, excitement had exploded among the three of them. They had watched as the long, sleek creature followed the same route the florist van had taken, then waited impatiently for the limousine to reappear, which it did exactly thirty-three minutes later. Kelly had taken pictures until the roll ran out, hoping to get a clear shot of the license plate. Whether she had or not remained to be seen and was the basis for much of the restlessness the trio shared.

"I saw a one and a three and a *G*," Mitch had said for the dozenth time as he left for his room only minutes before. As he had a dozen times, he'd frowned and said, "I think I saw a *G*. I don't know, maybe it was a *C*. And maybe the three was an eight. I just don't know. I couldn't see. The car moved too fast."

Will detected that Mitch was taking the failure personally. Maybe because it reflected badly on his skills as a detective, Will thought.

"It was dark. None of us could see," Will had told Mitch, knowing all too well what it felt like not to measure up to one's own expectations.

He wouldn't wish that feeling on anyone. Particularly not on Mitch who reminded Will of himself. Mitch Brody was running from something, too—running hard and fast and not too successfully. What that something was Will had no idea, no more than he knew what Kelly was running from. Yeah, he thought, looking over at her, the Golden Girl was running, too.

What would it feel like if, in her flight, Kelly ran straight to him?

Stop it, Stone! Neither Mitch's problems nor Kelly's are your concern. As far as comforting Kelly goes, she can comfort herself. That's what you had to do. That's what you've always had to do. For that matter, she probably has guys waiting in line to perform the service for her.

"What do you think?" Will asked, thrusting this last uncomfortable thought aside.

"What do I think about what?"

"About tonight?"

"I think we're on to something," she said. "The guy in the limo. We have to find out who he is."

She frowned.

"What is it?"

"Nothing," she said, bagging her camera and laying it on the floor out of the way.

"No, something's wrong. What?"

"It's the oddest thing. Something about him looks familiar."

"What?"

"I don't know." She shrugged. "I'm probably imagining it. You know how sometimes someone reminds you of someone else." She smiled. "I'd like to think that I don't go around rubbing shoulders with drug kingpins."

At the mention of her shoulders, Will's gaze dropped to the delicate curve of hers. In the ivory sweater, they looked all too inviting. Will looked away.

"Get some rest," he ordered.

At the sudden change in his tone, Kelly said, "Did anyone ever tell you that you can go from being nice to surly in seconds?"

"Yeah, well," he said, starting for the bathroom. "I told you before not to make me into a saint."

"Don't worry," she called after him. "I wouldn't waste the ti-me." She sneezed, chopping the word in half. A quick-fire succession of sneezes followed.

"And take something for that!"

"No!"

Will turned and planted his hands on his hips. "Stubborn, aren't you?"

"Yeah," she answered with pride. She fought to keep her eyes on his and not on the hips framed by his massive hands, hips that she remembered being pulled tightly against when they'd shared a bed. Last night he'd slept on the floor. Where would he sleep tonight? More important, where did she want him to sleep?

Will, too, fought to ignore the way tight jeans clung lovingly to a slim derriere, the way he remembered that derriere pulled flush against him.

"Go to bed," he ordered, as though he'd run totally out of patience. Which he had. With her and with himself.

AFTER WHAT SEEMED like hours of tossing and turning and listening to Will do the same on the floor, Kelly fell asleep. She'd hardly entered the blissful state, however, when she came awake instantly. Her first thought was that she was alone. Will had left her. Had he handcuffed her? The question sent panic hurtling through her. No, she realized with relief, she wasn't handcuffed. She wasn't— The thought ended abruptly as she heard something, a subtle movement, a sigh, coming from the direction of the window.

The drapes were pulled back as far as they would go, leaving Will silhouetted in the iridescent moonlight. Again, she longed for her camera, desperately wanting to capture the broad, muscle-bunched shoulders.

Hair that seemed to have grown an inch and looked intriguingly touchable as it trailed down the nape of his neck. The casual way he braced himself with only one hand flattened against the wall.

Yes, the camera could probably capture these things, but there was something more, something intangible, something that simmered below the physical surface. A strength of character—he'd have to be strong to endure what he had the past year. An intense loyalty— he'd have to be loyal to pay for a crime he didn't commit—his brother's crime. A bravery that was exceptional. How, then, could he speak of being a loser? How was it possible that he had no idea of his worth?

"What are you looking at?" she asked softly.

If her question startled him he didn't show it. Without turning around, he said, "The moon. It looks like a huge silver dollar pitched into the sky." Before Kelly could say anything, he continued, "That's what I missed most in prison—seeing the moon and the stars, hearing the sounds of the night, touching the darkness."

Kelly tried to imagine such a demoralizing loss of personal freedom, but couldn't. "You won't have to go back," she said as much for her benefit as for his.

Will said nothing for long seconds, then, "Some things are worth going back for."

The bleakness in the statement ripped at Kelly. "Some things like revenge?" When he didn't answer, she said, "Will?"

Don't call me that! he thought, but said, "Drop it."

But she didn't. "I'll help you get evidence to clear you, I'll help you prove Anscott's involved in illegal drug production, but I won't be part of a revenge plot that sends you back to prison."

"If you want out, get out," he said with such a lack of emotion that it frightened Kelly.

Fright immediately turned to anger, however. "You know I'm not getting out!"

"Then drop it."

Again, she ignored him. "What are you trying to prove?"

For the first time since their conversation had begun, Will angled his head in her direction. By moonlight, their eyes met. "I could ask you the same thing."

His words so startled Kelly that she could only stare. Finally, sitting up, she asked, "What do you mean?"

"Seems to me I'm not the only one trying to prove something."

"I don't understand."

"I'm running from the law. What are you running from?"

"I'm not running from anything," Kelly said, brushing back her hair. She was glad that the room was dark. She was afraid that Will would be able to tell she was lying.

"No, I don't buy that. The Golden Girl is running from something. If nothing else, she's running scared about failing. Are you afraid that you might actually do something that isn't perfect, that doesn't win a dozen awards?"

The accuracy of his accusation scared Kelly. "You don't know anything about me," she said in self-defense. She didn't want this conversation to go any further.

"Then tell me about you." Will could hardly believe what he was saying. From the beginning, he'd wanted no personal involvement with this woman. Yet here he was asking—no, demanding—the intimate details of her life.

Kelly could never remember feeling so vulnerable. She had to protect herself, so, again, she said, "I'm not running from anything."

If she had been relentless before, he was no less so now. "Why are you afraid of being left alone?"

"I'm not," she answered, hoping he wouldn't remember how she'd begged him not to leave her.

"The devil you aren't."

"Look," she said. "Just stay out of my personal life."

"What happened?"

"Stay out of—"

"Did someone walk out on you?"

"...my personal life."

"Who was it?"

"Dammit, Stone, I said to stay out of my life!"

"Who was it? A boyfriend, a husband?"

Something snapped in Kelly. "Everybody, okay? Everybody walked out on me. No one in my life ever had the decency to be there when I needed them. My mother died, my father was too busy traveling the world, my husband..."

As before, Will had a strong urge to protect her. "What about your husband?"

Smiling sadly, Kelly folded her arms about her legs, as though trying to hold herself together. "I chased off my husband before he could find an excuse to leave me. At least, that's what he told me I was doing."

"And was that what you did?"

Silence, then a truthful, painful, "Maybe."

"What makes you think he would have left you?"

"Given time, everyone does." It was both startling and therapeutic to give voice to thoughts that had long lived in her mind, to feelings that had long lived in her heart.

"Not everyone leaves," Will said.

"Yeah, sure," she said, not believing him, yet strangely believing him, too. Maybe, just maybe, there was one someone somewhere who'd hang around for the rest of her life. Someone who treasured relationships, who wanted, needed, another person in his life. Someone like Will? She pushed this staggering thought aside, saying "So, what about you, Stone?"

"What about me?"

"Let's put you under a microscope. Let's see what makes Will Stone tick."

"Nothing makes me tick."

"Ah, c'mon, you were more than ready to psycho-analyze me. You were more than ready to tell me I was running from something, more than ready to tell me I was trying to buy attention with perfection."

Will thought Kelly's last comment telling. Nothing had been said in regard to her trying to buy attention with perfection, though the possibility had crossed his mind. Thinking about how maybe he'd tried to buy attention with imperfection, he turned back toward the window, wondering, if it were a mirror, whether he'd cast any reflection.

"Go back to sleep," he said, roughly, wearily.

"No, you started this."

Still staring out at the moon, Will said, "Look, like I said, nothing makes me tick. You've got to exist before you can tick."

"What does that mean?"

"Just what I said. I don't exist." He gave a half laugh. "I have it on good authority."

"Whose?"

"My father's."

Before Kelly could question what she was doing, she slipped from the bed and moved silently toward Will.

"All due respect to your father, but you look real to me."

Her nearness startled Will, startled him and caused his heart to start beating a strange rhythm even before he turned to seek her out. Once he saw her, tangled hair and nightshirt-clad, moonlight drenching her in its platinum glow, his heart ceased its bizarre rhythm. That is, it ceased beating altogether right before it lurched into a breath-snatching cadence. His gaze took in everything: her hair, her eyes, the gentle swell of her breasts, but mostly, like a thief in the darkest night, he kept stealing glances at her lips. Her full, soft-looking, oh-so-tempting lips. Lips that he remembered kissing. Lips that he wanted to kiss again.

Kelly hadn't realized that she was standing so near Will. That is, until he shifted his body toward her, and his eyes moved over her. Then, his nearness, his presence was all she felt.

"Go back to bed," Will repeated in a husky voice.

Kelly didn't budge. Instead, she daringly held her ground. "Why?"

Will delivered the truth just as boldly. "Because if you don't," he said, his voice as thick as winter-chilled molasses, "I'm going to kiss you."

At his confession, his challenge, Kelly's heart danced madly in her chest. "That's impossible," she said, pushing him—herself—to the limit. "You don't exist, remember?"

Will knew that she was baiting him. A part of him resisted. Another part of him fell willingly into her trap. This part of him wanted to prove her wrong. Will Stone did exist.

And then, his eyes lowered from hers to the lips he was trying to ignore. A year's worth of abstinence, a week's worth of wanting, could no longer be denied.

With a low growl, he grabbed a fistful of her nightshirt and hauled her to him. The action, rough and abrupt, forced her to catch her balance by bracing her hands against his bare chest. She had time only to register the strength of his hand, the unleashed power in the thighs pressed against hers, before his mouth, like a storm-tossed wave searching for shore, crashed against hers.

Hard. His lips were hard, bruising, so needy that they elicited an immediate response from Kelly. She felt weak, giddy, yet curiously empowered. She also felt completely feminine in a way she could never remember feeling before. She whimpered at all the warm fluid feelings flowing through her.

Soft. Her lips were as soft as he remembered, far softer than any other woman's lips had ever seemed to him. So soft that they begged to be plundered. Her mouth flowered beneath his, inviting his tongue to enter, to flirt, to know her intimately.

At the touch of his tongue, the warm feelings in Kelly turned blistering-hot. Again, she felt she was falling, this time from the emotions blasting through her. She groaned and dug her fingers into his chest. Tight spirals of hair coiled about her needy, her greedy fingers.

Her passion ignited a fire in Will, a hot, burning, consuming fire that flamed the length of him, centering itself in one highly sensitive part of his body. In reaction, he groaned and buried his free hand, knuckle-deep, in her hair. He arched her neck so that she could better receive the sweet punishment of his mouth.

He wanted her.

The magnitude of this realization struck him like a lightning bolt, causing him to release her as unexpectedly as he'd seized her. Again, she stumbled, this time her eyes were wide with surprise, wide with disappointment. Her moist lips were parted and emitting tiny gasps.

"Go to bed," Will ordered. When she didn't move, he repeated, more harshly than he'd ever spoken to her, "Go to bed! Before we both regret what happens."

Kelly went back to bed, but not to sleep. As she lay there, she had plenty of time to think. Would she have been sorry if they had made love. The answer was consistently the same. No, she would not have been.

From his bed on the floor, Will, too, had trouble sleeping. He didn't waste his time pondering whether he would have regretted making love with Kelly. It really didn't matter whether he would have or not. He knew that she would have. A woman like her didn't take a man like him as a lover and not live to regret it. All things considered, though, she had made her point. Eloquently. She had proven that he existed. Nothing could have been more real than the kiss they had shared.

AT NINE O'CLOCK sharp the next morning, Will, Mitch and Kelly—she squeezed into the cramped back seat of the sports car—dropped the film off at Quick Pic. From there, they went for breakfast. If Mitch noticed that Will and Kelly hardly spoke to each other, hardly looked at each other, he said nothing, though there were times when Kelly thought he eyed them just a little too closely.

Like now.

She smiled through the steam rising off her coffee, crossed her legs, and made certain that she didn't brush against Will, though there seemed little chance of that with him sitting on the far side of the booth. She remembered vividly what had transpired between them the night before. And this morning. She suspected that Will regretted the kiss the moment she saw him. Or rather, the moment he refused to look her in the eye. She knew for certain that he did when she'd offered him the use of her comb and had been rejected. Using her toothpaste on the end of his finger was one thing, using her comb altogether another. The latter was an intimacy he apparently wanted no part of.

"I called this buddy of mine on the police force," Mitch said.

Kelly struggled to bring her mind back to the present.

Mitch continued, "I asked him to check on the Sunny Buttercup Florist—see if he could find out who owns it."

"Good. That may lead us to something important."

"By the way," Mitch said, downing the last of his syrup-soaked pancakes. "The consensus is that you've left the state. Nobody thinks you'd be stupid enough to hang around. Don't worry," Mitch added at Will's sudden concerned look. "I checked discreetly. In fact, the guy I asked knew that I'd once worked for you, so it seemed a reasonable question on my part."

"What does he think you're doing in Seattle?" Will asked, reaching for the syrup pitcher, but making certain that his hand didn't come anywhere near Kelly's.

"Working on a case," Mitch said in answer to Will.

Will nodded.

"Do all private detectives have police connections?" Kelly asked. "Or have I been watching too many movies?"

Mitch looked up, but said nothing for so long that Kelly thought he wasn't going to respond. How odd, she was just thinking, when he said, "I don't know about all private detectives. I, uh, I used to work with this guy." A hesitation followed, during which both Will and Kelly sensed that Mitch was trying to decide whether or not to say something more. In the end, his decision made, he said, "He and I used to be partners."

Partners? As in what? Kelly thought. *"I used to work with this guy."*

A thought jumped to mind.

"You mean you used to be a policeman?" she asked.

"Yeah," Mitch said, adding before either Kelly or Will could ask any questions, "I think the hour is almost up. Or it will be by the time we get back to pick up the pictures."

Kelly and Will took their cue. Mitch wasn't ready to tell them more. Perhaps in time.

Fifteen minutes later, however, Mitch and his past career had been forgotten for the more pressing issue at hand. Namely, the photographs. Eager though they were, the three of them managed to restrain themselves until they reached the car, but didn't even bother to climb inside before pulling the snapshots from the packet. As Kelly began to shuffle through them, both men peered over her shoulder.

"What are those of?" Mitch asked as he turned up the collar of his leather jacket in an attempt to combat the chill.

"Nothing," Kelly said, removing the first four photographs and placing them at the end of the stack. "Just a wedding I covered for a magazine. Here we are," she said, her voice growing excited.

"There's the van," Will said. "But you can't read the license plate."

"You can in this one," Kelly said, showing him the next snapshot.

"Great," Mitch said. "There's the driver."

The photograph, a close-up, revealed the driver to be a dark-haired, dark-skinned, mustached individual.

"I thought I heard him speaking Spanish," Kelly said.

"Damn!" Will said of the next photo. The limousine was nothing but a blur.

"Sorry about that," Kelly said, adding, "But never fear, we should have more of the limo."

They did. In fact, five more, but in each the license plate was illegible.

"Damn!" Will repeated.

"Damn!" Mitch echoed.

Kelly cursed, too, but it wasn't at the unreadable plates as much as it was at her incompetence. Will heard her agony. He placed his hand on her shoulder, reassuringly, and squeezed.

"It's okay," he said.

"No, it isn't," she said. "I should have gotten it."

"You don't always have to be perfect," Will said.

"Wrong. I do," she replied fiercely.

She felt Will's fingers at her shoulder, doing gentle things to her, things totally at odds with her self-flagellation. Up to this point in her life, she'd been rewarded only for succeeding. That Will was rewarding her—that's what his remarkably tender touch felt like—for failing was a novel occurrence. And a not altogether unpleasant one. She glanced up at him, stunned once more by his gentleness.

Their gazes locked, then slowly, as though his touching her had become painful, he removed his hand and rammed it into the pocket of his jacket.

"It's my fault," Mitch said. "I should have gotten the license number."

"It's neither one of your faults," Will said, his voice huskier than when he'd last spoken.

On the way back to the motel, Kelly studied the photo of the dark-haired man in the back of the limousine.

Noticing what she was doing, Will asked, "Does he still look familiar?"

Before she could answer, Mitch asked, "You think you know him?"

"Unfortunately, no. I'm not even sure he looks familiar now."

"Let me see," Mitch said.

Kelly handed him the photograph. He frowned. "You know, he does look sorta familiar."

Back at the motel, Kelly again picked up the photograph of the limousine. Regardless of what she'd told Mitch about no longer knowing if the man looked familiar, she couldn't shake the idea that she'd seen this man before. Had she or was she just imagining that she had? She threw the photograph back on the bed, where the others were strewn about.

"Yeah, I'll hold," Mitch said into the telephone receiver, after placing a call to his former partner. "Hey, Speedy, how's it going?" Mitch listened. "That bad, huh? Look, you got anything for me? Have you been able to trace who owns the Sunny Buttercup?'' Again, he listened.

As he did so, Kelly glanced over at Will, who sat on the edge of the bed studying the snapshots. She looked down at the pictures that had been laid aside. She picked up the ones of the Echieverra-Andriotti wedding and looked them over in a detached kind of way. These were not as good, she decided, as the ones she'd already mailed. Just as she'd suspected, there was nothing here worth sending to the magazine.

''You don't say,'' Mitch said. ''Yeah, I've heard of the company.''

Mitch's comment piqued both Will's and Kelly's interest. Will looked over at Mitch, as did Kelly, who started gathering up the photographs.

''Who owns the Sunny Buttercup?'' Will asked.

''Santico.''

''Santico?'' Kelly repeated. ''Isn't that one of the holding companies that owns Anscott?''

''Yeah,'' Will said, adding, ''the plot thickens.''

''Look,'' Kelly heard Mitch say into the receiver. ''See what you can find out about Anscott Pharmaceuticals. Yeah, like who owns it.''

Yeah, the plot was thickening, Kelly thought, glancing once more at the print of the black-haired man in the limousine. Once more the same question assailed her. Why did she have the feeling that she should know this man?

CHAPTER ELEVEN

KELLY SNEEZED. It was the only thing that had broken the silence since they'd begun another vigil at Anscott.

"Bless you," Mitch said, adding, "oh, I forgot to tell you. I called the Sunny Buttercup Florist, told the manager that I saw one of his vans with the license plate 331J—whatever—speeding, and the man said that the business didn't have a van with that license number."

"You think he was lying?" Will asked.

"No, I don't. I believed him. When you're a policeman, you learn to go with your instinct."

At Mitch's slip of the tongue, the question that had never been far from Kelly's and Will's minds resurfaced. Why had Mitch Brody left the police force? More important, why did he still think of himself as a police officer?

"I figure that the van is used only for transporting drugs," Mitch said. "And that the Sunny Buttercup logo is only a diversionary window dressing. Ten to one, the manager of the shop has no idea what's going on."

"Which eliminates him as being involved," Kelly said.

"Yeah," Will grumbled. "Now that leaves only the rest of the world as possible suspects."

Smiling, Kelly replied, "Actually, you can eliminate three more. You, Mitch and me."

Will looked over at her. She sat in the seat beside him. Even in the dark, he could see her grin...and her lips. Or maybe he couldn't see her lips at all. Maybe he could only *feel* them. Yeah, he thought, the memory of the kiss burning over him, he could feel them even now—pressed against his, his tongue curling with hers, her tongue making it plain that she wanted more of him. Much more of him. At this last thought, he felt his body's response. It was so powerful that the ache seemed to run from head to toe.

Kelly heard Will shift in the seat. She felt his desire, remembered his kiss and longed for things she could never remember longing this painfully for.

"Not everyone leaves."

Was that true? Kelly thought.

"You don't always have to be perfect."

Didn't she? Was it possible that someone could love her, imperfections and all?

"Look," Mitch said, pointing to a van moving down the road and toward the gate.

Both Will and Kelly abandoned their sultry thoughts for saner ones. They caught sight of the van just as it was passing by. The side of the vehicle bore the logo of MacMathson's Cleaning Service.

"You think it's another cover?" Will asked.

Kelly slipped from the car, as did the two men, Mitch from the cramped back seat where he'd insisted upon riding in spite of his long legs. The three of them watched as the van cleared the gate and started for the building. Would it drive to the back the way the Sunny Buttercup van had? No, it didn't. It pulled up to the front, where two men got out. Even in the distance, the trio could see cleaning equipment being unloaded.

"I think it's legit," Mitch said.

"I think it is, too," Will replied.

"I think we've just found a way of getting in," Kelly said, excitement underscoring her words.

The two men looked at her, she at Will.

"Remember I told you that the best way to break in was to make it appear that you weren't breaking in at all?" Before Will could answer, Kelly grinned. "How are you two at cleaning?"

THE RENTED VAN stood in the parking lot of the grocery store. Inside was a rented vacuum cleaner and floor buffer and sundry other items, principally some tools, which Will had insisted upon. Studying the floor plan of the drug company, he'd announced that he might know a way to get inside the security-protected room. Also in the van, packed down in ice, was a pound of hamburger meat which they had just bought. Both Kelly and Will felt as raw as the ground beef. Perhaps more raw.

The night had not gone well. More to the point, it had gone so slowly as to have set a new record for all the passage of time. Will and Kelly had tossed and turned, wanted and yearned, Kelly from the bed, Will from the floor, until, come morning, two moods had been less than terrific. Kelly, quick to lie to herself, held firm to the conviction that her mood had not turned sullen until they'd come to rent the van and cleaning equipment.

"Put all this on my tab," Will had said tersely.

"You bet," she had snapped back, trying not to notice the way his beard was filling out his face, attractively filling it out, or the way his bottom lip was fuller than she'd remembered it. Or the way that bottom lip had clung to hers.

"I mean it. I'll pay for it somehow." *Okay, Stone, she's attractive, but hardly the most beautiful woman you've ever seen. So give this whole want-to-throw-her-on-the-bed-and-ravish-her thing a rest, will ya?*

"Oh, I know you will, or I'll take you to small claim's court." *Okay, Cooper, give this thing a rest. For heaven's sake, he looks like a Neanderthal and acts even less civilized.*

"You've threatened that before!"

"I meant it before!"

"So be original!"

"Just pay your bill, okay?"

"Is anything wrong?" Mitch asked, coming up behind them.

Both Will and Kelly whirled around. Both shouted, "No!"

Mitch eyed his two partners with great speculation. He also eyed the gold wedding band on Kelly's finger.

Kelly noted the direction of Mitch's gaze. Something snapped inside her. The tension that had been building between her and Will since last night, the tension she'd been under for nearly a week now—for heaven's sake, she'd been taken hostage!—erupted.

"Oh, didn't Will tell you?" Kelly asked, her eyes shining as radiantly as the morning sun, as wickedly as a vixen. "We're married."

With that, she sashayed around the two men, jumped into the back of the van and slammed the door in two startled faces.

"The very thought of that, lady," Will had yelled after her, "is enough to make a man hang himself!" After a dramatic pause, he added, "High!"

TWENTY MINUTES and a lifetime later, after both van and car had arrived in the motel parking lot, Will, grumbling beneath his breath as he stepped from the sportscar, headed for the room he and Kelly shared, curled his fingers around the doorknob and opened the door. He stopped dead in his tracks. Kelly, who'd made it there minutes before, stood with her back to him, the telephone held to her ear. A feeling as cold as ice glazed over him when he heard her speak into the phone.

"Call them."

Will recognized the feeling. It had a name, and the name was betrayal. The coldness, like sharp-pointed icicles, jabbed at his heart.

"Yeah, I'll be in touch. Just call them, all right? No, I'm here with him now. Yeah, thanks, Rachel."

Will's feeling of betrayal turned to anger. The ice in his heart melted, replaced by a white-hot fire that leaped into flame. He snatched the receiver out of her hand just as she went to replace it. Startled, she whirled around... and found herself face-to-face with Will's stony expression, his grave-dead eyes.

He said nothing, but in the silence she heard the accusation as though he'd shouted it.

"It's not what it sounds like," she said.

"Isn't it?" he asked as he slammed the receiver back on the cradle. The crashing of plastic against plastic seemed to go on forever.

"No," she said, anger bubbling at his silent accusation.

"Then why don't you tell me what it is. Why don't you tell me who Rachel's supposed to call. Why don't you tell me who you're here with now."

Kelly's anger escalated. "In answer to your last question, a moronic jerk." She started to turn away.

Will grabbed her arm—hurtfully. "Answer me," he snarled.

In an action that Will had come to recognize as uniquely hers, Kelly tilted her chin. "All right. I'll give you an answer. I called Rachel because if I hadn't, she was going to get suspicious, which I suspect she already was. I certainly gave her enough clues early on to make her suspicious." At this, Will's eyes hardened. Kelly couldn't miss his reaction. "What did you expect, Stone? For me to just stand idly by and do nothing while you kidnapped me and dragged me off to Seattle? By the way, you're hurting me."

Will looked surprised that he was even holding her arm, much less that he was hurting her. He released her. The pain continued, though. At least in her heart. She could see, though, that Will was equally in pain. The easing of hers didn't matter to her, while curiously, the easing of his did.

"I called her to allay any suspicions she might have been having," Kelly continued. "It looks odd when you're sick and can't be reached at home, which Rachel had tried to do. I told her I'd been staying at a friend's, that I was better even though I hadn't fully recovered, and that I'd accepted a quick assignment that I just couldn't pass up. I told her I was in Seattle with the subject of my assignment. I also told her to call some key people to tell them I'll be heading out to Europe when I finish here. So that," she added, her anger returning, "is the extent of my betrayal, Will Stone!"

Will said nothing.

Kelly said nothing.

They just continued to stare at each other.

Finally, Kelly's anger, her hurt, spewed forth once more. "Damn you!" she cried, raking curls from her forehead. "How could you believe I'd do that to you after, after...after what we've been through. I thought we were partners, I thought we were friends, I thought we were..." The memory of his kiss raced through her mind. She wasn't exactly certain what that kiss made them. "I thought we were friends," she repeated, adding, "But then no one treats a friend the way you've treated me this morning. All you've done is holler and shout and carry on like a crazed grizzly bear."

"And I supposed you've been in the best of moods."

"As a matter of fact, I was in a good mood this morning."

"Like heck you were!"

"I was! For someone who'd listened to you grumble and groan all night."

"The floor was hard!"

"You chose to sleep there!" Kelly spat.

"And if I hadn't, you know damned well what would have happened!"

"Well, maybe it should have happened! Maybe we wouldn't be biting each other's heads off now if it had! Maybe—"

Whatever else she would have said was buried deep inside her throat, for, in a movement more fluid than a flowing stream, Will yanked her to him and covered her mouth with his. Actually, he did more than cover it; he pressed his mouth harshly, punitively onto hers. At the same time, with not an ounce of coyness, Kelly met his kiss with one of her own. It, too, was harsh. It, too, punished.

At the glorious torture she rendered, Will groaned, slipping his hands down her back and over the swell of her jean-covered hips, just the way he'd wanted to from the moment he'd hauled her back inside that service-station bathroom window. He cupped her hips, tugged upward until she stood on tiptoe and pressed her fully into the vee of his legs. He made no attempt to hide his arousal. Her body, so flush, so plush, against his was the sweetest pain he'd ever known. Sucking in his breath at every sensual stroke, he moved her up and down against the steel length of him.

Kelly moaned in reaction to his honest display of passion.

Dragging his mouth from hers, though he continued to rub her against him, he growled, "I want you!"

"I want you," she said, her breath coming as unsteadily as her heartbeat.

"Now!"

"Now," she confirmed.

"I'm tired of fighting."

"I'm tired of fighting, too."

"I'm tired of wanting you."

"I'm tired of wanting you."

"I'm tired of your lips driving me crazy."

"Do they drive you crazy?"

"Yes, they do. And so does your hair, and your sassy mouth, and your rear end."

He pressed more forcefully against the sweetly rounded object of which he'd last spoken. "I want you!" he repeated through gritted teeth.

In answer, she tangled her fingers in his hair and pulled his mouth back to hers. A frenzy of action began. Lips parted in a wet and wild mating ritual, encouraging tongue to curl with tongue, breath with breath. Kelly whimpered as his teeth bit gently, then not so gently at her bottom lip.

"Make that sound again, and I swear I'll take you here and now," Will growled.

"Promise?" she asked, her scratchy voice that of an impossible-to-resist siren.

"Yeah," he said, looking like a man who meant every word he'd just said.

As tempting as his offer was, something else tempted her. A memory she had of his bare chest. Reaching out, she began, one by one, slow by slow, to unfasten the buttons of his plaid shirt.

As the last button fell away, her eyes still meshed with his, Kelly ran her hands through the slit of the flannel shirt. Her palms connected with skin, with tightly coiled sprigs of hair, with nickel-sized nipples, which grew hard at her touch. Will made no sound. Kelly recognized his silence for what it was: a tribute to his self-control. When her mouth followed her fingertips, her lips kissing his chest, over and over, in a tantalizingly slow rhythm, Will groaned, ensnared a fistful of her hair, and dragged her mouth back to his.

His kiss was hard, even hurtful, and she loved it. She loved, too, how it made her feel—dizzy with desire, woozy with sensation. She grabbed his muscular shoulders for support.

Kelly knew that Will would be a lover of few words. Of that she'd never had any doubt. His silence mattered little, however, when he spoke so articulately with his body. At the moment, his body seemed to scream impatience. His mouth was still fastened to hers as he ran his hands beneath her bulky sweater.

"You feel so good," he whispered, his mouth leaving hers for the column of her upturned neck. He planted tiny kisses there, as he searched for and found the fastener to her bra. He nibbled at her earlobe as he slid his hands around her rib cage. His fingers slipped beneath the loosened bra, his thumbs only tempting inches from her breasts. He stopped.

"A year's a long time," he said. "Maybe I've forgotten how to touch a woman."

"I doubt it," Kelly whispered, as impatient to be claimed as he was to claim.

When he still hesitated, she edged her hand beneath her sweater, placed her hand over his and nudged it upward. She sighed as she filled his palm. Will growled, then eagerly found her other breast. Suddenly, his patience had endured all it could. Dragging the sweater over her head, he threw it to the floor. The lacy bra followed. As did his shirt. This time, when he pulled her to him, her breasts pressed against the solid wall of his chest.

"Yes!" she whispered, feeling the crinkly hair sweetly abrading her tender skin. She reached for his mouth again, to draw it back to hers, but Will stopped her. Anchoring her chin with his fingers, he forced her eyes to meet his.

"I haven't got a thing to offer you. I've spent the last year in prison."

"For a crime you didn't commit."

"Prison has a way of tainting you, making you guilty even if you're not. Even if I hadn't been in prison, I'm totally out of your league. I'm a drifter, for heaven's sake. I'm a loser, a—"

Kelly placed the tips of her fingers across his lips. "Don't ever say you're a loser again," she said.

"You're not. Not if you don't choose to be." She brushed, a finger across his bottom lip, then cradled the side of his bearded cheek. "For one hour in our lives, can't we forget the past and the future?"

"Promise me you won't have any regrets."

The way his thumb and forefinger dug into her chin, the way his eyes, dark and piercing, begged her, bore evidence of his need to hear her vow.

"No regrets," she whispered. "Ever. I promise. Now, you promise me the same."

"How could I regret—"

"Promise!"

"I promise."

They stood staring at each other, Kelly thinking what an odd couple they made—a man who believed himself a loser, a woman who controlled life by always performing perfectly.

Will, too, thought them a strange combination—a fugitive, a hostage. When he'd broken into her apartment less than a week ago, he hadn't envisioned this moment. He hadn't envisioned standing here wanting her so badly that he hurt in every cell of his body. Sweet heaven, he hurt! Sweet heaven, a year was a long time! Sweet heaven, the way she was rubbing against him was enough to make a man . . .

Will never finished the thought. Reaching for the zipper of her jeans, he scaled it downward, even as she fumbled with the zipper of his. In seconds, they had stepped out of their shoes and divested themselves of the cumbersome denim. Will removed his briefs but when Kelly started to remove the scrap of lace she called panties, Will, without a single word, halted her hand. He picked her up, laid her on the bed and followed her down.

Slowly, so slowly that both Will and Kelly thought their hearts would burst, Will slid the sheer lacy silk from her hips, which she raised slightly in order to aid him. At the sight of her, her leanness, her long legs, her femininity framed in curls as spicy-colored as her hair, Will groaned. He might well never ask for more than this.

A rush of hot feeling gushed through Kelly at the sight of him looking at her. His hunger, his approval, was the most powerful of aphrodisiacs.

"A year's a long time," he repeated hoarsely.

"I know," she said, reaching for him and drawing him down to her.

His body was a delicious weight against her. His back, smooth and dark, delighted her as she trailed her fingers up and down his spine, over and across his wide shoulders. She moaned as he kissed her mouth, her eyelids, the swollen nipples of her breasts, the last causing her to arch off the bed. Kelly was afire with a fever. She reached for him, her fingers grazing the hard strength of him.

He groaned again, shifted, plunged into her with a force he hadn't known he possessed. Kelly cried out at his powerful entrance. His mouth covered hers, while his hands cupped her breasts. With her legs wrapped around him, he stroked hard and fast . . . faster than he'd intended, faster than he wanted, but he couldn't stop himself. Kelly was so soft, so hot, that he was lost, deliriously lost, the moment their bodies merged.

The end came quickly for them both. Though neither regretted what had just happened, each was aware that some extraordinary something had just occurred. Some extraordinary something that had changed two lives forever.

CHAPTER TWELVE

ENJOYING THE STILLNESS of the moment, their bodies still soaked in sweat, Will and Kelly lay in each other's arms. Like lazy cats sunning themselves, neither seemed inclined to move so much as a single muscle. Similarly, neither seemed inclined to investigate too closely what had just happened. Both knew that something extraordinary *had* happened—they had each acknowledged this at the pinnacle of their passion—but now that acknowledgement posed a threat. A tender threat, perhaps, but a threat nonetheless. No, it was far better to just lie here and think nothing. It was far better to drown in the aftermath of pleasure, to soak up the sensual bliss of the nearness of each other's body.

"I'm sorry," Will said, substituting one troublesome thought for another. It also dawned on him that this was twice in less than a week that he'd apologized for something, and to the same person no less.

Kelly turned to look at Will. "For what?"

Turning his head so that their eyes met, he said, "For the quick performance."

"As you said, a year's a long time."

"Yeah."

"For me, too," Kelly said, adding, "I haven't been with a man since my divorce."

"What's your ex-husband like?" Will asked, surprising himself with the question. The truth was, though, that he was curious about what kind of man Kelly had been married to.

Kelly smiled. "He's nice—doesn't hate kids or kick dogs. He has a nice sense of humor, loves sports and has a brilliant IQ."

"What does he do for a living?"

"He's a professor at Berkeley. He has a doctorate in physics."

In other words, he was a mega-success, Will thought, once more feeling his inadequacy. He wished now that he hadn't asked.

"What about you?" Kelly asked as nonchalantly as possible.

"I don't have a doctorate in physics."

"That's not what I meant, and you know it."

"Have I ever been married?"

"Yes."

From quite early in their unconventional relationship, Kelly had wanted to know about the past and present women in Will's life. She'd told herself it was only part of her natural curiosity, but she wasn't certain her reason was that simple.

"No," he said, his voice once more flat.

"Why?"

"Never stayed in one place long enough. Never found a woman stupid enough."

Kelly raised up on an elbow. "Is that some more of your father's conditioning?"

Will reached out and caressed the underside of her breast. How odd, he thought, that he could touch her here, but couldn't touch her freckles, couldn't brush back her hair. How odd that just touching her in this simple way could cause a rebirth of sensations that had just been sated, and thoroughly, only minutes before.

"Let's just say that dear old Dad never wasted his time on compliments."

The way his rough knuckles stroked her breast made it difficult for Kelly to concentrate.

"I wish mine hadn't," she said, creatively drawing her finger down the center of Will's chest, across firm muscles and through engaging coils of hair. "How did you stay so fit in prison?" she said before he could respond to her statement.

"Exercise," he answered, but refused to let her off the hook quite so easily. "What do you mean you wish your father hadn't?"

"Compliments were the only things he ever had time to give me. Certainly never any of his time. I grew to think that all he ever wanted from me was an award-winning performance, which I stupidly thought would ultimately buy his attention. But it never did."

By now, her finger had skimmed his belly, toyed with his navel and had started lower. Will placed his hand atop hers. She looked at him.

"That doesn't feel good?"

"It feels too good," he said throatily, his body's hard and thick response confirming his words.

"There's no such thing as feeling too good, Stone."

As unexpectedly as lightning on a clear day, Will grinned. She'd seen him smile only once before and had thought it radiant then. She now thought it the most dazzling thing she'd ever seen.

"You're a real hedonist, aren't you, lady?"

She smiled, too, simply because she couldn't help reacting to his.

"There's nothing wrong with feeling good," she answered, though in her heart she knew that she was a bit of a fraud. She'd spent a great deal of her life pretending she felt good, pretending her daddy wasn't on the other side of the world, pretending that there weren't tears in her eyes. Sometimes she thought she'd even pretended with her husband, that his lovemaking satisfied her, perhaps even that she loved him. Had she pretended with Will? She thought again of the extraordinary thing that had just transpired between them, the extraordinary thing she didn't want to investigate too closely.

"Feeling is a dangerous thing," Will said, his voice full of the very feeling he was denouncing.

Kelly's smile had disappeared along with Will's. "Yeah, maybe you're right."

The clock on the nightstand ticked, but, for Will and Kelly, time seemed to have stopped entirely. Ironically, life seemed measured only in the one thing they were afraid to discuss—feelings.

It was as if feelings were an intimate luxury they couldn't afford, for no matter what they had just shared, one inescapable fact couldn't be ignored. They had no future.

FROM THE TIME that Mitch stepped into the room that afternoon, he sensed that something had happened between Will and Kelly, and it didn't take a genius to figure out what that something was. The fact that their bickering had stopped, coupled with the fact that they couldn't keep their eyes off each other, though each worked hard to do just that, only confirmed Mitch's suspicions.

Mitch squelched the urge to grin. Will wouldn't take kindly to any reminder that the hostage-taker had been taken hostage himself, though, from what he'd witnessed of Kelly's spunk and spiritedness, Mitch thought that Will never had much of a chance.

"Hey, are you with us?" Will asked at Mitch's almost-amused look.

"Yeah," Mitch said, returning his gaze back to the plan once more spread out across the neatly made bed.

"Now here's the drug-producing area of the company," Will said, pointing to the largest section of the plans.

The area was contained within U-shaped corridors, more squared than curved, that wrapped themselves around the sides of the building. Another corridor ran through the middle of the production area.

Will continued with, "The area appears to be a number of rooms, six, in fact, access to which is gained through this interior corridor and this door. All of the rooms may have individual security systems, though my guess is that there's a central system on this common door. Get through this door, or more important, gain entrance to this corridor, and you probably have access to all the rooms.''

"And you think you know how to breach the security system?'' Mitch asked.

"No.''

"But I thought you said—''

"I said I thought I'd come up with a way to get inside the area.''

"But how can you get inside the area without going through this door? This secured door?'' Kelly asked.

Referring to the blueprint, Will said, "See the wall space on each side of the door?'' He didn't wait for an answer. "We can enter through it.''

"You can't just walk through a wall,'' Kelly said.''Why not?'' Will asked. "If there's a hole there.''

Kelly's brows knit together. "You're going to cut a hole in the wall?''

"Why not? A wall's only a wall. You can cut, or saw, your way right through it, Will said.''

"The saw,'' Mitch commented in reference to the saw that Will had insisted they rent.

"The saw,'' Will confirmed, thinking of the metal cutters with which he'd hacked and cleaved his way to freedom through the top of the truck. Comparatively speaking, sawing his way through a wall would be as easy as falling off a log. "You can cut through anything if you have the right equipment.''

"But won't sawing be noisy?'' Mitch asked.

"Sure," Will said. "But who's going to be around to hear? The building's apparently vacated by six-thirty, seven o'clock, right?" This last he addressed to Kelly.

"Right. At least that's what the receptionist said when I called and asked her."

"You just called and asked the receptionist when the building was going to be empty?" Mitch asked.

"Sure," Kelly answered. "I told her I was with MacMathson's Cleaning Service and that we wanted to steam-clean the carpets, but that we weren't real sure when the best time was, that we needed the building to be empty."

"What if there's a guard inside that we don't know about?" Mitch asked.

"That's a possibility," Will answered. "If there is, we'll have to work around him. As far as the noise is concerned, the cleaning equipment will be noisy, too. We'll just have to camouflage any sawing sounds."

"And what if cutting through the wall triggers the security system? What if it's noise-sensitive?" Mitch asked, adding, "Look, I hate posing all the negatives."

"That's your job—to point out the negatives, to head any problems off at the pass," Will said. "And, to answer your question, we have no way of knowing what will set the security alarm off. We'll just have to keep our fingers crossed and hope no alarm goes off."

"And exactly what are we looking for tonight?" Kelly asked.

It was Mitch who answered this, "Designer drugs—Ice, Ecstasy, Angel Dust, anything that's manufactured for recreation, for the streets. We get a sample of anything that looks suspicious, get it out of the building and get it tested. By the way, I've arranged to get anything we find run through the police lab."

"How did you manage that?" Will asked.

"I told you I had connections."

"I'm impressed," Will said.

Kelly wasn't so impressed, at least not yet. She wanted to hear from Will's own lips exactly what he planned to do tonight. Looking at him, she said, "Now, let me get this straight. We get samples of any suspicious drugs, then get them and ourselves out. Right?"

Will hesitated just a little too long for Kelly to feel entirely comfortable. Finally, though, he said, "Yeah, we get 'em out, get 'em tested—"

"And then you'll have the proof that the police need to make an arrest?" Kelly asked. "And then our part in all of this is finished?" She left unspoken the question she most wanted to ask: And you'll walk away from any crazy scheme you might have of personally avenging your brother?

Again, Will was slow to agree, but only Kelly seemed to notice. Mitch rushed on with, "What about getting into the building itself? Is the cleaning service supposed to have their own key?"

Kelly reluctantly dragged her attention away from Will. "No, they pick up the key at the guard station." At Mitch's how-do-you-know-that look, she explained, "I called MacMathson's this afternoon, told them I was a new secretary at Anscott, and that I wasn't certain whether I was supposed to leave them a key at the gate or if they had their own. They said they picked up a key at the guard station."

"You'd make a good detective," Mitch said. "Oh, by the way, there's still no word on who owns Anscott. I'm beginning to think it's a phantom company that just appeared out of nowhere."

"Oh, it's real," Will said, recalling his brother's death all too vividly. As soon as he had a name, someone to hang the deed on, Will was going to make someone pay. Dearly. As far as he was concerned, proving the illegal manufacture of drugs was only the beginning. He knew that Kelly sensed this, though she was working hard to convince herself otherwise. He'd have to be careful. He didn't want her getting in his way.

"What about the dog?" Mitch asked.

"No problem," Kelly said. "I never met a dog who didn't like me, especially if I'm carrying a pound of ground meat."

"What if the real cleaning service shows up while we're there?" Mitch asked.

"They won't until nine o'clock," Kelly said, adding, "I asked about that, too. We'll be in by eight. That gives us an hour."

"But what if they're early?" Mitch said.

"We'll deal with it," Will said.

"What if the Sunny Buttercup van shows up?" Mitch asked.

"We'll deal with it," Will said.

"And what if the man in the limousine shows up?" Mitch asked, then answered, his voice chiming in unison with two others, "We'll deal with it."

"IF EITHER OF YOU want out, now's the time to say so," Will said as the van turned onto the tree-lined driveway leading to Anscott. It had rained again, though at present it had stopped, except for a light and lacy drizzle that left the asphalt road shimmering like a black gem.

Kelly, who sat in the passenger seat, glanced over at Will's profile. He'd been pulling away from her emotionally, even physically, ever since their lovemaking. He'd gone out of his way not to touch her, though, curiously, she found him watching her at every turn. She, too, watched him, however, and, though his ignoring her hurt, in her own way she supposed she was withdrawing similarly from him. Some instinctive sense of survival said that it was the best thing to do, that getting into a relationship with this man would be like getting into quicksand.

"I'm in," she answered, concentrating on what lay ahead, rather than on what lay behind.

From the back of the van, Mitch said, "I'm in, too."

All three wore gray uniforms with billed caps perched atop their heads. Though he couldn't even come close to explaining why, it miffed Will that Kelly, red curls wriggling out from under the cap, looked adorable. Then, too, it miffed him that he remembered all too clearly how those curls felt coiled around his eager fingers.

"Look," Will said, his voice curt once more, "I want to remind you two that this isn't a picnic we're going on."

"Naw," Kelly said. "You mean this isn't a fried-chicken-potato-salad-ants-crawling-everywhere outing?"

Will tried to give her a scathing look but it fell a little short of its mark. Something about the way she held her head reminded him of the sweet irresistibility of her neck.

"What we're about to do is illegal," Will pointed out.

"I say we shut up talking about it and do it," Mitch said.

"Yeah, Stone," Kelly said. "Let's live dangerously."

Less than a minute later, the iron gate and the brick guard station came into view.

"Let me do the talking," Will said, slowing the van.

Kelly sneezed, apologized, then groaned. "Uh-oh, it's the guard that's on duty when the Sunny Buttercup van shows up."

All three knew that chances of their running into the florist van had just increased.

"I gave you a chance to get out," Will said beneath his breath as he pulled the van alongside the guard station.

"Who wants out?" Kelly whispered back. "It's just getting interesting."

"Evening," Will said to the guard who stepped from his protective glass cubicle. The man, light-haired and dark-eyed, wore a military-style khaki uniform and a no-nonsense expression. A gun was strapped to his waist.

"This is private property," the guard announced. As though to confirm this, the dog barked in the background

"Yeah," Will said. "We know. We're the cleaning crew."

The guard looked skeptical. "What happened to Barney and Lou?"

"Both of them came down with food poisoning or something."

Again the guard expressed skepticism when he asked, "Both of them?"

"Yeah. Grabbed a bite of lunch somewhere yesterday. Bad chicken sandwiches. Both of them sick as dogs. Had to be hospitalized."

Still, the guard didn't look totally convinced. He stepped closer and peered inside the van. His gaze roamed over Kelly, then to Mitch in the back seat. "How come there's three of you?"

"Got to clean the carpets. Lou and Barney were supposed to have done it, but now we're stuck with doing it, plus we've got two other offices to clean tonight."

"Why doesn't the van have the company name on it?" the guard asked.

"It's new to the fleet. Look, man, I don't tell MacMathson when to paint the company name on his vans. You know what I mean?"

The fact that Will had spoken the name of the cleaning service made an obvious impression on the guard. Still, the man hesitated.

Kelly could no longer sit quietly by. "C'mon, give MacMathson a call if that's what it takes to get us cleared. I've got carpets to steam-clean, and the night's not getting any younger."

The guard gave her a quelling look.

So did Will.

Kelly was undaunted by both. "Look, I got the number right here," she said, fishing around in her uniform and finally producing a piece of paper. She called out a number, adding, "And will you step on it?"

Again, Will looked as though he could strangle Kelly.

Mitch looked as though he could use a shot of bourbon.

The guard stepped back into the cubicle and, for one brief moment, three people thought that he was reaching for the telephone. Instead, however, he opened a drawer, took out a key and handed it to Will. Three silent sighs filled the van.

"Go on," the guard ordered, as though he'd grown impatient with the whole conversation. It had begun to rain again and the raindrops splotched the guard's impeccably pressed uniform.

The key clasped in his hand, Will waited for the gate to open, then drove through. Turning on the windshield wipers, he glanced over at Kelly.

Before he said anything, she said, "It worked, didn't it?"

Will said nothing. He didn't trust himself to. More to the point, he wasn't certain that he could speak with his heart pounding so heavily.

Mitch could. "One question. Did you give him the right telephone number?"

"Of course," Kelly answered. "He had to have the number himself. The fact that we knew it, too, only legitimized us."

"I'll have to remember that," Mitch said.

"I challenge you to forget it," Will piped up, his heart still slamming against his chest.

It soon became apparent that one of their concerns—the dog—wasn't going to be a concern at all. Once on the property, they could see a fence dividing the exterior yard from the interior. The dog was confined to the exterior, making the property around the building safe to travel.

"Shucks," Kelly said. "I wanted to show you how to win and influence canine friends."

"Keep the meat close," Mitch said. "No telling what we'll find inside."

In seconds, Will pulled the van beneath a porte cochere, and the three of them started unloading the cleaning equipment.

"Mr. Personality might still be watching us," Will said, nodding toward the guard station. "So make it look good."

"C'mon," Kelly said, slipping her camera into a pail and dragging it and a vacuum cleaner toward the front door. "Let's do what we're here to do and get out."

"Don't tell me you're getting prudent at this late date," Will growled.

"Quit grousing and open the door." As she spoke, Will inserted the key and opened the door, which he held for Mitch, who carried in a load of cleaning equipment. As Kelly started through, she hesitated. Looking up at Will, she repeated her earlier question. "We're just getting samples of suspicious drugs and incriminating pictures, right? And then you'll call all this quits and let the police take over?"

"Right," he said, but again Kelly wasn't placated.

CHAPTER THIRTEEN

THE SAFETY LIGHTS within the reception area cast an eerie glow. In the subdued illumination, Kelly could make out a desk, abandoned at the end of the day with its stacks of paper and its mammoth switchboard. A tall plant stood in the corner and furniture—a sofa and two chairs—provided a comfortable waiting area for visitors. Kelly's immediate impression was that the room looked orderly and neat and very ordinary. She wasn't sure what she had expected. Would the waiting room of a drug company where unlawful activities were going on look this...normal? For the first time, she questioned whether they were on the right track. Maybe Will was wrong. Maybe Anscott wasn't involved in anything illegal. Maybe there was a perfectly good explanation for the florist van and the man in the tinted-windowed limousine.

"Check around," Will ordered as he turned on the overhead lights. "C'mon, move your rear," Will called to Kelly in a loud undertone.

"Yes, sir," she returned, snapping a couple of camera shots of the room before stepping toward a door that led off to the right. At the same time, Mitch moved toward a door that led off to the left. Kelly flipped on a light and said in the same hushed tone that Will had used, "It's an office."

"Same here," Mitch confirmed.

Will's only response was to open the door at the back of the reception area. "Let's check this out," he said, heading into a narrow corridor. Kelly and Mitch followed.

To their relief, it appeared the blueprint had been accurate. At least as far as the corridor was concerned. As shown on the plans, it was indeed shaped like a square *U*. Enfolding the building as though embracing it in its arms, it opened into two large rooms at the back, one an equipment room, the other a docking area. Just as expected, the bulk of the building lay within the confines of the U-shaped corridor. Just as expected, the door to this area, which lay opposite the reception room, was locked and protected by a security system that required the insertion of a card to deactivate it.

"The good news is that we're apparently alone," Will said.

"What's the bad news?" Mitch asked.

"The plans were altered. The door fills this entire side of the corridor. There's no wall on either side of it to cut through."

"What does that mean?" Kelly asked.

"That we have to devise a quick alternate plan," Will said, glancing both to the right and left of him. He started tapping on the wall in both directions. "Both of these walls lead into rooms."

"So, what are you going to do?" Mitch asked. "Cut into one of them?"

"I'm going to have to."

"Once inside," Kelly said, "it should have an opening into the corridor, shouldn't it?"

"If they didn't alter the plans again. According to the blueprint, each of the six rooms opens onto the interior corridor."

"Let's do it," Mitch said, glancing at his watch. "We've already been in the building ten minutes."

"My, my," Kelly commented, "how time flies when you're breaking and entering."

The sound of the saw ripped through the silence as its blade sliced through the sheetrock. Her adrenaline pumping, Kelly took photographs as Will cut a long rectangular slab out of the wall. White chalky chunks crumbled at their feet as the slab gave way.

"Timber," Kelly called when the piece of wall tumbled into the room.

Laying down the saw, Will stooped and, angling his tall frame, stepped between the wooden studs. He grabbed Kelly by the hand, saying, "C'mon, we're running out of time."

It was the first time they'd touched since their intimate interlude, and both were unprepared for the effect it had on them. Kelly's hand tingled, while Will's burned as though her fingers had branded him. He released her hand as soon as she'd stepped over the clutter on the floor. Kelly told herself that was what she wanted, for him to let go of her. Why then had she been tempted to cling to him, to entwine her fingers with his and never let go?

On the opposite wall of the room, above Will's and Kelly's heads, appeared an unexpected bright beacon of light. "We better use a flashlight from this point on," Mitch said. "We don't want to call any attention to ourselves."

"Good thinking," Kelly said. "When we find something to photograph, we'll hit the lights."

"*If* we find anything," Will said. "Have you noticed how squeaky-clean this place looks?"

"Yeah, well," Mitch said, "things aren't always what they appear to be."

"Would you look at this," Kelly said as Mitch scanned the room with the flashlight.

A large steel vat occupied the center of the room. To its right, crouching like some metal monster, was another massive bowl-like container with what looked like beaters attached to an overhead hood. Several other pieces of automated machinery, the function of which could only be guessed at, stood nearby. Next to the vat was a conveyor belt. The acrid smell of chemicals hovered in the air.

"Good grief," Kelly said. "It looks like a bakery."

"A squeaky-clean bakery," Mitch said, repeating Will's description. "There don't seem to be any drugs here."

"Let's check the other rooms," Will said, starting for the door.

Slowly, he cracked it open, then stepped out into the corridor, the inner sanctum. Then, a quick check of three other rooms, these fronted with waist-high walls of glass, revealed the same content—lots of phantom-shaped machinery, but absolutely no drugs of any kind, legal or illegal.

"There's probably a holding area for the drugs," Kelly said.

"Probably," Mitch agreed, "though that may be a real problem for us. There's no way we can go through an entire room of drugs in—" he checked his watch with the help of the flashlight "—thirty minutes. Especially since we don't know specifically what we're looking for."

"You're right," Will said.

Kelly could hear his disappointment, and she longed to comfort him. She knew only one way to do that. "What are you two doing? Giving up?" Before either could answer, she trooped back into the corridor. "C'mon, we've got thirty whole minutes."

As she issued her challenge, she wrapped her hand around the knob of the door of the adjacent room. She turned, expecting the door to be unlocked the way each of the other four doors had been. In this case, however, the door didn't budge.

"Well, isn't this interesting?" she said.

"What?" Mitch asked, shining the flashlight in her direction.

"The door's locked." In the sudden beam of golden light, Kelly saw that this room had no glass front. She also noticed a sign. "Hey, what does this say?"

Both Mitch and Will moved to stand behind her, Mitch focusing the flashlight on the square of cardboard. It read:

Special Government Project
No Unauthorized Personnel

"Interesting," Kelly repeated.

"From the beginning Anscott has done some special government-funded research on a variety of drugs," Will said. "That helps justify the high level of security."

"You really have done your homework," Mitch said.

"Yeah," Will said, trying the door and getting the same results as Kelly. "Anyone got any idea how we can get in?"

"Stand back," Kelly said, adding, "We need a file, a paper clip, anything with a sharp point that can be used to jimmy the lock."

Will glanced over at Kelly. "How come you know how to jimmy locks?"

"I'm a woman of many talents, Stone. What about my Swiss army knife? Do you have it with you?"

Will fished in his pocket and produced it.

"Great," she said, reaching for it. "Give me more light, will you?"

Mitch angled the flashlight, saying, "You sure I never arrested you?"

"Absolutely not. I'm too good to get caught. I'm— Got it!" she cried, handing the knife back to Will and opening the door.

Mitch flashed the light inside the dark room. It was unlike the others they'd been in. For one thing, it was smaller and not nearly as neat. It looked like a small lab, with beakers and burners and vials instead of the massive machinery they'd seen elsewhere. There was a desk cluttered with papers and folders in the corner of the room, while a huge island counter stood toward the front. Behind the counter, a green chalkboard ran the length of the wall. Kelly was reminded of her college science classes. This looked like the laboratory of an absentminded professor, not the hideaway of a criminal chemist making illicit drugs.

The same thoughts were probably going through Will's and Mitch's minds, Kelly thought, though neither verbalized them. Instead, Mitch turned on the overhead lights, saying, "If they thought it necessary to lock the room, let's take a good look around."

Both Will and Mitch walked through the room, looking here and there. Will picked up a vial containing a white powder, while Mitch smelled a beaker filled with a red liquid. He grimaced at the pungent aroma, then moved to another beaker, this one a quarter-full of a green liquid. Again, he smelled the contents. He started to put the beaker down, then, a thoughtful look on his face, he brought it back to his nose. He inhaled again.

Will, who'd observed his actions, said, "What is it?"

"I don't know." He sat the beaker down and reached for the vial that Will was still holding. Dipping the tip of his little finger into the white power, he brought his hand to his mouth for a taste. His eyes widened. "Do you know what this is?" Neither Will nor Kelly had a chance to answer. "Cocaine. The purest I've ever seen."

"Cocaine?" Will said, excitement lacing his voice. "You think they're peddling cocaine?"

"No. Surely it isn't that simple. Every Tom, Dick and Harry is peddling cocaine, and they don't need a setup this elaborate." A frown at his lips, Mitch reached again for the beaker of red liquid. He inhaled. Put it down. Picked up the beaker containing the green liquid. Suddenly, a strange look crossed his face. "Are these the only ingredients in the lab?"

Will and Kelly started looking around. "Looks that way," Will said. "What do you think?"

Mitch couldn't keep the exhilaration from his voice when he said, "What I think is that they're peddling something far more insidious than cocaine. Ever hear of a drug called Delight?"

"No," Will and Kelly answered in unison.

"It arrived on the scene about a year, a year and a half ago. Maybe two years now. Anyway, it's very complicated chemically. Appeals to a very sophisticated, very rich, clientele."

"What is this Delight?" Will asked.

"The best way to describe it is Mr. Cocaine meets Mr. Peyote, with a dash of Miss Wonderful thrown in."

"Peyote? Like the cactus?" Kelly asked.

"Yes and no. It's a cactus, but not the one from which mescaline is derived. This is a cactus grown exclusively in the south of Mexico."

"But its extract is hallucinogenic like mescaline?" Will asked.

"Oh, no," Mitch answered. "It's a dozen times stronger." He picked up the beaker of green liquid. "And I think this is it." He pressed the beaker under Kelly's nose. "What does this smell like to you?"

Without hesitation, she said, "Newly-mown grass."

"Yeah," Mitch said, a grin slashing his face. "That's exactly what we were told in the police force—the extract smells like newly-mown grass."

"But you haven't heard the good part yet," Mitch said, his blue eyes sparkling. "The cocaine and the cactus extract are blended with a high-powered drug that stimulates the pleasure center of the brain. This is what runs the cost up."

Kelly had begun to take photographs. "You think this red stuff is what stimulates the pleasure center?"

"Possibly."

"The ultimate high," Will commented.

"Yeah," Mitch said. "And when you OD, you die happier than you've ever been."

"So what do we do?" Will asked. "Take samples of these—" he indicated the beakers of red and green liquid, plus the vial of white powder "—and have them tested?"

"If we can't find the final product," Mitch said, starting to look around. "Which should be a capsule."

"Liquids in a capsule?" Will asked.

"That's another reason the drug is expensive. The liquids are crystallized, then ground into a powder. That's why it has to be done in a lab by chemists. The average Joe Blow doesn't know the slightest thing about the procedure."

Kelly was still snapping photographs as quickly as she could. "What time is it?" she asked.

Mitch checked his watch again...and cursed. "We've got less than ten minutes before the cleaning service is scheduled to arrive."

"If they're early, we're in deep trouble," Will said.

"Yeah, like in up to our necks," Mitch said, adding, "C'mon. Let's take these samples and get the heck out of here."

In seconds, three empty vials had been procured and samples taken. "I'll carry them," Kelly said. "You guys have the cleaning stuff."

"Guard them with your life," Will said. "Make sure the stoppers are on properly."

Mitch turned off the overhead light and switched on the flashlight. Kelly closed the door behind them. Dashing down the corridor, the trio slipped through the hole in the wall.

Both men hurriedly began to reload the van with the equipment. Once that was done, Will called again, "Let's go!"

"Where's the key to the building?" Mitch asked.

"The key? Where's the key?" Will mumbled, ramming his hand into the pocket of the uniform. "Here it is," he said, tossing the key to Mitch, who turned out the overhead lights and locked the door.

"Let's go!" Will repeated.

Taking great care, Kelly settled herself in the passenger seat of the van.

"Here, let me have one of the vials," Mitch said from the interior of the vehicle. Kelly handed him the vial containing the cactus extract, or what they hoped was the cactus extract.

Will started the van and pulled it from beneath the protective porte cochere out into the fast-falling rain. Adrenaline rushed through Kelly now that their mission had been completed—and possibly successfully. She also felt a chill. She hoped her cold wasn't worsening. Once this was over, she was going to give herself up to chicken soup and bed rest. The thought of all this being over, of Will walking out of her life as dramatically as he'd walked into it, stung as sharply as the bite of a viper, yet she knew it had to be.

Driving cautiously, but quickly, Will soon reached the gate, which he'd hoped would swing open at their approach. It didn't, however, for the guard, his back to them, was occupied with a telephone call.

Will cursed.

"Keep the vials out of sight," he said under his breath. "Assuming, of course, we ever get to pass through."

Kelly, anticipating this need, had already begun to slip the two vials between her legs. She draped her arm so that the stoppered tops weren't visible.

"What time is it?" Will asked.

"You don't want to know," Mitch replied.

As though to underscore the truth of this statement, Will saw a pair of headlights advancing toward Anscott. Both Mitch and Kelly noticed them, as well.

"Don't panic," Will said, giving the horn a beep.

The guard turned around, glared, then went back to his phone call.

"The jerk," Will said.

"This has got to be Barney and Lou," Mitch said.

"Miraculously recovered from food poisoning," Kelly said, adding, as she glanced over at Will, "How are you at driving through gates?"

"We're about to find out," Will said. "Mr. Personality has five seconds to open up. One. Two. Three. Four. Five."

Will revved the engine just as the gate began to swing open—slowly swing open. In the meantime, the pair of headlights drew nearer.

"C'mon, c'mon," Mitch coaxed the gate.

With a coolness that was admirable, Will pulled the van adjacent to the guard station and passed along the key.

"That was quick," the guard said, a smug look on his face, obviously pleased to have made them wait.

Will said nothing, and drove on past the station. He began to pick up speed. In seconds, they passed the cleaning van. Will accelerated and sped down the road.

"I'd say all hell's about to break loose," Mitch said.

"I'd say that smug look is about to be wiped off of Mr. Personality's face," Kelly said.

Will had no sooner turned onto the interstate than another van exited onto the asphalt road. The van bore the logo of the Sunny Buttercup Florist.

Mitch laughed.

Will smiled.

Kelly thought the ending to the evening perfect. She started to remove the vials from the anchor of her legs. At the same time, she sneezed—three times in rapid succession. Unbelievably, nightmarishly, one of the vials struck the camera and spilled its contents all over the pants leg of her uniform. Her reaction stunned even her. Fear, as ruthless as a biting-cold wind, surged through her, leaving her numb, leaving her immobile, leaving her a child once more.

HOURS LATER, Kelly lay in bed in the darkened motel room. The adult in her had forced the fear into a manageable corner of her heart, though she could not force the incident from her mind. She had failed Will. Just the way she had failed her father.

"Daddy, look at my report card," an excited fourteen-year-old Kelly had said. Her father had been home for a whole three days. More important, he'd told her that he would be home for two weeks. Two full weeks! That was more than she could ever remember his being home at one time.

"In a minute," her father had said, typing away at a magazine article that had to be at the publisher's by morning.

Already-typed pages of the article lay on his desk. Nearby sat a full cup of coffee, which Kelly had brewed just the way he liked it. In fact, after tasting it, her father had proclaimed it perfect. Perfect. Without error. Without mistake. That was the way she wanted to be for her father. More to the point, it was what she *had* to be.

"I made straight A's, Daddy. Mr. Prudue—he teaches science—said that my project notebook was the best he'd ever had turned in."

"That's good, sweetie," her father had mumbled, but she'd known that he hadn't really heard what she'd said. Maybe if she got closer, maybe if he could see the five A's, the five perfect A's marching single file in a black inky line on the report card, then she could capture his attention.

"Look, Daddy," she'd said, stepping closer, closer, closer.

The sound of the tumbling cup was indelibly etched in Kelly's memory. In retrospect, she believed she could hear the coffee splashing out, even hear it spreading all over the finished pages of the article.

"Look what you did!" her father had shouted. At the tears that gathered in her eyes, he had softened his tone, *"It's all right, Kelly. Daddy didn't mean to holler."*

But things hadn't been all right. When she'd awakened the next morning, he was gone. The housekeeper had told her that, during the night, he'd gotten an important telephone call and had had to fly to Africa—Nairobi—to cover an important story. Kelly hadn't believed that was the reason he'd left, however. Nor did she believe it for a long time thereafter. Ironically, almost two dozen years later, the child in her still believed that she'd driven him away with the accident, with her imperfection.

And now she'd failed Will. What's more, it was for the second time. The first time had been when she hadn't gotten a clear photograph of the license plate of the limousine. That failure, however, paled in comparison to her latest.

"I'm sorry," she said softly into the stillness.

She knew that Will was awake. She'd heard him tossing and turning on the floor. She'd seen him get up, pull on the plaid shirt, which he left unbuttoned, and move to sit in the chair by the window. This time, however, he wasn't watching the moon, but rather the steady drizzle of rain. She saw him angle his head toward her. She wanted to ask him why he wasn't in bed with her. She wanted to ask him why he was pulling away from her. She wanted to ask him why she was pulling away from him.

"How many times are you going to apologize?" he asked.

"How many times will it take to change what happened?"

She sensed his smile, that rare phenomenon that seldom visited his lips, but, when it did, it made such a spectacular showing.

"Unfortunately, life doesn't work that way. If it did, I would have changed a lot of mine," he said.

"I really am sorry," she repeated. "It was incredibly clumsy of me, incredibly stupid."

"Would you quit beating yourself up? Besides, it's no big deal."

At this Kelly sat up in bed and thrust her fingers through her hair. "No big deal?" She laughed, but the sound wasn't a pleasant one. "I may have just blown your chances of proving that Anscott was manufacturing illegal drugs. By now, they know the building was broken into. By now, whoever's behind the production of Delight has cleaned up the lab until you couldn't find a speck of dust, let alone a speck of anything illegal. Talk about squeaky clean!"

"You haven't ruined anything. We still have the vial of cocaine and the vial of cactus extract, and Mitch thinks the police lab can ferret out the pleasure stimulant by testing the spot on the uniform."

"You don't know that. He doesn't know that. He only said it to make me feel better." She sighed in self-derision. "I can't believe I was so clumsy!"

"Stop it!" Will's voice rang harshly, but not punishingly. Kelly wanted that voice to tell her that everything was going to be all right. She also wanted him to hold her, to kiss her, to make love to her just one more time. But he didn't. Instead, he stared at her until she could have sworn she was melting. Then, without warning, he said, his voice once more detached and filled with no emotion, "Go to sleep."

Kelly lay back down. Sleepless, she stared once more into the darkness, pondering mistakes; the man who was so near, yet so far away, and a moon that refused to shine on a night that cried.

THE TAP on the door was so slight that Will wasn't certain he'd heard anything. He'd just about decided that, indeed, he hadn't when the tap came again, this time louder. He pulled his long frame from the chair and, exercising caution, peered around the edge of the drapes. He saw Mitch, huddled in a leather jacket, standing in the rain.

"I'm sorry to bother you," Mitch whispered when Will opened the door.

"That's all right. I wasn't asleep."

"Yeah, that's my problem, too. I guess I'm just too keyed up." Mitch swiped at a wet strand of hair that tumbled onto his forehead.

"C'mon in."

"No, that's all right. I just wanted to tell you that I'm heading out to San Francisco. I want to get those samples to the lab as soon as possible. And, since I can't sleep, I might as well go now."

"What time is it?"

"Around three o'clock."

"You sure you don't want to wait until morning?"

"Yeah, I'm sure. Besides the sooner I get these to the lab, the sooner we'll know."

Even though he knew the answer, Will asked the question. "Do you think they can identify the drug from that dried spot?"

Mitch didn't hedge with Will, though he'd tried to spare Kelly's feelings. It was obvious that the accident had upset her deeply. "I honestly don't know. Let's believe the best until we know otherwise."

"Yeah," Will said, not at all accustomed to believing the best. It always seemed too risky.

"Well," Mitch said, "I'm heading out."

"Keep a record of your expenses—gas, food, whatever."

"Yeah, sure. Look, as soon as I have some news I'll let you know."

"Check again to see if you can find out who owns Anscott."

"Yeah, that's on my list." There was a slight hesitation, then, "Well, I'm out of here."

"Be careful," Will called quietly after Mitch as he started for the car. Mitch didn't turn around, but merely waved a hand in the air. Pulling open the car door, he started to crawl inside when Will spoke again, "Hey?"

Mitch, his arm hitched on the opening of the door, looked up.

"Thanks," Will said.

The two men stared at each other through the falling rain. "Hang tough," Mitch said finally, the words meant not only for Will, but also for himself. And then he was gone.

MORNING CAME with a marbled sky that mocked yesterday's rainy evening. Though he hadn't slept a wink, Will arose with a freshness he found surprising. Or maybe it wasn't surprising at all. He'd waited a long time—ever since he'd heard of his brother's death—to carry out the next step in his plan.

Dressing quietly—he mustn't wake her (even now, more than ever now, he refused to acknowledge her by name)—he stepped to her purse, which lay on the dresser. Though he hated his dependence on her money, there was no other way. He'd find a way to pay her back. That he promised himself. Digging through the contents of the purse, he found the traveler's checks. Although he'd have to forge her signature, he figured it didn't much matter. He'd served time for worse.

Will was on his way to the door when Kelly made a soft, little whimpery sound. He stopped, looked over at her and noted the curls that clustered on the pillow, across her forehead. One in particular captured his attention. The ringlet, crimson and coiled, spilled across her closed eyelid and onto the bridge of her nose, her freckle-dappled nose. As he had so many times, he had the urge to brush the curl aside. As he had done before, he told himself the act was far too intimate to even consider.

Then why was he walking toward her? On feet softer than a lover's plea? Don't, he told himself as he hunkered down beside the bed. Don't do something that you'll regret. But as he crouched beside her, as he looked down at her, a question formed: Would he regret it even more if he didn't brush the curl aside? At some point in the future, when this week was but a memory, would he regret denying himself this one sweet, forbidden intimacy?

The answer came quickly, unequivocally.

Reaching out with his forefinger, he tentatively grazed the curl. It looked shiny; it felt silky, like the little-nothing underwear she wore. It also seemed to cozy up against him, the way a cat rubs against a leg for attention, for affection. Will was totally lost, totally mesmerized, though not so lost as to lose sight of the fact that he mustn't awaken her. And so he didn't belabor the moment. With a fingertip, he gently drew the curl aside, to a place along the curve of her cream-colored cheek. He hesitated only a second, a second was all he dared, before pulling his hand away. He then stood and walked toward the door and out of the room. Even as he did so, he couldn't shake the feeling that he'd just done something astonishingly wonderful, something astonishingly foolish.

A FEW MINUTES before eight o'clock, Kelly woke up abruptly. She didn't even bother looking around for Will, or calling out for him. She knew she was alone. The deafening silence told her she was. The empty feeling in her gut told her she was. It was the same empty feeling she'd felt the morning after she'd spilled her daddy's coffee. She'd known he was gone even before the housekeeper had told her. No goodbye, no farewell, no sorry I'm leaving you again.

Yes, she'd been alone then.

She was alone now.

CHAPTER FOURTEEN

WILL WASN'T coming back, Kelly decided an hour later as she peeked through the slit in the drapes for the dozenth time. He'd taken the rented van, and, as far as she could figure, about two hundred dollars in traveler's checks from her purse. Okay, Cooper, call a spade a spade. He *stole* the checks from your purse!

Damn him! she thought, but she knew that the sentiment had nothing to do with his taking the money and everything to do with the fact that he'd left. She might have been able to convince herself that he and Mitch had gone somewhere—maybe even back to San Francisco—if the van hadn't been gone along with Mitch's car. Had Will returned it to the rental agency? Or, the thought suddenly hit Kelly, had he gone out alone on some crazy mission of revenge? But how did he know who to blame for his brother's death?

Good point, Kelly thought, stepping away from the window and once more beginning to pace the room. He had to come back. The game plan was for Mitch to call the motel, this room, when he knew something. Okay then, that settles it. He'll be back. He can't afford not to. Unless—

And so it went, over and over and over again. One minute she was convinced he was gone for good, driven away by the accident (totally illogical, she knew, but there it was!), the next that he'd come walking through the door at any moment.

Which was precisely what he did at eighteen minutes after ten o'clock. Kelly had just donned a pair of khaki slacks and an ivory sweatshirt and was running the hairbrush through her hair when the door opened. She hadn't even heard him approaching, hadn't even heard a key in the lock.

She looked up. Her hands, even the one holding the hairbrush, snapped on her hips. "And just where do you think you've been?"

Her pose looked for all the world as though it belonged to a wife confronting her just-returned husband, a fact that set Will's mind to spinning. What would it be like to be married to this woman? He couldn't believe he was even considering such an outrageous notion. He'd never considered marriage before, with any woman, and he wasn't the slightest bit interested in doing so now! He slammed the door behind him as though to punctuate this declaration.

"I think I've been out."

"You think you've been out?" Kelly repeated, knowing how absurdly stupid her reply was, but for the life of her, she couldn't think of another blasted thing to say.

"I believe that's what I said."

"Are you such an insensitive creep that you couldn't tell me you were leaving?"

"You were asleep," he said, shrugging out of the corduroy jacket and prudently dismissing images of her lying in bed, images of a curl that he couldn't get out of his mind.

"You couldn't have awakened me?"

He grinned—wryly. "What do you think I am? An insensitive creep?"

As she watched, he pulled his wallet from his back pocket and, crossing to the dresser, returned some money to her purse—a few bills and a couple of coins.

"I borrowed some money," he said.

"So I noticed."

"Don't worry. I'll pay it back...if I have to sell body parts to do it."

Kelly's thoughts ran rampant at the mention of body parts—a broad chest, muscular legs that entwined hers, a flat belly that fell away to... She chopped the thought off midstream, asking, "And just what, may I ask, did you buy for two hundred dollars of my hard-earned money?"

"What I bought is none of your business. And it didn't cost two hundred dollars."

"I beg your pardon. It's none of my business what you spend my money on?"

"That's right. It's none of your business where I've been. It's none of your business what I bought. In fact, nothing about me is your business."

"I don't believe you. Do I need to remind you that I didn't ask to be dragged along on this little excursion?"

"No, as a matter of fact you don't, but I'm glad you did remind me." He nodded behind him. "There's the door. Use it."

He knew what he was saying was razor-sharp and sure to inflict pain. What he didn't understand was why he was trying to hurt this woman...and why he seemed to be hurting himself in the process. All he knew was that some survival instinct told him that the longer he was with her, the harder it would be to say goodbye.

Kelly heard what he said. She understood what he said. She just couldn't believe that he'd said it. Nor could she believe how much it hurt. He'd used her and now was tossing her out on her ear. Hurt turned to anger.

"Did anyone ever tell you that you're a real piece of work? A real jerk? A real son of a—"

"Look, lady, you're free to go, okay?"

"Did it ever cross your mind that I might not want to be free to go? And why don't you stop calling me lady and call me by my name?"

Will ignored these last remarks. "Look, I'm not all that familiar with the procedure for taking people hostage, but I think the hostage-taker gets to decide when to free the hostage. I believe that's the way it works. Not vice versa."

Kelly threw the hairbrush onto the dresser, where it made a thwacking sound. She started toward Will like a she-devil on a mission.

"Well, that just shows how much you know, Will Stone. If you think that I've gone through everything I have—your breaking into my apartment and scaring me half to death, your dragging me here to Seattle, your handcuffing me—just to get tossed out before I even know the outcome... Well, you're sadly mistaken and crazier than I originally thought you were, which I might add, was fairly crazy."

She now, just as she had once before, stood nose to nose with Will. He was aware of the fresh, woodsy smell of her perfume. He was also aware of the way she'd avoided mentioning their lovemaking. He wondered how she categorized that. As something that never should have happened? A pleasant interlude to be enjoyed for what it was—two people wanting to make it with each other? For that matter, he wasn't certain how he categorized it, although he did know that he was having a hard time forgetting it. He was also feeling the need to strike again, because, beneath it all, he thought he knew the reason she didn't want to walk out the door. And he suspected that reason had nothing to do with him.

"What's wrong? Are you afraid you're going to miss out on that story? Are you afraid you're going to miss out on winning another award?"

Kelly felt as though she'd been slapped, which perhaps accounted for her reaction. Without thinking, putting all of her strength into it, Kelly struck Will full across the face with the palm of her hand. Even with the beard to cushion the blow, its strength snapped Will's head back.

His reaction was no less spontaneous than hers. With frightening speed, his fingers snaked out and grabbed her wrist.

Between one heartbeat and the next, the gates of both heaven and hell seemed to open. Hell because of the anger, the fury, that flashed through each of them, around each of them. Heaven because, no matter what the reason—a slap, the grabbing of a wrist—they were touching. And that was what each wanted more than anything else.

"Kiss me!" she screamed silently.

"Don't you dare kiss her!" Will told himself, abruptly releasing her.

She staggered backward, caught herself and said defiantly, "I'm staying."

"Suit yourself," he answered, turning his back on her as though she'd ceased to exist.

From the way he behaved the remainder of that morning and afternoon, Kelly thought perhaps she *had* ceased to exist. Will spoke to her only when he had to, and then only in monosyllables. When she asked him if he thought the van and the rented equipment—minus, of course, the uniform she'd worn—should be returned, Will, never looking up from his whittling, replied in the negative. She waited for him to elaborate, but he said nothing more, and so she dropped the subject.

During midafternoon, a patrol car, with two policemen inside, pulled into the parking lot of the motel. Will was the first to notice it. Easing from his chair as slowly as a cat stalking prey, he closed the drapes, then peeked out discreetly. Kelly, whose heart had begun to pound, not only for Will, but also for herself—after all she had joined the ranks of the criminal when she'd broken into Anscott—peered out the other end of the drapes. The van was parked nearby, two slots away from her car. If the police were searching for the van, it was only a matter of time until they spotted it. The patrol car, however, drove right past the van with total disinterest, then pulled back out into the street and disappeared.

Kelly and Will looked over at each other.

"That was close," she said.

"Yeah."

"You think the break-in was reported to the police?"

Will shrugged. "Who knows?"

That conversation marked the last of their civil dialogue. With each passing hour, two sets of nerves grew more frayed, until, by late afternoon, with the sun setting and night approaching, both Will and Kelly were fit to be tied. Will had even stopped whittling and had begun pacing the room. Kelly, who had been pacing, stopped long enough to study once more the photographs of the man in the limousine. She had just concluded, for the umpteenth time that the man looked familiar, when the telephone rang.

Both Will and Kelly raced for the phone. Will beat her by no more than half a second, grabbing the receiver and sitting down on the bed.

"Hello?"

"You sitting down?" Mitch asked without preamble.

"Is that a sit-down good news or a sit-down bad?"

"Try a sit-down excellent." Before Will could respond, Mitch said, "The lab made a positive ID of all three of the samples. Each is exactly what we thought it was. Looks like Anscott's up to its ears in the production of Delight."

Will grinned and, forgetting that he and Kelly were at odds, gave her a thumbs-up sign.

"They could determine the chemical content of the spot on the uniform?" she asked.

Will nodded, adding, "Anscott's making Delight."

"All right!" Kelly said, suddenly feeling higher than a kite. Her accident with the vial hadn't ruined everything.

"That's not even the best news," Mitch said, after hearing Will pass along the findings.

"What do you mean?" Will asked.

This last question captured Kelly's attention, and she moved to sit on the bed alongside Will. "What is it?" she asked.

"I think I've discovered who owns Anscott," Mitch said.

"What did you say?" Will's voice was incredulous.

"What did he say?" Kelly echoed.

"I think I know who owns Anscott." Mitch's voice rose in enthusiasm. "And you're not going to believe who it is."

"Who?" Will asked, his fingers painfully clutched about the receiver.

"Edward Andriotti."

The name had been spoken as though Mitch was presenting him with an early Christmas present. All he was giving Will, however, was a name that meant absolutely nothing to him. "Who is this Edward Andriotti?"

"Edward Andriotti?" Kelly asked, frowning. "What about Edward Andriotti?"

"You don't know who Edward Andriotti is?" Mitch asked, then answered his own question. "Sorry, I forgot you're not from San Francisco."

"Who is he?" Will repeated.

"What about Andriotti?" Kelly repeated.

"Lives on Knob Hill, owns half the real estate in the city, attends every social gala," Mitch said in answer to Will's question. "The kind of guy that everyone says they know even if they don't. We're talking old, old, old money here. We're talking squeaky clean."

"Then why do you think he owns Anscott?"

Kelly's expression turned to one of total shock. "Andriotti owns Anscott?"

"I'm not one hundred percent sure, but I'm ninety-nine point ninety-nine. While I waited for the lab results today, I checked up on Santico. Remember they own the Sunny Buttercup?" Not giving Will a chance to answer, Mitch moved on with, "I discovered that Santico owns several other companies, as well. To make a long story short, I called one of those companies, a security company, and got a talkative secretary who volunteered that she'd once been a guest at the wedding of Edward Andriotti's daughter. Her boss, who's apparently sweet on her, finagled an invitation for her. Apparently, it was the highlight of her life."

"But what's this got to do with—"

"Let me finish," Mitch interrupted. "Now, I asked myself, why would the boss of this two-bit company be going to such a classy wingding...unless this guy knew Andriotti in a pretty substantial way. So I checked on the guy. Before this low-profile company, he worked at two other small companies. He also used to work at the San Francisco branch of Anscott...as a security guard. And get this, the guy has a brother who works for Anscott-Seattle as a guard."

Will's heart was pounding. "Mr. Personality?"

"That's my guess. Now, here's the real good part. I called Edward Andriotti's Knob Hill home, pretending to be one of his Knob Hill friends, and was told that Mr. Andriotti was out of town on business for a few days. When I asked where, because I really needed to confirm his presence at a charity gala, I was told he was in... are you sitting down?" he repeated.

"Spit it out."

"Seattle."

"Are you serious?" Will said.

"What?" Kelly asked impatiently.

"Dead serious," Mitch said. "I think that Mr. Personality contacted Andriotti about the break-in, and Andriotti flew up to get rid of any incriminating evidence. In short, to clean house as fast as he could."

"Yeah," Will said, his heart beating a mile a minute. "That makes sense."

"Will someone tell me what's going on?" Kelly shrieked.

"Andriotti owns Anscott and he's here in Seattle," Will said to Kelly.

"He's here?"

"Yeah, here. And Mr. Personality, and his brother, work for him."

Kelly let what she'd just heard seep in. On one hand, it seemed preposterous, while on the other, it didn't seem preposterous at all. She wasn't quite certain about the why of this, except that something seemed to be falling into place in some far corner of her mind. Something that was still hazy and foggy, but there just the same. She stood, walked to the window and peered out. A million disjointed images went through her mind at lightning speed. She let them come.

A crisply cut, emerald-green lawn. A striped tent serving as a refreshment stand, a tent looking as though it belonged in the desert with a sheikh idling away his time inside. Waiters wearing tuxedos and bearing silver trays. A bride dressed in blinding white. Vows spoken in English and Spanish. The guard station at Anscott. The Sunny Buttercup van. Fleeting notes of what she thought was Spanish. A long black limousine with tinted windows. The fact that the hallucinogenic cactus used in the manufacture of Delight came only from Mexico.

Kelly's heart stopped.

"Oh, my gosh," she said.

Will looked up just in time to see Kelly race for the dresser. She began to plunge through the stack of pictures she'd taken at Anscott. She found the photographs of the man in the limousine. Yes, yes, it had to be! she thought, rummaging through the remaining snapshots for the ones she most wanted to see. They were at the very end, placed there because they'd been of no value. At the next to last photograph, Kelly's heart stopped again.

She looked up at Will, shock and elation warring for equal footing. "I know who he is."

"Wait a minute," Will said to Mitch, then to Kelly, "You know who *who* is?"

"The man in the limousine." Will's expression was encouragement enough to proceed. "He's Rodriqué Echieverra."

"Rodriqué Echieverra? The Mexican politician?"

"Rodriqué Echieverra?" Mitch asked. "What about him?"

"You tell me," Kelly said, stepping forward and presenting two pictures, one of the man in the limousine, one of the father of the groom. "I told you he looked familiar."

Even though he was staring at the incontestable proof of her statement, Will still had trouble computing what he was seeing. Finally, though, he had to accept the testimony of his own eyes.

"You're not going to believe this," Will said into the receiver to Mitch. The silence that followed his next words bore proof that Will had been precisely right.

WILL HAD LIED to her, Kelly realized an hour later as she raced her car toward Anscott. He'd also lied to Mitch, but that didn't soften the fact that he'd lied to her.

Once Mitch had recovered from the news about Echieverra, he, Will and Kelly had decided that he would return to Seattle. Then they'd determine what to do next. It seemed pretty obvious that it was time to reveal their cards to the police. It had also been decided that Mitch would fly back in order to save time. Kelly was to wait by the phone to hear from Mitch when his plane would arrive, while Will, because they'd eaten nothing since breakfast, went out to get a quick bite for them. At least, that's what he'd told her nearly an hour ago.

What an idiot she'd been! What idiots she and Mitch had been! Which was the first thing Kelly told Mitch when he called. His reply, when he heard what Kelly thought Will was up to, was to curse a blue streak. Which was exactly what Kelly was doing now as she down-shifted the car into gear and wove in and out of end-of-the-day traffic.

She had to stop Will from doing something stupid!

By the time she whipped the car off the highway and onto the asphalt road, twilight was descending. Shadows flitted about in the forest, while overhead an invisible hand seemingly leached the sky of color, leaving it a leaden gray that once more promised rain. Kelly, who now understood Will's reluctance to return the rented van, began to look for the vehicle. She suspected that he'd left it in one of the two or three places in which they'd parked while observing the guard station and the building. Cutting her lights so as not to give away her approach, she pulled the car alongside the first hiding space. It was empty. The second, however, was not.

Kelly inched the car into the thicket beside the obviously deserted van. She shut off the engine and opened the car door. A low branch of a spruce tree scraped against the hood of the car, making a scratchy noise that sounded eerie in the approaching night.

Hurry, she thought as she made her way through the forest. Had Will come this way? And, if so, how long ago? She kept moving, dodging trees in the dark forest, marking the guard station, keeping the building before her. The lights appeared brighter than usual. Had the area been placed under tighter security? Probably. Andriotti and Echieverra—she had trouble believing that these two men were behind the drug trafficking at Anscott—were no dummies. Security was probably tighter than tight, which left Kelly wondering just how Will was going to get inside the building. And what exactly did he hope to accomplish once he got there?

A sudden thought curdled Kelly's blood. Maybe he did have a weapon. After all, he'd bought something that morning, something that cost in the neighborhood of two hundred dollars.

Oh, God, please don't let him have a gun!

WILL HEARD the snarl of a dog the moment he dropped to the ground. Hell! He might have known that things had been going too well. He'd had no problem finding boulders that, piled one upon the other, had gotten him onto the brick wall. He'd even clipped the barbed wire without incident. Now, all he had to do...

The Doberman pinscher growled, revealing sharp, white teeth and a black attitude.

"Easy, boy," Will said, reaching slowly into the pocket of his jacket.

His fingers molded around the weapon he'd chosen to use should he be confronted with the canine. He pulled it from his pocket and aimed it at the dog. A quick flick of his wrist and a hunk of ground hamburger meat, which he'd found still iced down in the van, landed right at the dog's feet. Will saw the war being waged inside the animal: training versus temptation. Temptation won. As the animal gobbled down the food, Will sprinted across the dog run, bounded the fence and landed in the interior of the yard. Thanking Kelly for her farsightedness—she did, indeed, know how to win canine friends—he stayed in the shadows, willing his heart to be steady, willing himself to remember the gut-empty feeling he'd had as he'd knelt beside his brother's grave.

It was payback time. It was time to spill blood for blood. Nothing was going to stop him. This thought, this pledge to his brother, burned in his soul, lighting his way as he headed for the back of the building. This time, when he slid his hand into the pocket of his jacket, his fingers curled around cold steel.

As Will neared the dock area, he saw that the door was rolled to the ceiling. He slipped inside the shipping area and behind a crate, just as the sound of voices drifted to him. Shortly, two men, one with a heavy Spanish accent, appeared. Will wondered if this was the man he'd observed driving the Sunny Buttercup van.

"Let's get out of here, man," the Hispanic said to his companion. "The bossman is madder than a cornered rattlesnake."

"Is he always this testy?" the other man asked.

"*Si,* when things do not go his way, when people do not do his bidding."

The two men passed by where Will was hidden. In seconds, they disappeared out into the fast-falling night. Will heard an engine roar to life, saw headlights streak across the darkness, then the sound of a vehicle pulling away from the building.

Bossman? Was that Andriotti? If it was, it was too bad about his being angry, Will thought, slipping from his hiding place. Quickly, quietly, his gun drawn, he passed through the loading area and into the square corridor that wrapped itself around the building. Just as he hoped, there was a back door leading into the interior, and the laboratories. Was this door on the security system? There was only one way to find out. Will turned the knob, pulled and prayed that an alarm didn't go off. It didn't. Which encouraged him to step inside. Almost at once he heard another set of voices— one raised in anger. Another bore the traces of a Spanish accent.

"How do you know that anything was taken?" the man with the Spanish accent asked.

"I don't," another man said. This individual was clearly not pleased with the turn of events. "But we really can't take a chance, can we?"

Will stepped toward the voices. They seemed to be coming from the lab where the samples had been found.

"You Americans have no stomach. You panic too easily."

"And I suppose you would have done nothing?"

"Of course, I would have done something. I would have done exactly what you did. I just would not have panicked."

"And I suppose your esteemed career doesn't hang in the balance if we're caught manufacturing illegal drugs? Do you think you're going to win the presidential election from a prison cell?"

"You should have gone on the stage, Edward. You have a flair for the dramatic."

"And you have the arrogance of a politician."

For a moment, Will, who stood just outside the door, thought that a fight might break out, but in the end the Mexican, Rodriqué Echieverra obviously, laughed. "Touché, my friend. And is it not a good thing that our children get along better than we do?"

Will could sense that Edward Andriotti relaxed his stance. Perhaps the man even smiled. "You're right. But I still think that something might have to be done with Duggan."

"I told you the administrator should be one of us."

"He, and his innocence, have worked well in the past, but he's been getting too curious about the government-funded work. He was also curious about why the guard called me instead of him."

"What did you tell him about the break-in?"

"Just that the building was broken into, but that it didn't appear that anything was taken. I didn't mention that the door to this lab was unlocked."

"The police were called, *si?*"

"Yes, I played it just like a normal break-in, just like a routine vandalism, but I don't know..."

"There you go panicking again. It probably was a normal break-in, a routine vandalism. And, if Duggan needs to be dealt with, we shall deal with him. It is sad to say, but accidents happen."

"But what if all of this had something to do with *him?*"

This last was said in a manner that suggested references frequent enough that a name was no longer necessary for communication. Will wondered just who this unnamed man was.

"How could it? There is no way he could trace anything to us."

"He knew his brother worked for us."

Will's heart picked up its rhythm. Was he hearing what he thought he was?

"That proves nothing. Besides, he has problems enough of his own right now, problems like keeping on the run. Also, there were three of them who broke in. That does not sound like our lone wolf." Before Edward Andriotti could respond, Rodriqué Echieverra said, "Come, friend. As you Americans say, 'You are borrowing trouble.'"

A brief silence followed, a silence into which a dark voice drawled from the doorway, "Borrowing trouble, no. Bought it, yes. And at a real high price."

"WELL, WELL, if it isn't The Stone Man," Echieverra said, slowly shifting a red-tipped cigar from one hand to another. "I owe you an apology. I underestimated you."

Will looked straight into a pair of nutmeg-brown eyes, hard eyes, quick eyes, eyes that didn't miss a thing. "I owe you the same apology. But then, I should have realized that you would have followed the trial."

Pointing the gun at the two men, Will stepped into the small laboratory and looked around. The room didn't look quite the way it had the evening before. The vials, the beakers...all were in place, yet each contained different ingredients. No longer were there containers of white powder or green and red liquids.

Even as he surveyed the room, Will's attention never left the two men. Echieverra had thick blue-black hair that shone with an uncommon sheen, while his face, full and square-jawed, was only degrees away from being out-and-out handsome. He had a charismatic demeanor, which guaranteed success in the political arena, and which, together with his looks, unquestionably made him a favorite with the opposite sex. Yes, Will thought, Echieverra could probably attract any woman.

Edward Andriotti also probably had success with women. He looked like money—old money, classy money, the kind of money that could buy anything from crisp ski weekends in Aspen or Europe, to richly appointed yachts that sailed warm, blue seas. Andriotti could not be called a good-looking man but this didn't matter because his money bought the illusion that he was. Impeccably manicured fingernails, silver-streaked brown hair, styled to perfection, clothes by some designer whose name Will probably wouldn't have been able to identify, let alone pronounce.

"Yeah," Will addressed Echieverra. "It must have been real gratifying for you to watch the trial. To see someone else take the rap for a murder you committed."

Echieverra shrugged. "It has its rewards."

"Keep quiet," Andriotti said to his partner. Though he spoke softly, there was an underlying edge to his words.

The Mexican smiled broadly, revealing stark-white teeth that reminded Will of a certain Doberman pinscher. "Don't be a fool, my friend. The Stone Man knows everything. If he didn't, he wouldn't be standing here now."

"I thought you said he'd never trace anything to us," Andriotti said.

"So I was wrong," Echieverra replied nonchalantly.

"Yeah, well, you're wrong again," Will said. "I don't know everything. I have a few theories—prison gives you lots of time to formulate theories—but I need confirmation. It's one of the two reasons I'm here."

"And the other reason?" Echieverra asked quietly.

"Let's just say it's biblical in nature. Biblical as in 'an eye for an eye, a tooth for a tooth.'"

Andriotti paled. At the same time, a hardness crept into Echieverra's eyes and voice. This man was a scrapper, the kind who wouldn't go down without a fight.

"I take it you were responsible for last night's break-in?" Echieverra asked, slowly edging around the corner of the counter.

Will tightened the hold on his gun and said, "That's far enough. And, yeah, I'm responsible."

Even under the circumstances, with his heart pounding and his throat as dry as parchment, Will thought of the two people who'd been his accomplices. How odd that in such a short time two people whom he barely knew had become a meaningful part of his life.

"Don't you know that breaking into private property is illegal?" Echieverra asked as he dropped the cigar to the floor and methodically ground it out with his foot.

Will shoved the disturbing thoughts of Kelly and Mitch aside, urging himself to remember just why he was here. It was easy enough to do when he glanced at the cigar. It had to do with the way Echieverra snuffed out things, the way he snuffed out people.

With a feigned look of disbelief, Will said, "You mean that breaking into private property is illegal? Well, now, imagine that. I guess this Delight you're cooking up isn't, huh? Oh, by the way, the drug sounds like a gold mine."

"It is," Echieverra admitted.

"Will you be quiet?" Andriotti said.

"Take it easy, Edward," Echieverra said, crossing his arms across his sturdy chest. "It could be that Will Stone is a reasonable man. Not at all like his brother."

Will's jaw clenched at the reference to Stephen. "You figured out that we were brothers."

"It didn't take much to make the connection," Echieverra said. "Two men whose last name is Stone. Of course, your brother, the *cobarde*—the coward—that he was, fled before the police even knew of his existence. Actually, I admire your silent loyalty to him."

Will sneered. "I can't tell you what your admiration means to me."

"There's no need to be sarcastic," Echieverra said. "And even less need to turn down our offer so hastily."

Will could tell Echieverra was stalling for time, grasping for straws, but doing both with a finesse that was commendable. "What offer?" Will asked.

"A percentage of the action. Enough money to make you richer than you ever dreamed possible."

Will laughed harshly. "Let me get this straight. You're suggesting that I join you two?"

"Why not?" Echieverra said.

"What makes you so sure he hasn't already gone to the police?" Andriotti asked. A thin layer of perspiration had popped across his upper lip. Good, Will thought. The man was losing his composure.

"He hasn't. If he had, the police would have been crawling all over the place by now. Wouldn't they, Will Stone?"

"You're the one with the answers," Will said. "Just for the record, your offer turns my stomach."

"What a shame that you have such a delicate stomach," Echieverra said. "And how interesting that it is so selective. It stops short at selling drugs, yet fully embraces killing in cold blood."

In cold blood. The words had a chilling ring to them, causing Will to question for the first time if he had the strength, the guts, to carry out his grim plan. His answer came swiftly. Yes, he could kill in cold blood as long as he remembered the coldness of a corpse, the coldness of the earth that covered a coffin.

Again, Will struggled to steady his thoughts, to concentrate on his mission. He looked at Echieverra. "Tell me something, did my brother know what he was getting into?"

"Not in the beginning. By the time he figured out what was going on, he was knee-deep in it. He wasn't the brightest man I've ever known."

Will ignored the slur aimed at his brother. He felt good about having done so. It meant he was once more in control of his emotions. It meant that he was securely hidden in a blank, feelingless world.

"When he did figure out what he was into," Will said, "you tried to have him killed."

Echieverra laughed, a deep rich, reverberating sound. "Is that what you think? That, once your brother realized what the score was, we had him killed? Sorry to disappoint you. The simple truth is that he got greedy. He wanted more of the action than we were offering and he started stealing from us. That we couldn't tolerate.''

"For heaven's sake, Rodriqué, will you be quiet?'' Andriotti said as he whipped a linen handkerchief from the breast pocket of his suit and began to mop his upper lip.

Will felt as if a stake had been driven through his heart. He didn't want to believe what he'd just heard about his brother's guilt but he couldn't deny that the words could be true. In that moment, his brother truly died in Will's mind.

Still, Stephen's guilt didn't change the fact that his brother was his brother. Nor did it change the fact that these men had killed him, and that Will needed to hear the particulars of that death.

"So you set him up that day in the park, intending to have him killed.''

"We had no choice,'' Echieverra said.

"You're hanging us,'' Rodriqué Andriotti said, and this time a cold panic had crept into his voice.

Echieverra ignored his partner. "We intended to make it look like a drug buy that went bad. What we didn't expect was for your brother to get the upper hand...with a gun he'd stolen from us, no less.'' Echieverra smiled. "Nor did we expect you to come along and take the blame. In appreciation, why don't you let us pay you back for the time that you sacrificed?''

"And why don't you go to hell?'' Will growled.

The smile at Echieverra's lips faded. "Your brother was stupid, your brother was greedy, your brother was a loser. I guess losing runs in your family."

Something snapped inside Will, something hot and primitive, something that allowed a torrential flow of the emotions he'd been trying so hard to keep at bay. He felt anger at his father—*"You're never going to amount to a damned thing!"* He felt the humiliation, the disgrace and dishonor that only a son can feel at disappointing the man who'd given him life. He felt rage at the man who stood before him, at the man who was condemning him to more of the same disgrace and dishonor.

"Go ahead and kill us," Echieverra taunted. "Personally, I don't think you're man enough. I don't think you're winner enough."

Steadying his right hand with his left, Will aimed the gun directly at Echieverra. How cocksure the man looked! Just the way his father always had.

"You're wrong, Echieverra," Will drawled. "I'm through being a loser."

Will's finger began to pull the trigger, ever so slowly....

"Kill them!" Will could hear his brother crying. *"They killed me. I was weak, but I was too young to die, to die, to die..."*

...slowly...

"No," Andriotti begged, his handkerchief-laden hand pathetically reaching out to Will.

"Kill them," Will heard something deep inside himself saying. *"They'll find a way to buy their freedom if you don't pull the trigger."*

...slowly...

"I don't believe you're capable of that kind of violence," Will could hear Kelly saying.

...slowly...

"You're a loser...a loser...a loser..." Will could hear his father taunting.

"No!" Will howled like the tormented creature he'd spent his life being.

And then the shots rang out. One. Two. Just enough to even his brother's score, just enough to honor a graveside promise.

KELLY, who'd just entered the building via the route Will had taken, stopped short at the silence-splintering sound of gunshots. Her heart came to the same abrupt, and sickening, halt.

"No," she whispered in feeble defiance against what she knew to be the truth. She was too late. Too late to avert what possibly had been the inevitable. Too late to save Will from himself.

CHAPTER FIFTEEN

FROM HIS BUNK, his hands stacked beneath his head, Will stared out at the world through the spaces between steel bars. No longer could he see the moon or the sun. No longer could he hear the birds or the rain. Instead, he saw only his cell, heard only the muffled noises of other prisoners, noises which all too often turned to angry shouts or desperate cries. As hard as it was to believe, in the span of a week he'd forgotten how traumatic incarceration could be. Everything had come surging back, however, the minute the door had slammed shut behind him.

That had been three days ago, three long days. Since then, he'd spoken to no one but his lawyer. Actually, he hadn't even wanted to talk to him, but he knew he had to. What he really wanted was to be left alone. Maybe then he could make some sense out of what was happening to him. For a man who'd tried hard not to feel anything, he was suddenly inundated with feeling. Principally feelings of confusion and fright. Over and over, he heard the two shots that he'd fired. Over and over, he saw the look on Kelly's face, first when she'd rushed headlong into the laboratory at Anscott, later when the police had carried him away in handcuffs. She had looked as bewildered as he now felt.

"Hey, Stone?"

Will glanced up and met the gaze of a guard. He liked this man, mainly because he was considerate. He hadn't treated him as though he were a subspecies of human being. But then, everyone here at the San Francisco jail had been decent, not like Froggie back at Folsom.

The guard inserted a key into the cell lock, twisted it with a noisy rattle and yanked open the door. "You're a free man," he said.

Free man. Will had waited a long time to hear these words. How ironic that he was hearing them at a time when he'd never felt more captive. Furthermore, he felt a total stranger to himself.

Why hadn't he killed Echieverra and Andriotti? He'd intended to. There had never been any doubt in his mind about avenging his brother. Why then, hadn't he carried through with the plan? Why had he simply fired two shots, symbolically one for each man, into the ceiling of Anscott?

He'd asked himself these questions a hundred times, beginning as he'd waited for the police. Will himself had called the cops. He'd known that he would be arrested. After all, he was an escaped convict...and he'd just broken into Anscott brandishing a gun. He'd taken great pleasure in seeing a squirming Echieverra and Andriotti arrested, too. Within a day of their apprehension, all three had been extradited to California,

Echieverra and Andriotti to await trial, he to await possible freedom.

As he'd awaited his freedom, he'd continued to ask these questions. Each time he did, he came up with the same answer. Will knew that he'd been angry with the world for more years than he cared to count. Maybe the truth was that he'd been angry with himself for buying into his father's evaluation of him. Perhaps he'd realized as he'd stood there, his brother's murderers before him, that, while he'd always be his father's son, it was time for him to be his own man...and that meant deciding for himself if he was a loser.

"You're a loser only if you choose to be."

Kelly's words came back to haunt him, just the way they repeatedly had over the past three days. It had been her words that had stayed his vengeful mission. It had been her words that had brought about his new philosophical awakening. She and she alone had given him something that he'd never had before: a belief in himself. Oh, it wasn't clearly defined, far from it, but the fragile beginnings were there. She'd also given him one other thing: the desire for a future. Both these things, a budding belief in himself, a desire for a future, scared him. What did one do with a future when one had already discounted it?

"Hey, Stone, did you hear me? You've been exonerated. The bad guys are going to trial, the good guy is going free."

Slowly, Will pushed to a sitting position on the edge of his bunk, then, a quick look around at his sterile surroundings, he stood and stepped toward, and out, the door.

"Good luck," the guard said, holding out his hand.

Will shook the man's hand and mumbled a heartfelt, if self-conscious, "Thanks."

"Collect your things out front," the guard said, adding, "Oh, by the way, someone's waiting for you."

Will's heart kicked out a loud thump, and he immediately chastised himself for it. It was probably his lawyer. It certainly wasn't *her*. Furthermore, he didn't want it to be her. He no longer tried to explain to himself what had happened between them. It had simply happened, a mad and magic moment out of time.

In minutes, all of his possessions in a paper sack, Will emerged into the waiting room. Mitch stood and, a smile at his lips, walked toward Will. Though Will wasn't disappointed to see this man who had become the closest thing to a friend he'd ever had, he realized that a part of him wished it had been Kelly standing there.

You fool! Will chided himself.

"I told them to call me when they were getting ready to release you," Mitch said.

"Thanks."

Will had followed Andriotti's and Echieverra's arrest in the newspaper. San Franciscans had been stunned to learn of the dark, sinister underside of one of their favorite sons. Their neighbors south of the border had been no less startled. Will had been right about Echieverra. He was a scrapper, a man who wasn't going down without a fight. He'd hired the biggest and best legal names to represent him, but even cynical Will couldn't help but believe that justice would prevail this time. There was too much evidence stacked against Echieverra and Andriotti. Will would do his part. He'd testify at the upcoming trial.

"C'mon, let's get out of here," Mitch said.

"Yeah," Will said, thinking that, if he never saw the inside of a prison again, it would be too soon.

Mitch led the way to his car, and within minutes they were on their way out of the parking lot. Will didn't look back.

"What about a thick, juicy steak?"

Will looked over at Mitch, who negotiated the car with ease. "That sounds like an offer I can't refuse. But I'm buying."

"No," Mitch said. "This one's on me."

"No," Will said, adding, "They gave me my prison severance pay." He grinned. "They also offered me the obligatory suit."

Mitch took in the red-plaid shirt, the jeans, that Will still wore. He, too, grinned. "I take it you passed on that last item."

"I figured dirty was better than ill-fitting."

Mitch's grin faded. "You're welcome to some of my things."

Will's grin disappeared, as well. He realized that this man had touched him, deeply. "Thanks, but I can make do."

Sensing Will's need for independence, Mitch let the subject drop. In due time, both men were seated at a booth in a small diner. Neither man spoke much as he ate, neither feeling any need to fill the silent void with chatter.

Will couldn't help but note that though Mitch had ordered milk he couldn't keep his eyes off the foam-topped mugs that passed their table.

Mitch couldn't help but note that Will hadn't once brought up the subject of Kelly. Mitch wondered when would be the best time to tell Will that she had called that morning. Somehow, he didn't think now was the time.

Once they'd devoured the meal, which Will had paid for, and were again in the car, Mitch brought up another delicate subject. "What are you going to do now?"

The swiftness of Will's answer surprised him. "I'm going to find me a place to live and pound the pavement for a job."

"Then you're going to stay here in San Francisco?"

"I might as well, at least until the trial. I'd just have to come back for it. Actually, San Francisco's as good as any place . . . better than most."

A sudden thought occurred to Will, though perhaps it wasn't so sudden, after all. Maybe the thought had been at the back of his mind all along. Had he decided to stay in the city because of a red-haired, green-eyed woman? The possibility of that disturbed him, because, whatever his future held, she had no place in it. Of that he was certain. She could do better than him. A lot better.

Will glanced over at Mitch. He knew his friend had asked something, but he had no idea what that something was. "Sorry, what did you say?"

"I said, where are you going to stay tonight?"

"At the Salvation Army or the YMCA. Don't worry about me. I'll find something."

"Look," Mitch said, hesitating as though he knew the subject had to be brought up with the greatest of care. "Why don't you stay with me?" He countered the objection he heard coming with, "At least until you can find a place of your own."

"I don't know."

"I won't kid you," Mitch said. "My place isn't the Ritz Carlton, but the sofa does open up into a bed. Not the most comfortable bed in the world, but a bed nonetheless."

Will grinned. "Have you ever slept on a prison bunk?"

"Can't say that I have."

"If you had, you wouldn't apologize for the sofa."

"So does that mean you'll stay?"

Will paused, touched by his friend's generosity of spirit. "You're sure?" Will asked.

"I'm positive," Mitch answered with a wide grin, and Will had the oddest feeling that Mitch was relieved. Could it be Mitch didn't want to be alone? Because of the ludicrousness of the notion, Will immediately dismissed it.

Nodding his head, he said, "Thanks, Mitch. It will only be until I find something."

"Right. Only until you find something."

MITCH WAS RIGHT. His apartment, three small rooms over his one large-roomed agency, wasn't the Ritz Carlton, but it was neat and clean. Well, sorta.

Gathering up the clothes strewn about furniture and floor, Mitch said, "Make yourself at home."

Will set his paper sack of possessions on a table beside a lamp with a soiled shade. He looked at the cubbyhole kitchen, which the landlord probably referred to as cozy, while the living area, with the sagging sofa that opened into a bed, looked as though it had been furnished secondhand, possibly even thirdhand. Even so, Will would have been tickled to call the apartment his own, and it did have one undeniable thing in its favor: It wasn't prison.

Picking up a framed photograph, Will studied the image of a blond-haired young boy wearing a blue baseball cap. The photograph caused Will's mind to turn to thoughts of Kelly, though he told himself the connection from photograph to photographer was logical enough. Even so, he brushed the thought aside. "Is this your son?"

A pile of clothes in his arms, Mitch glanced over and said, "Yeah. His name's Scott. He lives with his mother."

The tone of Mitch's voice, polite, didn't encourage further comment.

"Have you heard from Kelly?"

Although the question was never far from his mind, Will hadn't intended to ask it. In fact, he'd promised himself he wouldn't under any circumstances. So what the heck was he doing breaking his vow?

Mitch stopped his crude efforts at housekeeping and faced Will squarely. "She called this morning. Said she was on her way to Europe. Some assignment or something. My guess is that she's somewhere over the Atlantic right now." There was a hesitation, then, "She, uh, she didn't leave a message for you."

The news that she was leaving the country didn't take Will by complete surprise. After all, she was devoted to, even obsessed with, her job. After all, he'd postponed, and rather spectacularly, the execution of that job. No, he wasn't surprised. What was he then? Disappointed? Yeah. No. He was hurt. Dammit, he was hurt! He had no right to be, but he was. After all they'd been through, she hadn't even cared enough to send him a hello, a hope-you're-out-of-prison-soon, a go-straight-to-hades-for-all-I-care.

"Sorry," Mitch said.

"Don't be. She doesn't owe me anything."

It crossed Will's mind that she'd gotten the only thing that had any meaning for her: a story. This realization hurt anew and so deeply that it gutted his stomach.

What he wouldn't give to throttle her!

What he wouldn't give to take her in his arms!

What he wouldn't give for a swift-acting shot of whiskey!

KELLY PUSHED the button above her seat and, when the stewardess answered it, she asked, "Would it be possible for me to have some cocoa? With maybe just a dash of whiskey in it?"

The stewardess smiled. "Can't sleep, huh?"

The woman didn't know the half of it, Kelly thought, but said, "I'm afraid not."

"Let me see what I can whip up."

"Thanks," Kelly said, sighing as she crawled back beneath the folds of the woolen blanket. She couldn't seem to get warm. On the plane, or, for that matter, anywhere else. She'd been cold, bone-deep cold, for days. Ever since she'd heard the two gunshots ring out.

Even now she could hear the sinister sounds blasting through the silence of Anscott. For those horrible seconds, she had stopped living. She couldn't even remember traveling the distance to the laboratory. All she remembered was entering it to see both Echieverra and Andriotti alive and well, if pale with fright, and Will... She wasn't certain how Will looked. Maybe as surprised as she that Echieverra and Andriotti were alive. Maybe even angry with himself that they were. Undoubtedly confused by the unexpected turn of events.

The coldness had continued as she'd watched the police take Will away. Handcuffed. Shackled. As though he was a dangerous fugitive from justice. Fugitive. Yes, he was that. Dangerous. Only to himself, she'd thought then, but later she realized that she'd been wrong. Will Stone was dangerous to her well-being. He personally threatened her in a way that no man ever had. Simply put, he did things to her heart that she didn't want done to it, that she couldn't afford to have done to it.

And so, the coldness had remained. She'd spent the next two days in bed, trying to convince herself that the viral cold in her head was responsible for the coldness in her body, though she knew, even at the time, that she was lying to herself. The coldness was the result of fear, fear at the power this man had over her. In the end, she did exactly what she knew she would do: She ran. From the country. From Will. From herself. She smiled mirthlessly. How odd that it was now she who was on the run.

"Here we go," the stewardess said.

"Thanks," Kelly said, reaching for the mug. As she did so, she looked, for the hundredth time, at the third finger of her left hand. She had removed the gold wedding band from her hand, but she couldn't remove it from her memory. The absence of the ring made her feel colder yet.

"You're not taking a chill, are you?" the stewardess asked.

Kelly smiled and lied. "No, I'm fine."

She took a sip of the bracing liquid. Its warmth flooded her, along with fiery memories, memories of Will's kiss, memories of Will's caress, memories of Will's body moving over and into hers. Again and again, she'd tried to explain their interlude of lovemaking. It had lasted only an hour. Only an hour out of all of the hours of her life, and yet no other hour was sharper or clearer. No other hour spoke so heatedly to her heart. No other hour seemed so real. In fact, it was almost as if she'd never truly been alive before. And the thought of never being that alive again frightened her.

And that, she thought, was the crux of the issue. She was lousy at relationships. Worse, she was a destroyer of them. Her job was the only thing in her life that brought her lasting satisfaction. The images that she captured on film were permanent, constant, faithful. They were there every time she looked at her photographs.

She wondered, though, as she settled down with her warm blanket and cocoa, if Will had been released yet. What would he do now? Would he remain in San Francisco? Would he keep in touch with Mitch?

And what, if anything, had their week together meant to him?

CHAPTER SIXTEEN

IT WAS a funny thing about the future, Will discovered. It took care of itself—minute by minute, hour by hour, day by day. Within the first week of moving in with Mitch, Will found a job doing carpentry work for a shop specializing in custom-made cabinets. The following week, he found a place of his own, a one-room efficiency apartment that he could barely afford on his limited budget. Again, he had the momentary feeling that Mitch was sorry to see him go. For all that he and Mitch were growing closer by the day, there was a part of Mitch that remained a mystery to Will, just as Will continued to remain a mystery to himself.

In a very real sense, he still felt on the run, from emotions he couldn't explain, from a fear that didn't make sense, but existed anyway. The fear basically had to do with the feelings he continued to experience. All kinds of feelings, everything from the fullness of heart at watching a sunset to the profound sense of satisfaction at finishing a piece of woodwork. He wanted to share these feelings, this new self he was becoming, with Kelly. Kelly? When had he started thinking of her by name? And did she ever think of him at all?

September became October, and the city grew cold with winter. On the first Monday night of the new month, of his new life, Will began to teach a volunteer class in woodworking under the auspices of a community project designed to help inner-city kids. These kids reminded Will of himself at their age—underprivileged, rebellious, begging for someone to notice them in a positive way.

At first, Will wondered if the six-week program would make any lasting impact on these troubled young lives, but then he remembered the short time he had spent with Kelly, time that had changed his life forever. She had believed in him, believed in his innocence, and had helped him prove that innocence to the world. He'd told himself that he didn't care what people thought about him, but he had cared, just as these kids cared. In the weeks that followed, every time he helped a child discover something positive about himself, Will likewise discovered that same positive something in him.

One thing he discovered without the help of the kids or anyone else. One night, when memories were all he had to keep him company, he discovered that he was in love with Kelly. Interestingly, the realization didn't frighten him. Instead, it gave him a peace he'd never known before.

MITCH'S LETTER caught up with Kelly on the eve of her flying to Africa for the last leg of her assignment. At the sight of the worn envelope, which looked as if it had traveled as much of Europe as she had, Kelly's heart skipped a beat. Eagerly tearing into it, hoping to learn anything about Will, she read with greedy haste. Much of the letter dealt with the status of Echieverra and Andriotti and the upcoming trial scheduled for the first of the year. Then Mitch hoped she was well and having a good time in Europe, and when would she be home? Get in touch when she did return to the city, and the three of them would get together.

The three of them?

She read on:

Will is settled into his own apartment and has a job. Guess it doesn't surprise you that it has to do with carpentry. He'd strangle me if he knew I was telling you this, he'd die if he knew I knew this, but his boss said he had the most gifted hands he's ever seen. Will's also working with inner-city kids, teaching them woodworking, and, frankly, I think playing teacher agrees with him. By the way, you wouldn't know him without his beard.

The letter went on for another brief paragraph. All through it, Kelly hoped for a message from Will, but there was nothing, not a hello, not an I-miss-you, not a do-you-ever-think-about-the-week-we-spent-together? Disappointment crowded in around Kelly. She told herself that it was foolish to feel disappointed, but nonetheless she did.

That night, unable to sleep, Kelly slipped from bed, turned on a lamp and searched through her luggage for the packet of photographs she'd hidden away. Few in number, they were photographs of Will, photographs which she'd taken at odd, unobserved moments during their time together, photographs she'd intended to use in a pictorial story of a fugitive. Why hadn't she sent the photographs to a potential buyer? She didn't know, except that, somehow, doing so took advantage of Will in a way she couldn't bring herself to do. Not even if selling the photographs, or showing them in a display, meant another award.

The first photograph showed Will gazing out the motel window as he'd done so often. Once again, Kelly was struck by how photogenic he was, by how attractive he was—even if he was wearing a beard that made him look more than a little wild. Kelly traced the tips of her fingers across the beard's image. She could feel its bristliness. She could feel the beard deliciously chafing her cheeks, delightfully abrading her breasts. Her eyes dropped to Will's hands. Yes, those hands were gifted, not only at woodworking, but also at knowing just where, and how, to touch a woman.

He touched more than your body, though, didn't he, Cooper?

No.

Oh, yes, he did. He touched your heart. Don't bother to deny it, Cooper. It would be stupid to, for it's as obvious as the freckled nose on your face. It's also obvious that you're—

Don't say it!

Okay, I won't. I won't tell you what you already know. I won't tell you that you're in love with Will Stone.

ON THE LAST DAY of October, a cold, rainy afternoon, the transmission on Mitch's car went out. It was the final straw. The day had been one of the worst of Mitch's life. He'd lost a client, whose money he really needed, he'd had lunch with his ex-partner, Speedy Talbot, an activity that had only served to remind him that he himself was no longer a cop, he'd tried a dozen times to get in touch with his son to wish him a happy birthday, but couldn't get anyone to answer the phone. Finally, he'd reached his ex-wife, who'd politely—yeah, let's be polite if nothing else—told him that his son wasn't there, that he'd gone on an overnight camp-out with her new boyfriend. Another man was taking his son camping on his birthday. And now, adding insult to injury, and to the tune of an exorbitant towing charge, his car had given up the ghost.

Clutching a paper sack to his chest, Mitch cursed, and rammed the key into the lock of his apartment. He was soaked to the skin from waiting for a trolley car. He could never remember wanting a drink so badly. Ever since he'd spent the week with Will and Kelly, he'd been sober. At first, he'd promised himself that he'd get through the Anscott investigation before taking another drink. Afterward, it had been a matter of pride. In the beginning, with Will staying with him, the temptation had been a little easier to avoid. With Will gone, temptation knew no bounds. After today, he was tired of fighting it.

He wanted a drink!

And, dammit, he would have one!

Heedless of the puddles he was leaving behind, Mitch crossed to the small table in the kitchen and plopped down the sack. The action caused the wet paper to slip, leaving the liquor bottle exposed. Reaching for the first thing he saw, a jelly jar now passing as a glass, he slammed it down on the table, grabbed the bottle and started pouring out the liquid before the bottle was fully uncapped. Liquor splashed onto the table. Mitch didn't even notice.

He emptied and refilled the jar, over and over and over, until his pain began to dim, until the world began to glow with a rosiness that he'd missed. An hour later en route to the sofa, Mitch stumbled and fell. Somehow he managed not to spill a drop of the liquor either in the fall or in his clumsy attempt to get up. Finally, he hauled himself onto the sofa—wet clothes and all!

And from that vantage point, he continued to drink. His mind dark, and slipping toward darker, he now drank straight from the bottle. He imagined now that the answers to his questions could be seen in the bottom of said bottle. There they were. He could see them floating around.

Who had Scott gone camping with? Andriotti and Echieverra. Dammit, why had Connie let him go with those men?

How much did a transmission cost? A million, zillion dollars.

And didn't anyone care that he was innocent of the bribery charges? No, no one cared. Especially not whoever had set him up to take the fall. He knew who that someone was. It was either Santa Claus or the Easter Bunny, and, as soon as he was sober, he was going after the son of a . . .

The thought trailed off as Mitch fell into a drunken stupor.

"HEY, STONE, you have a phone call," a male voice bellowed.

Will frowned. He and three other tenants shared a hall telephone, but this was only one of a handful of calls he'd ever received. Checking the clock—it was nearly nine—he laid aside the bills he'd been working on. Each week since he'd landed a job, he religiously mailed whatever he could afford to Kelly's address for her to apply to his outstanding account. He'd similarly tried to pay Mitch for his services, but Mitch had insisted that Will owed him nothing. Mitch's generosity freed Will to set aside money for a gravestone for his brother. It would take time to pay off Kelly, and to collect enough for a gravestone, but he'd eventually do both. Yes, Will was feeling pretty good about himself these days.

Opening the door of his apartment, Will stepped out into the drafty hallway, where he saw the receiver dangling almost to the floor.

"Hello?"

There was a pause, then a soft-spoken, "Will?"

Images of sassy red curls and sexy lips flashed through Will's mind. He'd often wondered how he would feel when, and if, he and Kelly ever connected again. Frightened? Relieved? Angry? In truth, he felt none of those emotions. What he felt was that "alive" feeling again, as if the world had just stepped into sharper relief, as if colors had just become brighter, as if the rain striking the roof suddenly did so with greater force.

"Will?" Kelly repeated.

"Yeah, I'm here."

"Look," she said, "I'm over at Mitch's—"

"Mitch's? I thought you were in Europe."

"Actually, I was in both Europe and Africa, but I just got back to San Francisco this afternoon."

"Out on another Pulitzer-Prize-winning assignment, huh?" There was a time he would have asked the question with sarcasm, but not now. Perhaps it was a tribute to his own growing emotional strength. Now he found himself genuinely wishing that Kelly was emotionally strong enough not to need to strive for this kind of perfection in her life.

Kelly ignored his question, asking instead, "Can you come over?"

Will recognized the serious tone of her voice. "What is it?"

"Mitch is drunk. I mean dead-drunk. He's passed out on the sofa. I've tried to budge him, but I can't."

For a reason he didn't stop to analyze, Will wasn't surprised at what he was hearing. "I'll be there as soon as I can."

"Will, he hasn't said a word, he hasn't moved a muscle. He doesn't even know I'm here. You don't think he's...unconscious or something. I mean, I know he's in a drunken stupor, but . . . but . . . I can't get him to come to at all.''

"Don't panic. He's all right. Just put on some coffee." When Kelly said nothing, he asked, "Okay?"

"Okay, but you're coming now, aren't you?"

Will could hear Kelly's fear, and, as always, he wanted to take her in his arms and tell her that everything would be all right. "I'm on my way. Go make that coffee."

With that, he hung up the phone.

Kelly, too, recradled the phone, looked over at Mitch, who lay precisely as she'd left him, and started for the kitchen. Trying not to think at all, about Mitch's being drunk or about having just spoken to Will—he sounded wonderful!—she rummaged through the cabinets until she found a coffeepot and a tin of coffee. Liberally dumping the dark-roasted grounds into the pot, she added water and set it to perking over a blue-red flame.

Crossing once more to Mitch, she knelt beside the sofa and took his hand in hers. "Mitch?" she called softly, but got no response.

"C'mon, Mitch," she whispered, brushing the damp sprigs of sandy-blond hair back from his forehead. "Talk to me."

Whether it was her entreaty or the aroma of coffee beginning to fill the apartment, Mitch groaned, blinked, opened one eye.

"Kelly?" he slurred.

"Yeah," she said with a small grin.

"You'reinEurope." The three words came out as one.

"No, I'm right here with you."

"Fall."

"What?" Kelly asked.

"Itookthefall."

Kelly frowned, giving him a quick once-over to see if he had any bruises. "Did you fall?"

"SantaClaus . . . EasterBunny."

Kelly's frown deepened. "I don't understand."

"Watchoutforthem. Watchout..." He slipped back into a drunken darkness.

Kelly was still sitting at Mitch's side when Will, who found the door unlocked as had Kelly, entered the apartment. With the rain, she hadn't even heard footsteps on the stairs. At the expected, yet unexpected sound, her gaze rushed to meet Will's. For a moment, she had the dizzying sensation that the world was spinning out of orbit.

Mitch had been wrong, Kelly thought, she would have recognized Will anywhere, anytime, even without his beard. He'd had his hair trimmed, too, though its edges continued to brush the raised collar of his raincoat, though perhaps that was only because his hair was soaked. Even without the facial hair, he looked as rugged, as uncompromisingly male as he always had. Maybe even more so with his shaven, strength-filled jaw so visible.

She looked tired, Will thought. The kind of tired that a long sleep would have little effect upon. She looked emotionally tired, as though the past weeks hadn't been all that easy for her. A part of him wanted to comfort her, while another part of him selfishly hoped that the weeks had been trying for her. He hoped that she hadn't been able to stop thinking of him any more than he hadn't been able to stop thinking of her.

Brushing back her hair from her eyes in a gesture painfully familiar to Will, Kelly rose from the floor and said, "He came to for just a minute, but he was incoherent. Although he did recognize me."

"His clothes are soaked," Will said, slipping out of his own moisture-slick raincoat.

"I know. He must have been out in the rain."

"First things first," Will said. "Bring me some coffee."

Kelly complied and in seconds set a steaming mug on the table beside the sofa. Will knelt on the floor and lightly tapped Mitch on the cheek.

"C'mon, buddy, let's come back to the land of the living."

When Will got no response, he gave his friend a slight slap. Mitch moaned and swatted at the hand disturbing his blissful oblivion.

"Sorry," Will said. "It's time to face the music . . . and the headache."

"Goaway," Mitch slurred.

"Nope," Will said. "Not until you drink some of this coffee."

Mitch told him what he could do with his coffee.

"I don't think that's possible," Will said, "so why don't you take just one swallow of this."

"I don't want . . ."

"What don't you want?" Will asked, trying to keep Mitch talking.

"To be sober. Sober sucks."

"Yeah, well, you might have a point. Nonetheless—"

"Scott'scamping...can'teventakemyson... camping."

Will braced an arm around Mitch's neck and forced him to a semisitting position. Bringing the mug to Mitch's lips, he forced down some of the coffee. Mitch choked.

"Here, try it again," Will said, urging down more of the brew before Mitch had time to object. Most of this hit its target, Mitch's stomach, before Mitch could stop it.

He groaned in protest. Another swallow, followed by yet another groan, followed by yet another swallow. Mitch's mouth began to loosen. "Scott'sbirthday. He went...camping."

"That's good," Will said.

"No, he went...without me." Suddenly, Mitch's eyes focused. "How much does a transgression cost?"

"What?" Will asked.

"Transgression...no, no, trans-*mission*. How much does a transmission cost?"

"I don't know, buddy. Probably a bundle."

"Yeah, a bundle...mucho dinero." He took another forced sip of coffee, then gave a mirthless laugh. "I know how much a transgression costs."

"You do?" Will said.

"I do," Mitch answered. "My job." He looked up at Will with beseeching eyes, eyes that suddenly swam in tears. "Why did they do that to me?"

"Do what?" Will asked.

"Say I took a bribe. I didn't. I swear. Santa Claus and the Easter Bunny set me up..." He trailed off, as though he knew what he was saying didn't make sense. "No, they weren't the ones." He looked back at Will. "Who set me up for the fall? I can't remember."

"What're you talking about?" Will asked, frowning.

"He mentioned the fall before," Kelly said. "And Santa Claus and the Easter Bunny."

"No, no, someone else," Mitch said. He looked up at Kelly, saying, "Who would do that to me? And why would Connie believe..." Mitch trailed off abruptly. "I think I'm going to be sick."

In a display of uncommon strength, Will practically carried Mitch to the bathroom. Afterward, Will stripped the wet clothes from him and settled him in bed.

"Go to sleep," Will said, turning off the lamp and starting from the room.

"Will?"

Will turned, barely able to see his friend in the dim light of the bedroom.

"I didn't take the bribe."

Will had no idea what his friend was talking about, but he knew without a doubt that whatever it was was serious. He knew one other thing, as well. If Mitch

Brody said he didn't take a bribe, then he didn't take it.

"No, I know you didn't," Will said.

"You do?" Mitch asked incredulously.

"I do," Will said softly. It seemed to be the lullaby that Mitch needed to send him off to sleep.

When Will reentered the room, he found Kelly in the kitchen, where she was pouring herself a mug of coffee. At the sound of his approach, she turned toward him. Once more, the world seemed to tilt on its axis. Had it been so very long since they'd spent a week together? In a way, it seemed like only yesterday. In another, it seemed as if it had been forever.

"He's asleep," Will said.

Without asking, Kelly poured Will a mug of coffee and, carrying both mugs to the table, she sat down.

"I vaguely remember, about a year, year and a half ago," she said, "seeing something in the newspaper about a police officer being accused of taking a bribe. But then, it seems to me the charges were dropped—unsubstantiated—or something. I just remember the officer quit the force, which I thought odd if the charges had been dropped. Do you think that was Mitch?"

Will, who'd dragged out the chair across from Kelly and sat down, drew the mug to his lips for a slow sip. "I'd say that's a real possibility."

"But why would he quit if the charges were dropped?"

"Maybe they were, maybe they weren't."

"I'm not following you."

"What if he were given a choice—leave the force with honor or be prosecuted?"

Kelly curled her fingers around the warm mug. "I see what you mean," she said reflectively. "Yeah, that would make sense. That would also explain why this Connie person left him. She thought he was guilty, even though charges were never pressed. Who is she, anyway? His wife?"

"His ex-wife. At least that's what I gather. He's never mentioned her but once and then not by name. He just said his son lived with her."

"His son is this Scott who's gone camping?"

"Yeah."

Both sipped their coffee.

Suddenly, her eyes typically spewing fire, Kelly said, "You know, that really chaps me. How anyone could believe that Mitch could do something like that! And his ex-wife should be strung up by her heels! I mean, I know I haven't known Mitch for a long time, but you don't have to know a person a long time to know him well. And Mitch just isn't capable of that kind of duplicity. No, indeedy, he isn't capable..." She trailed off at the grin that nipped one corner of Will's mouth. "And just what's so funny, Will Stone?"

"You. I had forgotten how full of spit and vinegar you can be."

And what else have you forgotten? her eyes seemed to say.

Nothing, his replied. *Not your kiss, not the way you felt in my arms, not the way you felt beneath me.*

Kelly read everything his eyes spoke. The part of her that had wondered just what their week together had meant to him now had its answer. She was relieved—no, overjoyed. At the same time, fear cut a wide swath through her once more. Darn it, she was no good with relationships! Standing, she carried her mug to the coffeepot for a refill.

Will noted that her mug did not need refilling. It was almost full. He also noted a resurgence of his own fear. The two of them were from different worlds. Could they possibly make it together?

"Did you get the money I sent?" he asked, wanting desperately to change the subject.

She glanced back at him, but her gaze didn't quite meet his. "Yeah." She then added, "But you didn't have to."

"Oh, yes, I did. Oh, yes, I do."

This time her eyes did meet his. He saw a devilish gleam jump to life in the dark green irises. He heard the same devilry when she said, "I feel it only fair to warn you that I've added an additional charge for mental anguish."

A hint of a smile claimed Will's lips again. "Have you now? Well, I feel it only fair to warn you that I've deducted similar charges."

"You're charging me for mental anguish?" she asked, fighting to keep her lips from twitching.

"You bet. When an escapee takes a hostage, he's entitled to certain things."

"Such as?"

"Someone who, just once in a while, does what he says."

"Then you should have taken some namby-pamby hostage."

"Is that what you wish?" Will asked. "That I'd taken someone else hostage?"

The question had been asked in that low, kind of growling voice that he sometimes had, the voice that emptied Kelly's lungs of all air. The need to run consumed her again, and she pushed back her chair, saying, "What I think is that I need to go. I'm tired. Dog-tired." As she spoke, she grabbed her coat and started for the door.

"Why didn't you send off the story about me?"

Kelly halted, turned around and said, "What makes you so sure I didn't?"

"Did you?" When she hesitated, he repeated, "Did you?"

"No," she said, brushing back her hair from her eyes. "Look, Stone, don't read anything into it, all right? I already have enough trophies."

"I didn't think you could ever have enough. I thought that was how you proved your worth. I thought that was how you made people like you—by proving how perfect you are."

Maybe he was right, Kelly thought. Maybe, though, she was tired of being perfect. Maybe she was tired of trying to be something she'd never had any hope of being. The truth was, at the moment, she felt much less than perfect. She felt scared again. So very scared!

Once more, she started for the door, this time hastening her steps. Suddenly, Will's fingers wrapped around her upper arm. He whirled her around. Instinctively, her eyes went to his.

"I've got to know something," he said in a sexy voice.

"What?" she asked breathlessly.

"Do your lips feel the way I remember them feeling?"

"I—I don't know," she whispered. "How do you remember them—"

"Soft," he interrupted. "So soft they drove me crazy. Did I only imagine that?"

Kelly was beyond saying anything. She simply stared, the lips he'd just spoken of parted to allow the escape of a tiny half breath. That half breath grew thinner yet, when he started to lower his head—lower and angle it.

His mouth brushed hers, once, twice, then settled into a kiss so gentle that Kelly thought she was dreaming. Surely nothing in life could be so tender, so...so absolutely perfect. This was real perfection, not her shallow, repeated attempts to keep buying attention.

All too soon, Will slowly but resolutely pulled his mouth from hers. "Yeah," he whispered. "I remembered right."

The taste of his mouth lingering like the sweetest of candy, Kelly spoke from the heart, "You scare me, Will Stone."

"Yeah, well, lady, you scare me, too."

CHAPTER SEVENTEEN

A WEEK LATER, Mitch stood at a meeting of Alcoholics Anonymous and announced before the group of strangers that he was an alcoholic. The only thing that got him through the painful and humiliating ordeal was Will's presence.

"I don't know how I'm going to get through tomorrow, and the next day, and the next," Mitch said on the way home that evening.

"You don't have to get through tomorrow," Will said, emphasizing the AA creed. "All you have to do is get through today."

Will thought the advice equally appropriate for his own life. After seeing Kelly again, after kissing her again, he was in more of a quandary than ever. He wanted to go on seeing her. He wanted to go on kissing her. He wanted to tell her that he was helplessly, hopelessly in love with her. He sensed that she felt something for him, something that she was fighting. Perhaps, considering her divorce and the reasons for it, she would have fought her feelings for any man.

Was it even remotely possible that he, Will Stone, did have something to offer Kelly?

"WHEN ARE YOU and Kelly going to stop dancing around each other and get together?"

The question, boldly direct, took Will completely by surprise. He and Mitch were having dinner together. Almost a full week had passed since they had attended that first AA meeting, two weeks since Will had last seen Kelly.

"Don't pretend you don't know what I'm talking about," Mitch continued. "And don't act surprised that I do. It's as plain as a wart on a frog."

Will answered just as directly, just as boldly. "If it's that plain, then it should also be plain that I'm all wrong for her."

"Is that so?"

"That's so," Will said, downing a large swallow of coffee. "Now let's change the subject. Are you sure you had no idea who set you up?"

Mitch said nothing.

"You suspect someone?" Will asked.

A look of anger darted across Mitch's face. "Suspicion won't hang anybody." When Will started to speak, Mitch interrupted with, "Look, maybe I don't know a thing. Maybe I only wish I did. At any rate, could we just forget this? I was burned—caught with 50,000 dollars in my account—and that's that. In the larger scheme of things, it doesn't matter one red cent." With that, he downed in one swallow the milk remaining in his glass. "It's you and Kelly we should be worrying about."

Will shook his head. "There is no Kelly and me. We're from different worlds. I'm from the wrong side of the tracks."

"That may be true, buddy, but it doesn't change one basic fact." When Will arched an eyebrow in question, Mitch said, "The lady's in love with you."

"THE LADY'S in love with you."

Like a refrain, the words played over and over again in Will's mind later that night. He paced the floor of his tiny apartment, he went for a walk in the cold night air. Nothing seemed to clear his head, which seemed as foggy as the streets he walked. Was she in love with him? And if she was, didn't he have all that graver a responsibility to her? He couldn't let her waste her life on him.

There you go again, that alien voice said to him from out of the cold night.

"Go away," Will muttered, huddling deeper into his jacket.

No way, mister. Not until I've had my say. Okay, so you are from the wrong side of the tracks, the wrong side of life. You've, nonetheless, got one thing to offer her that nobody else can. Ah, I can see I've got your attention.

"You've got nothing," Will said, the words carried off by a stinging-cold breeze.

You might not be good enough for her, Stone. Frankly, I think that's debatable, but for the sake of argument, say it is true. It still doesn't change one ba-

sic fact. Nobody's ever going to love her the way you do. And you know it.

Will walked the deserted streets, uphill and downhill, through the park where he'd first seen Kelly. With each step, the alien voice seemed less alien, its words filled with the golden sage sounds of wisdom... and hope... and every good thing that Will had ever thought beyond his grasp. By the time he reached his apartment, he knew one thing with a certainty that couldn't be denied. The voice was right. No one would ever love Kelly the way he loved her!

Before he could consider what he was doing, he grabbed the telephone book lying on the hallway floor, madly dashed through its pages, and found Kelly's phone number, which he dialed with the speed of a flash fire. As the phone began to ring, Will's heart began to pound. What was he going to say? Just blurt out the fact that he loved her?

Ring.

No, he couldn't do that. What then? Ask her out? No, that would be anticlimactic after what they'd been through.

Ring.

Okay, maybe his first thought was right. Maybe he should just come clean and admit that he loved her. Get it out of the way right up front, let her know where he stood right from the start.

Ring.

But what if she... It suddenly dawned on Will that he wasn't going to get a chance to tell Kelly anything.

She wasn't at home. Slamming the receiver back on the hook, he cursed, wondered where Kelly was, and wondered if he'd ever find his courage again.

ASLEEP ON the sofa bed, Will didn't hear the fingernail file as it was inserted into the lock of the door and jiggled ever so slightly. Neither did Will hear the turning of the doorknob or the opening of the door. A faint rattling sound, that associated with metal, momentarily filled the room. Will sighed and changed position. The intruder halted, waited, and, when Will didn't make another sound, tiptoed forward.

Timing was everything, the intruder thought, kneeling at the side of the sofa bed. One end of the handcuffs securely around the intruder's own wrist, the shadowy figure fastened the other cuff around Will's wrist—the one that peeked from the blanket. At the same time, a hand went across Will's mouth, catching him in the midst of, "What the—"

"Do as I tell you, and I won't hurt you," a feminine voice whispered into Will's ear.

Will thought the voice sounded scratchy-soft, like grosgrain ribbon. He also thought it sexy. Maybe the sexiest voice he'd ever heard.

"That's it," Kelly whispered. "Just take it easy."

She could feel her own heart pounding furiously and she would have sworn she heard Will's thumping just as wildly.

"I'm going to take my hand away and, when I do, I don't want to hear a sound out of you. You got that?"

Will made no response.

"You got that?" she asked, her warm breath brushing against Will's ear.

He nodded.

Slowly, Kelly eased her hand from Will's mouth. He shifted to a sitting position and started to reach for the nearby lamp.

"No, leave it off."

Will obeyed, adding, "What do you want?"

"To talk."

"Couldn't we talk without these?" he asked, rattling the handcuffs joining them together.

"We could, but we wouldn't. We've done a good job of avoiding it so far... Oh, and by the way, I'm doing the talking, and you're doing the listening."

Will hid a smile. Yeah, this was the sassy, cheeky woman he'd once taken hostage, though now he sensed that the sassiness, the cheekiness, might be nothing more than bravado, and that underneath shimmered a wealth of insecurities. Maybe the handcuffs were her way of assuring that she didn't back out before she'd said what she came to say.

"So talk," he said, fighting as always the urge to take her in his arms.

"Okay, I will," Kelly said, almost angrily. "There I was minding my own business—"

"When?"

"The night you broke into my apartment. Anyway, you stormed into my life that night, then a week later you stormed out."

"I thought that was what you wanted . . . for me to get out of your life and leave you alone."

"I do . . . I did . . . you're talking!"

"Sorry."

"Anyway," Kelly said, "you stormed into my life, and it hasn't been the same since." She raked her fingers through her hair, dragging Will's handcuffed hand behind hers, a fact she didn't even seem to notice. "I want my life back, Will Stone! Or at least a facsimile of it!"

"So, what's stopping you from getting your life back?" he asked softly, sexily, in that voice that sent shivers skittering down Kelly's spine.

"You know darned well what's stopping me! You know darned well that something happened between us, something more than you, Tarzan, taking me, Jane, hostage! You know darned well that both of us have been running scared ever since."

Her crisp words came to an abrupt stop, suddenly making the silence in the room seem deafening, making her heart roar in her ears. She had just crossed the Rubicon. There would be no turning back now.

"I'm tired of running, Will."

The way she said his name squeezed his heart just as always. That, combined with what she'd just said, threatened to crush his heart completely.

"Then stop running, Kelly," he said.

Kelly glanced up quickly, her eyes finding Will's in the moonlight-streaked room. "You've never spoken my name before."

"I know," he said.

What did his finally speaking her name mean? She knew that his doing so now was significant. Did he, too, want to stop running and, if so, what lay in store for them if they did? Her lack of answers once more bred frustration, even anger.

"I'm not perfect, Will, and, frankly, I'm tired of trying to be. I'm tired of trying to earn people's love through perfection, because no matter how many awards I win, I never feel it's enough to keep the people I love near me. And you know what the irony is?" She didn't even come close to giving him a chance to answer. "My father never really cared if I was perfect. That was never the real issue. The real issue is that, for whatever reason, he was too caught up in his job, his life, to give me any more of himself than he did. Then along came Gary. Poor Gary. I made him pay for the sins of my father." She sighed. "And, furthermore, I'd probably make the same mistake if I married you."

At the mention of marriage, Will's heart missed an entire beat. "No, you wouldn't," he said, his voice filled with emotion, "because you're no longer that little girl who so desperately needs her father. You now know that he wasn't perfect. If he had been, he'd have recognized his daughter's needs and tried to meet them.

If he didn't have to be perfect for you to love him, why should you have had to be?'' When she said nothing, he added, ''Love doesn't demand perfection, Kelly. If it did, you wouldn't be in love with me.''

The word *love* hung in the air like the headiest of fragrances. Kelly felt it filling all of her senses, filling all of her heart.

''Is that what I am?'' she asked softly.

''Isn't it?'' When she gave no answer, his hand sought hers. Even though the handcuffs were a hindrance, his fingers entwined with hers. ''Isn't it?'' he repeated.

''Yes,'' she whispered, the one word so quietly spoken that Will had barely heard it, but heard it he had—not with the ear, but with his heart.

Will tugged, sprawling Kelly across his chest. She thought he was going to kiss her, she wanted him to kiss her, maybe more than she'd ever wanted anything, but he stopped short of it, their lips but a mere whisper apart.

''Say the words,'' he demanded roughly.

''I love you,'' she said, the confession nothing more than a sliver of sound. Then, of her own volition, she added, ''I love you, I love you, I—''

His mouth covered hers, hard and fast and with a furious hunger. He kissed her not like the loser he'd always felt himself to be, but like the winner she made him feel. He kissed her like a man who'd turned his back on the past and was heading toward tomorrow.

Rolling her to her back, he pinned her beneath him.
Pulling his lips from hers, he stared down into her face.
In the moonlight, he could barely make out her features, which he began to trace with his fingertips, her
cheeks, her chin, her eyelids, her lips. Once he reached
her hair—he dragged her hand in the wake of his just
as she'd done earlier—he brushed it aside gently, lovingly.

"I'm only going to say this once and never again for
the rest of our lives," he whispered. "I know you could
do better than me, probably a lot better—"

"Will."

"Hush. I know you could do better than me, but I
love you more than I love life itself. I love you more
than anyone will ever love you, Kelly Cooper. And I'll
always try to be there when you need me. I'll never
leave you...and I'll damned sure never let you push me
away."

His words brought tears to Kelly's eyes. "No, you
won't leave," she whispered, trying to caress his face
with a hand that was securely fettered to his. The awk-
ward attempt led her to say, impatiently, "Would you
please cough up the key to these handcuffs?"

"What key?"

"You don't have the key?"

"I didn't even know what happened to the handcuffs."

Silence.

Suddenly, Kelly giggled.

Just as suddenly, Will laughed.

"Gee, I guess you're going to have to be my hostage for the rest of the night," she said.

"How about for the rest of my life?"

"Bingo," Kelly whispered just seconds before Will's hungry mouth once more found hers.

*   *   *   *   *

Be sure to watch for Mitch Brady's story in:
#568 Proof Positive *by Sandra Canfield,*
the spin-off from Snap Judgement.

Look for Proof Positive
in October 1993, wherever Harlequin
Superromance Books are sold.

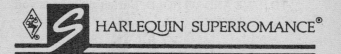

COMING NEXT MONTH

#546 AFTER THE PROMISE • Debbi Bedford
Despite all his knowledge and training, Dr. Michael Stratton could
only stand by helplessly as his small son, Cody, battled for his life.
But something good might come of this—Cody's illness had
thrown Michael and his ex-wife, Jennie, together. While others
worked to heal his child, Michael could heal his marriage.

#547 SHENANIGANS • Casey Roberts
Paul Sherwood was a man with a mission: to take over ailing
cosmetics giant Cheri Lee. Lauren Afton was a woman with a
goal: to save her mother's self-made empire. Lauren knew she was
a match for Paul in the boardroom, and she had a sneaking
suspicion they'd also be a pretty good match in the bedroom....

#548 THE MODEL BRIDE • Pamela Bauer
Model Jessie Paulson had been on the jury that convicted
Aidan McCullough's father of murder, yet now the verdict was
beginning to haunt her. Aidan, too, was haunted by his father's
conviction. Not only had it uncovered a past best left buried, it
was standing in the way of his future with Jessie.

#549 PARADOX • Lynn Erickson
Women Who Dare, Book 5
Emily got more than she bargained for when she decided to start a
new life in Seattle. Her train crashed and she woke up to find
herself in the year 1893, at the home of rancher Will Dutcher.
Trapped in time, Emily had to discover a way to return home. But
how could she abandon the man she loved?

AVAILABLE THIS MONTH:

#542 WORTH THE WAIT
Risa Kirk

#543 BUILT TO LAST
Leigh Roberts

#544 JOE'S MIRACLE
Helen Conrad

#545 SNAP JUDGEMENT
Sandra Canfield

Following the success of WITH THIS RING and
TO HAVE AND TO HOLD, Harlequin brings you

JUST MARRIED

SANDRA CANFIELD
MURIEL JENSEN
ELISE TITLE
REBECCA WINTERS

just in time for the 1993 wedding season!

Written by four of Harlequin's most popular authors, this
four-story collection celebrates the joy, excitement and
adjustment that comes with being "just married."

You won't want to miss this spring tradition, whether
you're just married or not!

AVAILABLE IN APRIL WHEREVER HARLEQUIN
BOOKS ARE SOLD

JM93

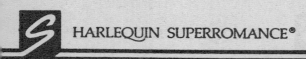

HARLEQUIN SUPERROMANCE®

WOMEN WHO DARE DRIVE RACE CARS?!

During 1993, each Harlequin Superromance WOMEN WHO DARE title will have a single italicized letter on the Women Who Dare back-page ads. Collect the letters, spell D A R E and you can receive a free copy of RACE FOR TOMORROW, written by popular author Elaine Barbieri. This is an exciting novel about a female race-car driver, WHO DARES ANYTHING . . . FOR LOVE!

Mail this certificate, designated letters spelling DARE, and check or money order for postage and handling to: In the U.S.—WOMEN WHO DARE, P.O. Box 9056, Buffalo, NY 14269-9056; In Canada—WOMEN WHO DARE, P.O. Box 621, Fort Erie, Ontario L2A 5X3.

Requests must be received by January 31, 1994.
Allow 4-6 weeks after receipt of order for delivery.

D-086-KAT-RR